BROTHERHOOD OF THE BADGE

DALLAS BARNES

ROUGH
EDGES
PRESS

BROTHERHOOD OF THE BADGE

This book is dedicated to the men & women who carry a badge & a gun in service to others. Becoming a police officer is a life changing experience, never to be forgotten, nor for the faint of heart. Police officers carry deadly weapons. They have a sworn duty to protect the lives and property of others. A decision to use deadly force is irreversible and timeless. Few other professions have such demands or responsibilities. Becoming a cop is a choice...being a cop is a privilege.

AUTHOR'S NOTE

Although based on the writer's experiences as a police officer this book is a work of fiction. Names, characters, and locations are the product of the writer's imagination and are used fictitiously. Any resemblance to real persons, living or dead, is purely coincidental.

All references to the LAPD, both the department and the officers thereof are fictional representations. Departmental policies, protocols, and procedurals are fictitiously presented to protect the integrity of actual operations.

In two hours and twenty-six minutes she would be dead. Dawn Hill was nineteen years old. She had been in Los Angeles for fourteen months. She came to L.A. to become an actress. Instead, she became a whore. A former high school cheerleader, Dawn, like thousands of other young women, was drawn to the City of Angels like a moth to a flame. Blonde hair, blue eyes, and a figure few men ignored, along with a seductive smile, made Dawn a candidate for a career in Hollywood, but dreams and reality were proving to be a tough match.

Dawn came to Los Angeles from Fresno, California. A reluctant family provided the resources for a one room apartment in the city's sprawling San Fernando Valley. Dawn quickly learned nothing happened in Hollywood without an agent. She talked to eleven of them. Eight of the agents asked her to bare her breasts. After the eleventh request she agreed. She fled the office when the man insisted on touching her.

Dawn met Nathaniel Wyde, better known as Nation Wyde, sitting at McDonald's a block from her apartment. Dinner was a Big Mac with fries. It had been the same for months. Money was fading which meant, when gone, a reluctant embarrassing return to Fresno. Nation Wyde, a handsome young Black man approached with a tray. "Haven't I seen you on TV?"

Dawn smiled. She was flattered. "No, afraid it wasn't me."

"But you are an actress." Nation sat down across from her. Dawn had no idea he had been waiting, looking for the profile he had learned to recognize. She was what he called a Pigeon; the type reacting to a few crumbs. Nation Wyde was handsome, polite, friendly, and to Dawn's delight, he professed he was an actor. At least that's what he said he was. Nation rattled off six prime time series he had small appearances in. Dawn was impressed. He did not mention his arrest for pimping, grand theft auto, carrying a concealed weapon, and assault. Dawn was pleased to learn Nation lived in the valley only blocks away. It was another lie. Nation lived 14 miles away in LA's ghetto with his aging mother.

Nation claimed he was only three years older than Dawn, but the truth was he was twelve years older. Dawn didn't seem to care. She was no longer alone in the City of Angels. Now she had a friend. A willing seduction followed two days later. The same day he moved in with her. Nation tactfully convinced Dawn to pose nude for pictures with the promise he could quickly turn them into money. "Hey, every girl in Hollywood does this," Nation assured. "Mary Tyler Moore, Salma Hayek, Mylie. It's art, Baby."

After the nude pictures, and with money still a challenge, Nation introduced Dawn to Chuck Ross, a middle-aged overweight executive with Moonbeam records. Ross needed a date, a trophy for his arm, and he was willing to pay. It was a corporate retreat in Las Vegas. Nation was paid twenty-five hundred for the introduction after showing Dawn's nude pictures. Nation told Dawn he was paid a thousand. Dawn, broke and desperate, agreed. She flew to Vegas where she was provided with a suite on the thirty-second floor of one of the Signature Towers at the MGM Grand. She was there two days. She was seduced by Ross and two others.

Money came but went quickly. Dawn and Nation were living the good life in Hollywood. The best restaurants, new clothes and more, as Nation arranged more and more dates. They became a blur for Dawn. She found herself playing a role of innocence. The men she was dating were complimentary and generous while Nation kept promising, "Just one more time," every time, he announced another date.

Dawn was returning from a date in Puerto Vallarta, Mexico when an excited Nation Wyde shared the news. Everything was set. They were both to have major roles in "Naked Justice", a major multi-million-dollar motion picture to be shot in the Virgin Islands. Nation claimed he knew the director. All they needed was a buy in of ten thousand and they'd both be in the picture. "Hell, girl, you'll be a star."

Dawn's excitement turned to disappointment. "We don't have that kind of money."

"I know someone who does," Nation argued. "All you got to do is drive a car. It's the First Federal on Wilshire Boulevard. I'll go in and make a major withdrawal. Baby, we'll be in the movies."

"Rob a bank!" Dawn was shocked. "I can't do that."

"You wanna be in this movie or not? We got no money. This could make us both rich. No more of this freaking dating."

"You could get hurt. We'll go to prison." Dawn was alarmed.

"I'll use a toy gun. I know the bank. Inside and out. I can be in and out in minutes. Do you know how many bank robbers in LA aren't caught? Google it?"

Dawn, her inner thighs still sore from the Mexico trip, reluctantly agreed. The next day they drove to the bank for a walk through. There was a no parking zone flanking the front of the bank. There were no guards, just bullet proof glass shielding the tellers behind the line of counters. Three desks outside the shields provided access to the aging bank manager, a female loan officer and a new accounts clerk. Nation had learned from Google that banks train their staff to cooperate with robberies. Better to lose money than to lose lives. "We park right here, and I go in. We'll give up the car a couple blocks away. I'll wear a mask, Baby, then we're off to the islands."

After searching Google again Nation learned most banks had significant cash in from weekend business deposits. Nation targeted Monday. Dawn emailed friends and family, telling all she finally had a part set in a motion picture and would soon be leaving for the Virgin Islands. Nation needed a gun. He went to nighttime Melrose Avenue. He talked to five people before he connected with one who knew where he could buy handguns. Nation bought two. One, a chrome 380 caliber automatic. The other, a heavier Blue Steel forty-five caliber automatic.

When Nation returned and unwrapped the towel hiding the two guns, Dawn grimaced. "I don't want a gun. You said you'd use a toy gun."

"We're going to have a lot of money," Nation argued. "I want you to be safe. We'll get rid of them right after."

"I've never even shot a gun," Dawn confessed.

"And you won't have to," Nation assured.

The day came and Nation left early to go rent a car. At least that's what he told Dawn. Reality was different. He walked two blocks to the wide parking lot of a supermarket where he waited until he spotted an elderly gray-haired woman park a red Dodge. Nation Wyde waited until the stooped old lady disappeared into the market.

"Yeah, grandma, you don't need a four hundred horse powered Dodge. I'm gonna do you a fucking favor. Just call your insurance man, he'll send you plenty of money." Nation's early criminal skill set, and arrest starting at age 12 involved GTA, Grand-Theft-Auto. 12. Nation smiled as he slid in behind the wheel of the car.

Dawn was nervous but she convinced herself to look at it as if it were a role she was cast in. She would be the daring beauty who drove a getaway car. Plus, banks had lots of money. Weren't they all insured? Anxiety turned to excitement. For wardrobe Dawn picked a pair of faded tight-fitting jeans and a form fitting sleeveless turtleneck blouse. She stood at a mirror in the apartment's bathroom and fine-tuned her makeup. She smiled at the image in the mirror. "Mirror, mirror on the wall, who is the most daring of them all?"

Dawn's cell phone buzzed. "Hello."

"It's me, Babe. Got a nice red Dodge for us. Get ready, we're on our way to being rich."

"I'm ready," the cheerleader from Fresno purred in reply. Dawn was ready but it was forced. She had thrown up in the bathroom bowl shortly after Nation Wyde left to get the rental car. She decided she would tell him after the robbery. She was pregnant. A pregnancy test from the corner drugstore proved it. She was careful with the men she seduced but it was different with Nation Wyde. She was certain he would share her excitement. Perhaps marriage would follow.

Sixteen miles away, twenty-eight-year-old LAPD Officer Brian Culpepper sat in his patrol car reading a digital report on the computer screen mounted below the dashboard. Culpepper had been assigned to an L Car. He was working alone, taking report calls in the Wilshire Area. He didn't like the assignment as a report writer but he had drawn the short straw at roll call. Usually, he'd be teamed with James Wilder, in a two man A Car, answering hot calls, but the older officer assigned the L Car had called in sick. Brian was hoping, it would be a one-day thing. Fate would prove him right. Brian Culpepper had been an LAPD officer for six years. He was an attractive, single, combat veteran of the conflict in Afghanistan. A migrant from Springfield, Ohio, the Marine Corps had introduced Culpepper to California. His first impression of the LAPD came when he and two other Marines got into a fight with six sailors in a topless bar on Santa Monica Boulevard. Bursting into the brawl in the dim lit bar room two LAPD officers, batons flailing, quickly took command of the situation. Culpepper found his arm twisted up into the middle of his back and hand-cuffed before he could resist. All were laid out on the floor. There was little doubt they were going to jail.

The two LAPD officers assessed the damage, broken glass, a table, and a broken chair. The officers collected monies from the battered service men. "I was in the corps in Iraq," the older of the two officers announced. Culpepper studied the man. The man's chrome name tag on his uniform shirt read, Whittaker.

"My partner was Navy Air. Me, the Marines. My partner and I work together, because together we're stronger. We kick ass." Whittaker's eye's drifted over the row of combat-ants whose heads were bowed like repentant high school students. "Assault and battery, disturbing the peace, destruction of private property. We put you in jail like the deserving felons you are, you're headed for a dishonorable discharge. You get the message?" Silence answered from the rank of service men. Again, Whittaker's eyes swept over them like a burning laser. "Because you're in service to my country this is your lucky day. Now, get your asses out of my city before I change our mind."

Culpepper was impressed. Immediately after his discharge he applied. The LAPD hiring process required passing a comprehensive written exam, an oral interview, a psychological face to face with a shrink, and a demanding physical agility test, all followed by six months of intense academy training followed by a one-year probationary period. Culpepper, a Marine Corps veteran, found the regimen more challenging than his boot camp training in the Corps, but once completed he knew he now belonged to an exclusive Brotherhood. He was now nearing a point in his police career, with four years of service in two different patrol areas, when he could apply for promotion. He wanted to be a detective. No, he was going to be a detective. Bosch, a highly rated television series about an LAPD detective had convinced him. Uniformed patrol was the back-bone and foundation of all police work. If you couldn't make it as a uniformed cop, you sure as hell weren't going to make it as a detective. Culpepper had decided he'd make the best of his day on the L Car; anyway, Bosch would be on tonight.

Another important dimension of Officer Culpepper's life was Deputy District Attorney Pamela Moss. Culpepper had met Pamela in the cafeteria at the County Courthouse. Ironically, it was once again the crowded table syndrome. It was Brian who welcomed the attractive, dark-haired, shapely young woman to his table.

"Do you mind?" Pamela had asked, pausing nearby with her lunch tray.

"Not at all. Please," Brian said. He was betting Pamela was a defense attorney.

"You here on a case?" Pamela asked as she sat down across from Brian.

"Assault with a deadly weapon. Department one twelve," Brian said. "We're selecting a jury."

"You're defending?" Pamela asked, straitening in her chair. She had assumed Brian's suit and tie meant he was an attorney.

"No." Brian smiled. "I'm the arresting officer."

"Oh, you're a cop."

"And you're a defense attorney? I hope not on my case?"

Pamela smiled. "Close, but no brass ring. I am an attorney, but a deputy district attorney."

"You don't look like a district attorney."

"And you don't look like a cop."

"So, I'm sitting here with a district attorney. Single or married?"

"Does it make a difference?" Pamela asked between bites of her lunch.

"Might make a difference to your husband?"

Pamela paused and smiled. "I haven't met him yet. And you?"

"Single. Not in a relationship."

"Me too. All work and no play."

"Have you ever dated a cop?"

"I don't even know your name."

"Culpepper. Brian Culpepper."

Pamela reached a hand across the table. "Moss, Pamela Moss."

Brian took her hand. It was warm with polished manicured nails.

"Nice to meet you, Pamela Moss. Would you like to go hiking with a cop this Saturday? Josiah National park?"

Pamela paused from her eating, raised her eyes to meet Brian's casual friendly look. "Yes, I would like that."

In the days and weeks to follow, they were both cautious with their relationship as it grew, but they both knew it had become exclusive and serious. They enjoyed talking about their love of justice and the nuance of law and law enforcement. Without realizing it they were both gaining invaluable insight to a dimension of law and order neither had ever known.

Brian often asked about the legality of police procedures, and Pamela used Brian for impartial insight into cases finding their way through LA County's courts. More important, however, was simply their love of just being together.

Brian was the first to confess it with words. He was at the door, kissing Pam goodbye before heading for the station and another day patrolling the streets of Los Angeles. "I love you, Pamela Moss," he said, cradling her face gently in his hands.

They kissed and then Pamela spoke, "And I love you, Brian Culpepper."

It was Monday morning in Los Angeles and it seemed to Culpepper the city's four million residents had all decided to come out at once. The streets were crowded with both an army of pedestrians and a never-ending fleet of cars, trucks, and busses. The sun was shining, and the air was full of the sounds of the city.

Brian was driving west on Wilshire Boulevard in his black and white patrol car when he saw the red Dodge sedan parked in the red no parking zone in front of the First Federal Bank. There was a young blonde woman sitting behind the wheel of the car.

Brian eased his patrol car to a stop beside the car. Obviously, the woman was waiting for someone to return from inside the bank. Deciding it was not worth a citation, Brian looked at the young blonde in the Dodge. She seemed to be avoiding eye contact.

"That's a red zone, miss," he said through his open passengers' window. "You're going to have to move. If you're waiting on someone just drive around the block and come back."

Dawn Hill's heart was in her throat. She was in a panic. Nation Wyde, wearing an over the head rubber mask of former President Donald Trump and black leather gloves to foil the countless security cameras, was still in the bank with a gun. Now an LAPD officer was parked beside her. The loaded .45-caliber automatic pistol lay cradled in her trembling hands.

"Did you hear me?" Brian called again from his idling patrol car.

Dawn screamed as loud as she could and raised the pistol. She pointed it at Culpepper and pulled the trigger time and time again. The succession of eight shots filled the air with concussions as hot expended shells fell into her lap.

The rain of bullets ripped through Culpepper's patrol car filling it with shattered glass and pieces of jagged hot steel. As quickly as the shots began, they ended. The woman was still screaming and pointing the gun at him.

Shocked, breathless from a bullet that had slammed into his protective vest, Brian ignored his ringing ears and blood running down over his face. He grabbed his .40 caliber Glock from his belt holster, aimed at the woman, and fired a succession of five shots. Two of the .40 caliber bullets struck Dawn Hill on the forehead just above her eyes. Her head jerked violently as blood splattered the inside of the Dodge. Another hit in her left shoulder. The remaining two shots pierced her neck. Blood spurted from her nose and mouth. She fell forward with her face against the steering wheel. The horn began a loud blare.

Brian, keeping his gun aimed at the woman, pushed the patrol car into park. His heart was racing. He grabbed his radio mike, tried to catch his breath before speaking. "Officer needs help! Shots fired! Seven-Lincoln-34. First Federal. Wilshire and Spaulding!" It was a shout. Immediately, a calm solemn female voice answered on the radio. "All units, officer needs help! Shots fired. First Federal, Wilshire and Spaulding."

Stomachs tightened in police cars across the 502 square miles of the City of Angels. Eight patrol cars in the vicinity flipped on emergency lights and siren to speed toward the scene. Inside the bank, Nation Wyde, gun in gloved hand, wearing a MAGA ball cap over his head-covering mask of former President Trump, stood in front of the bank managers' desk. He heard the sharp gunfire outside. So had the balding bank manager, who discreetly tripped a silent robbery alarm.

"Please don't kill me," the manager pled. Nation knew he had to flee. His eyes searched frantically. An elderly woman gave him the answer when she entered through a side double glass door from adjoining Spaulding Avenue. Donald Trump bolted for the door.

Brian, gun aimed at the woman in the Dodge, opened his car door, lowered himself and slid out of the car. Street traffic stopped behind him. In the center lane, morning traffic continued to flow by. Some drivers noticed, glanced, but continued. The horn on the Dodge continued its steady blare. Irritated with the delay more horns were sounding from cars lining up behind the patrol car. Sirens joined the course of horns with their electronic yelps echoing in the concrete canyons as they approached in the distance.

Brian rounded the back of his patrol car and eased toward the Dodge. Dawn's blonde hair was crimson and matted with blood. Her face was against the steering wheel. The horn continued its blare. Brian looked to the bank. He expected at any moment armed suspects would be bursting through the door, headed for this getaway car.

Sirens were closer now. Brian looked at the blonde, her wounds, the blood. It was obvious she was dead. He reached to her shoulder and pulled her away from the steering wheel. The horn stopped. Brian's stomach convulsed. Police cars screamed to a stop around his car. Officers with shotguns scrambled out.

Brian lowered his pistol. He was gasping for breath. He knew he had survived. He reached and wiped at blood running down his face. He wondered if he had been hit. Was he going to die? It all felt surreal. His jaw was hurting from gritting his teeth. He took a quick look around. Were there others?

A growing collection of those on the busy sidewalks were stopping, , staring, pointing, and watching. Most held open cell phones, raised aimed, cameras recording it all. The tangle of arriving police cars with lights and sirens, were now blocking traffic in both directions on the wide six-lane street.

A uniformed cop, with a 12-gauge shot gun laid a hand on Brian's shoulder, it was Jim Wilder, his usual partner. "You, okay?"

Brian managed a nod without taking his eyes off the dead blonde. She was slumped behind the wheel. Her head cantered; mouth open with a tongue sticking out. Her eyes were open, staring blankly.

"Shit," Brian said, recognizing how young she looked. He

gasped, not realizing he had been holding his breath. He looked to his feet. The .45-caliber automatic pistol lay on the surface of the street.

Sirens were loud as more police cars arrived. Tires screeched as they slid to a halt. Sergeant JD Kent, a muscular Black man, was among those first on the scene. JD was the assistant watch commander. He and Brian knew each other well.

JD reached Brian; his own gun drawn. He glanced at the bloody body of the blonde then to Brian, who stood with his gun held in both hands. Blood was tracing down his face from his hairline. "You okay?"

"She shot me," Brian said in disbelief.

"Give me your gun," JD's order was firm as he reached for Brian's weapon. He could see Brian was trembling.

Arriving officers, guns in hands, seeing JD with Brian, stormed by headed for the bank. Others were already inside. JD uncocked Brian's Glock automatic, set the safety and pushed it into a rear pocket. Then pulling a plastic glove from beneath his gun belt, without putting it on, he wiped the blood from Culpepper's forehead.

"Stand still," he ordered, brushing glass shards from Brian's hair. "Glass cut. Not bad. Go wait in my car. I'll get an ambulance ordered. And breathe."

Brian nodded agreement, took a final look at the bloody young girl, and turned away.

"Lady Killer," a loud accusing male voice shouted from the crowd of curious onlookers. Brian heard it, paused for a moment to look back. A chill made him shudder. He tried to spit but couldn't. His mouth was dry. He felt tired.

The crowd on the sidewalk was growing larger, moving closer, offering shouted questions and comments.

"She dead?"

"Look how young she is."

"Why'd you kill her?"

"They shot her for parking in the red?"

"Pigs, assholes!"

"Fucking lady killer!"

The number of digital cameras aimed at the cops was growing, many now live streaming to the Internet. Brian walked on, head lowered, to JD's car.

An ambulance arrived, its siren winding down as it wormed its way through the tangle of police cars jamming the street.

Two LAFD paramedics joined the army of cops around the Dodge and the bloody blonde. All wanted to see.

"Watch the gun on the pavement," JD Kent said. "And don't touch the car."

Gloved hands opened the car door as the two paramedics eyed the girl's bloody body. One reached and searched for a pulse on the girl's neck. He already knew she was dead.

The paramedic looked to his partner and shook his head. "Nothing." The shattered bloody face before them had death written all over it.

The lead paramedic glanced at his watch and wrote on a clipboard. "Time of death, 10:50 AM."

"Put out a code four," Sergeant Kent ordered a nearby officer.

"And you," he said to another sergeant arriving on the scene, "get some uniforms organized. Get the crowd moved back, both sides."

The paramedics moved to Brian who sat waiting in the front of the sergeant's car. The door was open. "Let's have a look at you."

From the sergeant's black and white, Brian could no longer see the girl, but what he had seen, and the names he had been called, were not about to be forgotten. Sensing threat, real or imagined, he felt strangely naked without his gun.

The paramedics wiped the drying blood from his face with sterile gauze. They found a cut on his scalp above the hairline, carefully finding and removing more glass shards from his hair.

"Looks like a glass cut. Bleeding has stopped. Can you stand up for us?"

Brian pushed out of the car. His hands were trembling. He tried hiding them behind his back, but the paramedics found and examined both. They patted him up and down gently, front and back, looking for wounds. "Any pain?"

"No, I, I'm okay," Brian answered, then asked, as if hoping the horror he had just seen was somehow not true. "The girl, how's the girl?"

"You wearing a vest?" one of the paramedics asked.

"Yeah."

The paramedic twisted Brian's mandated digital video camera from its mount near the center of his chest and raised it for him to see. The small video camera had been shattered by a bullet. "Guess there wouldn't be any film at eleven."

Brian moved a hand over his heart where the bullet had impacted. He had yet to feel pain from the bruise that was to follow.

"You're a lucky man," the paramedic smiled.

Brian said nothing. He didn't consider himself lucky.

Two uniformed officers approached.

"Gonzales from Metro," one announced. "Sergeant wants us to take him to the station if he's okay. If not, he goes with you."

"Superficial glass cut discovered left hairline," the paramedic pointed. "It's small and clotted. Discovered what appears to be a bullet impact center of the chest. No complaint of pain or injury. Vest and camera caught it." The paramedic offered the damaged camera. "Bullet not present. Probably at the scene somewhere."

He looked at Brian. "The choice is yours. We trans you to General for a complete exam, which we recommend, or..." He gestured to the waiting officers.

"I'll go with them," Brian said.

2 ALL THE KING'S MEN

Brian was quiet in the back seat as the two Metro officers drove away from the scene of the shooting. He knew department policy dictated he not to talk to anyone until the OIS, the Officer Involved Shooting Team, interviewed him.

The two metro officers knew the drill too. They were quiet driving the city streets to the Wilshire Area Station. Brian felt awkward in the back seat of a police car. His empty holster added to the feeling. He was surprised at the voices on the police radio coming from across the area and the city. There was a mix of male and female all sounding calm, professional, routine.

"Seven-Adam-28, see the woman, a missing person, two-one thirty-seven, West Sixth."

"Three-Adam-9, a 484 suspect, there now, the Comet Liquor, nineteen-thirty-West Adams, your call is code two."

"Seven-Adam-28, Roger."

"Seven-Adam-three-nine, a mailman is reporting strong odor coming from a residence with uncollected mail, at Fourteen-twenty-six, West Jacob Way, possible DB. Postman claims the occupant is a senior in poor health. He's waiting at the scene."

How could they not know, Brian wondered? Didn't they give a fuck? What was wrong with the world? A young woman had just been shot to death. She was all bloody and shit, and she shot at him! Nothing was normal or routine anymore.

Although Brian's shock and growing PTSD wasn't processing it, more than a third of the city's nine thousand cops and three thousand support personnel had heard, and they cared.

The world was listening too, as live streaming digital images continued from at the scene, adding thousands of viewers at first, then hundreds of thousands, and finally the compelling images went viral, beyond count.

For most of those seeing and hearing, it wasn't that they didn't care; it just wasn't personal. Most would grimace, maybe shake their heads, and go on with their day. In Los Angeles, like most major metropolitan cities in the country, cops shooting someone to death was no longer news that lasted more than a day, maybe two. For the city of Los Angeles, the shooting death of Dawn Hill was about to change all that.

At Wilshire Station, Brian, with his empty holster, solemn look, and two-man Metro cop escort, drew curious looks from the detectives in the squad room as he was escorted to an interview room.

Everyone knew who he was. He was the poor bastard who had just shot someone. Business in the busy Monday morning squad room stopped and fell quiet, except for the telephones that continued to ring unanswered. All stood silent. The days when an officer involved shooting was something to be celebrated among the ranks were long past. Now, everyone knew, Brian's life, and perhaps his career, was about to be turned into what most cops described as *a huge pile of shit.*

The interview room, usually reserved for suspects, was small, soundproofed with once-white panels on the walls, and furnished with a scarred, aging, wooden table and three padded chairs. A mirror on one wall reflected the harsh light in the room.

Brian knew it was a two-way mirror. There would soon

be unseen faces on the other side if they weren't already there. The room, although basically clean, had a lingering smell of unwashed bodies.

Brian pulled out one of the chairs and sat down. He unconsciously fingered the tear on his uniform shirt where the bullet had hit his protective vest. He was beginning to feel the bruise beneath.

"Can we get you anything?" one of the Metro cops asked, standing at the open door.

"No, I'm good," Brian said. His mouth was dry, and the words were strained.

"Well, we gotta go. You put yourself first in this," the older of the two said as he studied Brian.

"It's got a good shooting written all over it," the second officer added as they pulled the door closed. The silence that followed was heavy.

Nation Wyde, after bolting out the side door of the bank, pulled off his MAGA cap and the over-the-head vinal mask of former President Trump. He drew curious looks from those passing on the sidewalk but ignoring them he hurried on.

Nearly a block away, he deliberately slowed his walk until he spotted a trash can outside a restaurant. Several speeding police cars approached, electronic sirens yelping.

Nation's heart rose into his throat. He froze, deliberately looking at the passing police cars. Every nigger worth a fuck knew if you looked away, like you were innocent, you would get jacked up and put down hard, but the police cars roared by without slowing.

After another glance around, Nation pushed the mask, gloves, and gun deep into the trash can. He hoped his disguise in the bank worked. Hell, the videos may not even be able to establish he was a Black man, but for the moment, he was a motherfucker who was wishing he were miles away.

17

Shit, it had all gone south, and the motherfucking bank hadn't given up a dime. Rich motherfuckers. He wondered how long he had before fucking Dawn would give him up. Bitch probably already had. Fuck her. She was the one that turned it all into a fuck fest.

He had to get his ass south of the Santa Monica Freeway, back to the ghetto where a man could be among his own. Fucking police would be soon stopping every nigger downtown. A tandem city bus approached and slid to a hissing stop at the corner. An illuminated sign above the driver's front window announced *Crenshaw & Slauson*. Nation Wyde bolted for the bus.

At the First Federal bank on Wilshire Boulevard, a horde of detectives and other investigators had joined the officers at the scene. Robbery-Homicide, the Wilshire Robbery team, OIS, SID, Use of Force investigators, and more.

More being the FBI, with a team who had come from their nearby office.

They had learned of the shooting on a police radio they monitored. The FBI agents quickly lost interest when they learned of the young girl being shot to death and that the bank had not been robbed. Suffering no loss, it simply became an attempted robbery.

The scene, especially with its growing crowd filled with threats and cursing, had bad press written all over it. They promptly decided the situation all belonged to the LAPD.

"Send over copies of the reports, would you?" they asked one of the robbery teams and quickly disappeared.

Two Coroner's deputies arrived and began their grim task. After their preliminary on-scene investigation, they would take custody of the body. Before touching anything, like the now horde of investigators ahead of them, they began with multiple digital photos from every possible angle, from wide, up close, and dirty including the Dodge, as well as Brian's bullet-riddled patrol car.

Next came careful measurements, again from every angle. The handgun the girl dropped to the pavement beside the driver's door of the Dodge and the shell casings from her lap had already been collected by the LAPD OIS team.

Along with the medical report setting a time of death and probable cause, left behind by the LAFD paramedics with the gun and casings, all were laid out, displayed and photographed by the coroners' deputies.

The tempo of the swelling crowd of curious changed dramatically. Harassing and threatening uniformed police officers in the performance of their duties had somehow evolved into an acceptable predictable national practice. The allure of digital cell phones recording police procedures coupled with urban geographics were growing the crowds of curious, brought biased, aggressive, ill-willed attitudes rooted in radical, political ideals fed to them by social media, biased political broadcasts, and a collection of splinter groups claiming their freedom and liberties had been lost and threatened by all government authority. Cops, they claimed, were stealing their liberties, their guns, and all too often their lives.

They gathered quickly, like bugs around a bright light. Insults and shouts fueled the incitements. Breaking and demanding, this now regular behavior, had become a growing danger to first responders everywhere. This day it was happening at the intersection of Wilshire Boulevard and South Spaulding in the City of Angels.

A thrown bottle, arcing high, tumbling from deep in the crowd, fell smashing onto the windshield of Brian's patrol car, shattering it with a loud cracking sound. A roar of approval came from the ranks of the crowd. Soon more bottles followed. Officers scattered as they fell to the pavement, sending glass flying. A roar of approval came from the crowd.

"Get your helmets!" JD Kent shouted. The once methodical, carefully paced crime scene investigation went into a rush to get it done and get the hell out of there. More cans and bottles impacted the Dodge. The coroner's deputies and cops took cover.

Two uniformed officers hurriedly brought a wheeled gurney from the Coroner's wagon to the driver's side of the Dodge. The deputies began the awkward task of lifting the girl's dead bloody body from behind the steering wheel.

The crowd howled and booed. Another crash sounded. Flame flashed and smoke billowed into the air as one of the parked patrol cars was set aflame. Again, the crowd roared approval. Cell phones waved in the air like a swarm of large angry bugs.

The agitated crowd formed a street wide semi-circle around the band of sixteen officers and detectives. Despite orders and warnings to stay back, the sound of window glass shattering made all stand frozen. The sound was followed by ar plume of smoke reaching into the air.

A store front had been shattered. Shouts and cheers filled the air.

"Seven-William-Twenty," JD Kent barked into his hand mike. "Get LA Fire out here. patrol car and store front on fire. We need help. Advise command to call a tactical alert. Awwwww!..." JD cried. A glass bottle hit his shoulder, breaking, splattering him with hot sauce and rice. "Sono-fabitch," he said with his mike still keyed. Again, the crowd's approval filled the air.

Four helmeted officers, armed with batons, surrounded the cowering Coroner's deputies who now had the covered body of the girl belted on the wheeled gurney. The four-some pushed through the crowd of curious, angry, shouting, insulting, young and old, to the waiting Coroner's van. Reaching it they found the rear doors of the gray nonde-script van had been pulled open and the inside looted.

Sheets, masks, plastic gloves, and an assortment of papers, along with a second gurney lay in the street. All were ignored as the body was lifted and pushed inside. A brick clanged as it bounced off the side of the van. Once the body was inside, the two deputies scrambled in, turned on emergency lights and drove slowly, pushing the van through the mob, fists hammering side panels and windows as it moved away.

The van escaped the crush and sped away. A r brick tumbled through the air. It struck one of the officers, hitting him between his helmet and neck. He went down hard. The crowd roared. Fire truck sirens yelped in the distance along with more police cars.

Deputy District Attorney Pamela Moss was in her office on the sixteenth floor of the LA County courthouse. A half-eaten sandwich, a Diet Coke and a collection of papers and open law books cluttered her desk. She was cramming for an argument over admissible evidence scheduled for an afternoon appearance in department one-oh-six.

A muscular tattooed biker with a shaved head would be sitting there brooding and awaiting the continuation of his trial for the rape of his third wife's fourteen-year-old daughter. Earlier in the day, when Pamela first arrived in the courtroom, the shaved head was already sitting hand-cuffed at the defense table inside the bar.

Two uniformed armed county marshals stood some distance away near a closed-door masking holding cells. They were the only four in the quiet courtroom. Pamela had long ago learned to arrive first and leave last. A tactic she'd picked up at UCLA's School of Law—not from a professor, but from a graying Black woman who cleaned classrooms.

Pamela had lingered to finish copying notes from a large whiteboard. The woman was already at work with a broom and a trash cart at the back of the room. "Try it. First in, last out." The woman smiled at Pamela. "You may just find you like it."

The tactic became a practice for Pamela but entering the courtroom this morning, the consequence had proving different. The two marshals who had brought the biker into the room, both recognized her and paid little attention as they continued with their conversation.

It was different for the Bald handcuffed biker. He turned, watched as Pamela approached carrying her armload of books, cellphone, a briefcase, and a Starbucks coffee. She was dressed in a black jacket, a matching above the knee skirt and heels. Her shoulder-length brunette hair was pulled into a twist and pinned behind her head. She had put careful effort into looking good, but as always, stopped short of any attempt to look too good. Courtroom rule number one for women.

She caught a menacing look from the biker as she pushed through the bar to reach the prosecutor's desk.

"Hey, sweet cheeks," the biker whispered so the marshals would not hear. "You wanna come over here and suck my cock?"

Pamela stopped, shocked. She stared at the man for a moment in disbelief, then asked, "What did you say?"

The biker smiled, looked away. "I didn't say nothing."

Pamela moved, dumped her burden of items onto her desk across from where the handcuffed biker sat. She gathered her cell phone and turned to the man, stepping closer, pushing it at his face. "Say it again," she ordered. "My sisters on the line. We both heard you. And it's recorded."

The heavy muscular biker grimaced, twisting his chair away from Pamela. It screeched loud on the floor in the quiet courtroom.

"Hey, everything okay over there?" one of the marshals called. They were both looking, evaluating.

Pamela offered them a smile. "All's good," she assured. Then in a softer, lower, tone, meant only for the biker's ears, she leaned closer to the back of his neck. "I look forward to playing this for the jury. Sure, you don't want to add anything else?"

The biker didn't answer.

Somehow Pamela's hour-long noon recess had transformed itself into a now fading 15 minutes, most of which would be consumed by a bathroom break and a grooming checkup. Asking for a comfort break during trial was against everyone's policy but the defense.

She was clearing her desk when John Harps, another deputy district attorney stepped into the open door to her office. He leaned a shoulder on the door frame. He was a handsome single man, a bit older than Pamela, and constantly trying to charm her into accepting an invitation to dinner. Pamela's relationship with Brian Culpepper, an LAPD cop, was something she and Brian had both decided to keep low profile and discreet. There were no policy prohibitions on either side of their professions and departments, but there was just something about a cop and a deputy DA dating.

"Hey, working girl," Harps called from the doorway. "You hear what's going on down on Wilshire?" He was eating an apple.

Pamela granted him a quick glance then resumed jamming papers into the briefcase on her desk. "Tell me, Johnny Appleseed, what have you heard while I've been in here preparing to defend our city against the forces of darkness?"

"You know what they say," Harps said, crunching another bit from his apple. "You can always ask someone else." He stepped to move away.

"Okay, okay," Pamela called. "I'm sorry. What's going down on Wilshire?" She knew portions of Wilshire were part of Brian's beat, but Harps had no need to know why she was curious.

"Police shooting and rioting," Harps said, pausing in the doorway. "They're still fighting fires. Channel 5 is carrying it. It's all over the net. Shocking, huh?" He added sarcastically, "Means we're going to get a wave of criminal complaints coming our way."

Pamela was concerned. She knew Brian's taste for adventure and his devotion to duty would have him at the scene whether called there or not. "That's unfortunate," she said, granting Harps a quick smile as she gathered her briefcase from the desktop. "Riot or not, I've got a rapist waiting on me in one-oh-six."

She had already decided to go to a restroom down the hall and make a call to Brian's cellphone. She wanted to make sure he was safe.

"After you send this biker to the joint, you want to allow me to buy you dinner?" Harps queried.

Briefcase in hand Pamela moved for the door. "Think of the money I'm saving you by saying maybe someday."

Harps nodded, tossed his apple in a skilled basketball-like style to land perfectly in the trashcan beside Pamela's desk. "You not married, are you?"

"Not yet," Pamela said as she pushed by him.

Alone in the quiet employee restroom, Pamela sat her briefcase on a countertop and pulled her cell phone from a pocket on her suit jacket. She had Brian's number on speed dial. She punched the number and moved the phone to her ear.

Seventeen city blocks away a cell phone, laying on the vacant front seat of LAPD patrol car 33982, signed out by P-3, Officer Brian Culpepper, at 0750 hours, began to vibrate. The unanswered vibrating cell phone would soon be enveloped in fire. A flaming open can of paint from a nearby looted hardware store had been tossed into the car's back seat. It was one of the two police cars that would be burned, and it was thirty-eight seconds from having its near full gas tank explode which would result in the destruction of the car and everything in it, but Deputy District Attorney Pamela Moss had no way of knowing.

"You've reached, Brian Culpepper," a recorded message said in Pamela's ear. "I can't take your call right now. Leave a message at the tone and I'll return your call as soon as possible." His voice made Pamela smile. How professional she thought. An electronic beep sounded. "Brian, it's Pamela. I heard what's going on. I'm concerned.. I'll be in one-oh-six until we recess about four. When you get a chance, call me Kisses, bye."

Detectives Mark Connelly and Steward Baxter from the OIS, the Officer Involved Shooting Team, had been with Officer Brian in the interview room of the Wilshire Area

Detective squad room for nearly three hours. Brian had been escorted on a bathroom break and provided a Diet Coke. He was nervous, but candid, and seemingly in control of the truth.

The two detectives, older by at least a decade, had gone over the details of the shooting with Brian time and time again, looking, searching for inconsistences, minute details, facts, not as Brian represented them, but proven facts they had found with their investigation at the scene.

The physical evidence they collected told a story that could not be denied, they told Brian none of the conclusions they had made. They weren't there to talk with him, they were there to listen to him talk. When the interview began, Brian was told it would be recorded, audio and video. He was also advised departmental policy dictated as a sworn LAPD police officer he had no right to remain silent. In the performance of his duties, he had used his gun to take a human life. If he claimed a right not to talk and remain silent, he would immediately be suspended without pay and ordered to surrender his badge and gun.

During the interview, Brian tried to read Detective Baxter's notes, which from where he sat across the table made for little success. Baxter and Connelly seemed to be playing good cop, bad cop with him and although he knew it, it was proving effective. It was Connelly who had escorted him to the bathroom, bought the Diet Coke, and made small talk about a dog he had just bought for his two kids. Back in the interview room Baxter pressed for details while Brian, without realizing it, was now looking to Connelly every time he answered.

"So," Baxter said after pausing to review his notes, "one more time. What did the girl say after you pulled alongside her?"

Brian knew he had already answered the same question several times. He was careful to word his answer the same as before. "She didn't speak." He looked at both men to impress his candor. "She just sat, staring straight ahead. My front window was down. I called to her, I don't remember

25

my exact words, but it was something like, that's a red zone. If you're waiting on someone, drive around the block."

"Did she move the car?"

"No."

"What did she say?"

Brian shifted in his chair. He sat with one hand resting on the table. His fingers curled shut as he spoke. Baxter made a note of it. "She never said anything. After I spoke to her, she started screaming, stared straight ahead, and then she turned, looked at me, raised the pistol and fired."

"How many shots were fired?" Again, it was Baxter asking.

"I don't remember."

"An estimate?"

"More than one."

"What was she shooting at?"

"Me. I saw the muzzle flash, heard things breaking in my car. I suppose I ducked; I don't know. I grabbed my Glock, aimed, and fired."

"How many shots did you fire?" Connelly asked.

"Three."

"How many hit her?" Baxter pressed.

"I don't know."

"Why did you shoot this woman, Officer?"

Brian wet his lips before he spoke. The fingers on the table tightened even more. "I was in uniform, in a patrol car. She fired a gun at me. I felt, no, I knew my life was in danger, as well as of others in passing cars and on the sidewalks. I shot her to protect myself and others."

Baxter granted a nod and flipped his notebook shut. He exchanged a look with Connelly and straightened in his chair before his eyes returned to Brian. "Do you have anything else to add?"

Brian pulled his hand from the table. He sat silent for a moment before answering. Then he exchanged a sober look with both men. "I wish it hadn't happened."

Baxter nodded acceptance, pushed out of his chair to gather his jacket from the back of it. The move implied it was over. Brian watched as they prepared to leave. He was uncertain what was next. It was Connelly who spoke.

"We'll submit the results of our investigation to the Shooting Review Board. They'll decide within the next week to ten days. You'll be summoned to the Board for the decision. Until then we suggest you treat the matter as confidential. That works best for all concerned. You will be placed on administrative duty. I'd guess the front desk, equipment survey; it's up to your watch commander."

Brian pushed to his feet, wiping his damp palm on a uniformed trouser leg. He intentionally extended his hand across the table, first to Baxter. "Thank you."

Baxter took his hand. It was a firm exchange.

"What becomes of my gun?" Brian asked.

Baxter evaded a direct answer. "It will be admitted as evidence as part of the investigation until the Board makes their decision. Until then, borrow one, buy one; you still have a badge."

Brian nodded and looked to Connelly, then extended a hand. Connelly granted a sober fleeting smile as they shook. "Thank you for your candor, Brian. Truth always finds its way."

It was over. The two detectives stepped out of the room and walked away, leaving the interview room door open. An announcement to all the interview by OIS was over. Brian sank into his chair. He felt weary and uncertain, but he decided to get up, get out, breathe, shake it off, and get clean. He pushed out of his chair and unbuckled his gun belt with its empty holster. He slung it over his shoulder. It was as if, somehow, the empty holster was announcing to the world that he was the shooter. He was the one who had shot and killed a girl. It didn't matter that she had shot at him. He knew when the shooting was discussed, and it would be, talked about, analyzed, criticized, by every cop in LA, plus the world. Brian Culpepper would be the shooter. He was the one the crowd called the Lady Killer.

Emerging from the interrogation room, Brian found the detective squad room quiet. The desks lining the room, most with computer screens, sat empty. A single team, jackets off, sat at a computer, engrossed, reading data on the screen. If they noticed Brian they didn't react. He was glad. He glanced at his watch. It was nearly five PM. He headed for a hallway exit.

Brian's plan was simple. He'd go to the locker room, change into civies, and get the hell out of there. It was as if some shadow was haunting him, following him. He looked forward to the isolation his apartment could offer. He would go there, call Pamela, shower, and eat something . He wasn't sure what he would tell Pam, if he told her anything. Did she know? How would she? The department would insulate him from the media. They would provide details of the shooting, but they would not reveal the *shooter's* name.

The station was active. PM watch was now on duty. It was comforting for him to see something normal. Brian reached for his cellphone as he walked the station's rear hallway toward the employee locker room. He reached for the pocket on his trouser leg where he normally carried his cell phone. It was empty. It had to be in his patrol car. He remembered laying it atop the front seat. He moved toward the locker room as two cops from the PM watch approached, escorting a handcuffed young Hispanic. Brian nodded to them as they passed. Their faces were familiar but he didn't know their names. "Hey," one of the officers called, pausing momentarily with their arrestee to glance back at Brian. "Aren't you Culpepper?"

Brian slowed his walk looked over his should, acknowledging the question with a nod.

"You're the shooter," the officer announced with a smile, , "the lady killer." It was if he were looking at a celebrity.

3 TRUTH OR CONSEQUENCES

Brian pushed open the door to the locker room. The voices and faces exploded as if it were a surprise party, and for Brian it was. There were seven of them waiting. Jim Wilder, his patrol partner and friend, Sergeant JD Kent, their field supervisor, Clark Kent, his partner, Meat Ball. Josh Davis, Phil Kramer, and David Ross, better known as Doc. Ross had been a medic in the Navy. They cheered, patted Brian on both shoulders, shook his hand. "You're the man! Look at you, dude. A mere scratch. It's quick draw Culpepper, the Lady Killer."

They gave him no choice. They had waited on him after they were EOW—End of Watch—and Brian knew it. The day had been shocking, long, painful difficult, and somehow lonely, but now, in the midst of these men, if only for the moment, it faded.

They were more than friends, or partners, or someone you knew at work, they were kindred spirits, they were cops. Although now dressed in an assortment of less than stylish casual civilian attire masking their profession. "OIS treat you like shit?" Wilder asked. "I hear Baxter is a real piece prick."

"You were in there all afternoon. Did they feed you?" Meatball questioned.

"Yeah," Brian said.

29

"Well, I'm freaking starving," Wilder announced. "How about I pick up some nachos supreme down at that Mexican dump on seventh and come over to your place?" he said to Brian.

"I'm not really hungry, dude," Brian said with a smile.

"Like we give a shit," Wilder said. "I'll eat yours too."

"My wife likes Taco Bell," Meatball announced. No one seemed impressed.

Brian looked to Sergeant JD Kent. "Someone bring my shop in?" Their police cars all had an inventory control number, assigned for tracking vehicle's service and mainte- nance. Cops called them *shop numbers*.

JD shook his head. "Sorry. Your car got torched."

"My cellphone was in the car," Brian was shocked. "They burned it?"

"Seven-Adam-sixty-three, lost theirs, too," JD said.

"We went on tactical alert after you left. Two police cars burned. Four businesses with broken windows. Seven arrests."

"Arrests," Wilder mocked. "I thought looting was the new national pastime."

"They looted the ladies' wear shop couple doors down from the bank," Doc added. "Took the two good looking mannequins wearing lace panties they had in their front window."

"Those bastards," Wilder snarled. "I got a hard on every time I drove by there."

Ignoring Wilder, Clark Kent said, "City will buy you a new phone. They got insurance."

"Bastards," Brian muttered, remembering the agitated angry crowd. "That was my only phone."

"You wanna take mine?" Wilder offered. "I'll get it back when I come over."

"I don't know any of my numbers," Brian said. "When someone called, I just press save."

"Yeah, life's a bitch," Wilder said. "You survive getting shot dead by a forty-five, and you wanna bitch about losing your cellphone."

Brian offered an open palm to Wilder. Wilder placed his cell phone in it. "Be there about seven. Old lady's working PMs tonight." They all knew Wilder was married to an LA County deputy sheriff assigned to the county jail. "I gotta feed the dogs and then it's beaner delight."

The small talk faded as most finished putting on shoes and shirts, stuffed off-duty guns beneath their shirts, bitched about the Lakers, the weather, and the ever-increasing price of beer.

All called out a shout to Brian as a goodnight before they disappeared out the door.

JD Kent followed Brian to his locker. "You okay?"

Brian could see from the sergeant's face it was a serious question. He reached to his hairline and the glass cut that was now barely irritated. He nodded. "Yeah, I'm good. Vest saved me." Brian took off his soiled, torn shirt and vest to hang them in his locker.

"Had a near miss when I was working Seventy Seventh," JD offered, leaning a shoulder on the row of tall lockers. "Found a bullet hole in the sleeve of my shirt after a three-ninety decided to empty his gun at our car when we pulled up on him. We had to kill him."

Brian nodded. Lifting a .32-caliber automatic from his locker, he pushed the off-duty gun into his beltline. The feel of the gun was comforting, reassuring, as if his role as a cop was restored.

"Point is," JD continued, "I didn't get hit, but it still hurt. You know what I mean?"

Brian's eyes found JD's. "Yeah, I know what you mean."

JD patted Brian on the shoulder and moved away.

The air in the station parking lot felt cool and crisp beneath a layer of clouds. The evening's gathering darkness had brought on the collection of intense flood lamps. Rain, Brian guessed. He welcomed it as he walked to his waiting black 4-wheel drive GMC pickup. Big, dirty, mud-covered tires made the truck set higher than most. Brian reached up, opened a door, and clambered in behind the wheel. Getting further and further from the shooting was reinvigorating him. The idea his neighbors at Rock Mount Apartments would know nothing of his day and he knew nothing of theirs was a welcome thought. He offered a wave to the PM watch officer assigned to the parking lot gate as he drove out.

It was 17 miles from Wilshire Area Police station in downtown metropolitan Los Angeles to Brian's apartment near Venice Beach. It was often a crowded slow tedious drive, but Brian argued to all—*It's worth it.*

His apartment complex was eight blocks from the beach and once you were at the Venice beach, well it was quintessential iconic California. Bronzed suntanned bodies in string bikinis, sandy beaches, and the ocean.

Venice Beach was always crowded, which was part of the allure. Easy to get lost in. There, Brian Culpepper enjoyed riding his bike down to the beach at night to walk to the water's edge. There, he would listen to the gentle slap of the waves while feeling and tasting the air and counting stars that seemed to reach down to touch the sea.

Thinking about it, Brian considered going down to the beach. Maybe, he thought, he'd invite Pamela. She loved the beach as much as he did. He didn't have her telephone number. It had been lost with his cellphone, but he knew the District Attorneys' office had a 24/7 Deputy DA on duty. The DA deputies were available for questions about the law, assistance with drafting search warrants or any assistance a field cop or detective might need in the performance of his duties. Brian would simply call the duty deputy and ask him to have Deputy District Attorney Pamela Moss call him on the cellphone borrowed from Wilder. It would seem businesslike to the deputy.

Without giving the matter much thought Brian had decided he wasn't going to tell Pamela he had shot and killed a woman. Actually he had to confess, he hadn't shot a woman, he had shot a girl. He realized he better tell Pamela, but it wasn't going to be tonight.

Maybe, he thought, wheeling his pickup into the gated basement garage of his apartment complex, Pamela may not want to venture out. He knew during a jury trial she could be, and had been in the past, all work, and no play.

The inner court of the Rock Mount Apartment complex was illuminated with dancing reflective light from its sprawling pool. The tropical plants rimming the decking were masked in heavy shadow. Brian emerged from the stairs near the shallow end of the pool. Lights from the apartments in the three-story complex helped erase the darkness. It was a warm night and with windows open the faint sound of music and television voices drifted over the courtyard. Brian felt better as he rounded the pool to his first story apartment. Reaching his door Brian pushed in a key. As he turned it the door swung open. It was unlocked. Shocked, he stepped into the open door. Deputy District Attorney Pamela Moss was standing, pen in hand, at a countertop divider that separated the kitchen from living room. She looked to Brian, sharing his surprise. She dropped her pen and hurried to him, throwing her arms around his neck. Brian's arms encircled her. They kissed before she spoke. "I was leaving you a note. Remember that thing Alexander Graham Bell invented, called a telephone? I called you three times. I was worried. Why didn't you call me?"

"I'm sorry. I lost my cell." Brian kissed her forehead. He was feeling a wave of relief. The woman he loved was in front of him. He could feel her body against his. The press of her breasts against his chest. Her legs pushed to his. Brian snaked a cell phone out of his pocket, held it up. "Borrowed this from Wilder. I was going to call the duty deputy to get your number."

"You don't know my number?"

"Your number is ten."

Pamela smiled, kissed him again before looking into his eyes. "I heard what happened down on Wilshire. You, okay?"

Brian wondered how much she had heard. Did she know he was the shooter? Did she know he had killed a girl? He decided to cover it. "Can we talk about it tomorrow. It's been a long day."

Pamela nodded agreement. "Same for me. I've been here almost an hour. I was writing you a note. I've got court at eight in the morning."

"Do you want to stay? Wilder is bringing Mexican food."

"Sounds good," Pamela agreed pulling away from him to gather her purse from the countertop divider. "But so does winning my case."

"You won an award by driving over here tonight," Brian said.

"What's my award?"

Brian answered with a smug smile as Pamela moved for the open door.

"We'll see." She smiled.

"Wait I don't have your number."

Pamela paused in the doorway. Brian moved to her. She kissed him on the cheek and was out the door. "Call the duty deputy," she called over her shoulder. "And throw my note away."

"Love you," he called after her. The echo of her heels clicking on the decking was his only answer. Brian closed the door.

———————————

Brian Culpepper was not the only cop having a long day. The FBI may have shrugged and said, "Send us copies," to the detectives from RHD, Robbery-Homicide-Division, responding to the shooting and attempted robbery on Wilshire Boulevard, but with one dead as the result of the OIS, Officer Involved Shooting, they were taking it very seriously. The death of the girl and the resulting civil unrest told all concerned there could be no loose ends. A six-man bank team was now well into the night searching for Nathaniel Wyde. It was in every sense of the word, a

Nation-Wide search. Forty minutes after they arrived at the bank on Wilshire Boulevard a technician from Latent Prints identified prints lifted from the stolen red dodge. They belonged to Nathaniel Wyde. The discovery of the prints was reinforced with CCTV images from eight cameras from retail shops lining south Spaulding. The detectives laughed hard when they watched the video images of former President Donald Trump emerge from the bank and run south on Spaulding. When Nation Wyde finally paused and pulled off his over the head mask his identity was no longer in question. The hunt began.

Armed with a collection of addresses, photos, and the names of relatives, the six-man robbery team began kicking in doors in LA's ghetto. Nation Wyde narrowly escaped arrest walking toward his grandmother's house on West Fifty-Eight street. He was a short half-block away when three unmarked police cars pulled to an abrupt stop. He watched in stunned silence as six white men stormed up the steps. "You better get you Black ass outta here, Boy," a graying stooped neighbor with a can warned as he labored past Nation in the shadows. Nation turned and hurried away. He was to spend the night sleeping in an abandoned car.

Brian went to the note Pamela left on his kitchen counter. He read it carefully, several times.

Brian,

I waited here for over an hour. Where are you? I'm worried. You haven't answered my calls. I love you, but if we are to have a future it must be me first, cops second. Call me.

Love - Pam

After reading the note Brian folded it carefully and slipped it into a time worn Bible he kept in a bedside night-stand. The Bible, a childhood gift from his grandmother, brought a rush of memories, doubts and anxiety. *Truth may not always seem the answer*, his grandmother's knurled hand had written on an inside cover, *but anything else is a lie. Don't lie.*

Brian agreed with what he had read. The truth he had been dealt this day, truth he had to tell time and time again had been more than painful. It had morphed into a blanket of oppression that was beginning to haunt his every moment. His doorbell sounded. He welcomed it. He pushed the Bible back in the nightstand. Did real cops need a Bible to prop them up? He thought not. The doorbell sounded a second time. Maybe Pam had second thoughts and returned. He glanced at his wristwatch. It was twenty after seven. Wilder and his Mexican food Brian concluded. Not only food but booze. Wilder would be bringing a six pack. He never went anywhere without it. He moved for the door.

Crossing to the door Brian smiled. There seemed to be an unwritten law among cops when they drank. The talk could be candid and open, and once the drinking was over it was never mentioned again—unless brought up by the individual who mentioned it in the first place. As he reached for the doorknob, he hoped Wilder had brought two six packs.

Brian opened the door without hesitation. "It's unlocked," he said and then fell silent. His first emotion was shock., and then he felt foolish, because he'd been so certain who he'd find outside the door. Brian knew who the man was. He didn't understand how he knew, but he knew. He was surprised he felt so little fear. He wished he could think of something to say. He could not. He just stared.

The man who stood outside the open door was in his mid-forties. His hair was matted with the rain that was now falling. His glasses were dotted with droplets of water. Brian couldn't tell if the man was weeping or not. His white shirt wet with rainwater was clinging to his shoulders. He held a blue steel .45 caliber automatic pistol aimed at Brian's chest in a trembling hand. The heavy pistol was cocked. "I... I've come to kill you," the man said, wiping water from his chin.

Brian said nothing. His teeth were clamped tight. He held the door and stared.

"I was at my shop today when they came to tell me," the man continued. "They said she was dead. Shot and killed by the police. My little girl," he sobbed. The pistol wobbled in his hand. "I saw it all on the internet. She was all bloody. They said the cop that shot her was named Culpepper. You know you're on the internet, Culpepper?"

Brian remained silent. Tears were welling in his eyes.

"She was going to come see us next weekend," the man added. "Did you know that?"

"No, sir," Brian answered meekly. The rain was heavier now, slapping the smooth deck in the courtyard and dancing on the surface of the lighted pool.

"What did you know about her?" the man demanded. "You killed her. What did you know?"

Wilder was driving, squinting at the rain-covered windshield of his Jeep as a less than effective wiper swept back and forth leaving blurred streaks behind. "What's the lyric?" he asked with a glance at Clark Kent sitting on the passenger's side. "It never rains in California?"

"There it is," Clark Kent said pointing.

Wilder nodded, wheeled the Jeep down into the basement garage of the Rock Mount apartment complex.

"Why the hell aren't you older?" the dead girl's father growled. "Goddamnit, why aren't you older?"

Brian didn't answer. He wished the man would lower the gun and come in out of the rain. The man didn't hate him, and Brian knew that. The man wanted to, but he couldn't. He was doing what he had to do, and Brian understood that.

"You know," the man said, "Dawn was never disrespectful to me or her mother. Never." Rain was running down his face to drop from his chin. He switched the gun from one hand to the other. "She was a good kid. No matter what happened, she was a good kid."

"Goddamned rain," Wilder complained as he and Clark Kent emerged from the lighted dry stairway into the shower wetting the inner court.

"Do you know how old she was?" the man with the gun demanded.

"No, sir, I don't," Brian answered.

"Jesus Christ!" Wilder blurted as he and Clark Kent rounded a wide leafed tropical plant to find the man, gun in hand, aimed at Brian just ahead of them. Wilder dropped the bag of Mexican food and grabbed the Glock automatic carried in his waistband.

The man with the .45 aimed at Brian heard Wilder shout, "Drop the gun."

The command reverberated in the courtyard's hardened wetness. Wilder raised his gun, going into a two-handed squat combat stance.

"Don't!" Brian shouted.

The rain-soaked man seemed confused, shocked. He looked at Wilder, then to Brian.

Clark Kent tossed the sack of six packs he carried. The beer cans thudded against the cement decking. Clark Kent grabbed for his gun.

"Drop it!" Wilder screamed even louder this time. A female wearing a bathing suit opened the door of the apartment next to Brian.

"Don't move," Brian pleaded, reaching out toward the man.

The man looked to Brian. Water traced from his hair

down over his face. He raised a hand to wipe at it. He squinted through his fogging glasses. A volley of shots filled the courtyard with sharp explosions. The man wheeled, arms flailing he dropped the gun. He clutched his punctured abdomen and staggered, with a drunken gait, away from Brian's doorway. A scream came from the bathing suit in the doorway.

Wilder and Clark Kent stood, guns poised, watching. Brian stepped from the doorway, mouth open in disbelief, arms reaching. The man moved away; arms wrapped around his abdomen as if to hold the heavy flow of blood inside him. He turned, nearly fell, staggering toward the pool.

"No!" Brian shouted. He bolted for the man., but before he could reach him the man stepped over the lip of the pool and fell with a heavy face-smacking splash into the illuminated blue water. A crimson cloud billowed out around him as he sank unmoving, lifeless, toward the bottom.

Brian splashed into the water seconds behind the man. Wilder tossed his gun and dove in after them.

Clark Kent pushed his off-duty gun into his waistband and knelt on the wet decking to reach for the limp blood-stained form as Wilder and Brian pushed him to the surface.

Kent grabbed a wet collar and pulled. "I got him," he said, pushing a hand under an armpit and lifting. He struggled to get the bleeding form up onto the deck. A shoe came off and floated away.

Breathless and soaked, Wilder and Brian climbed out. The courtyard was beginning to fill with the bold and the curious on all three levels of the complex. Brian knelt beside the man. He could see he was dead. His mouth and eyes were open. Blood gurgled from his mouth and ran down his neck. His pupils were large, dark.

Wilder fell onto his back beside them. He was choking and gagging. "Sonofabitch," he gasped; water poured from him to mix with the man's blood.

The curious were staying well back, pointing, peering, talking as they gained courage. "Hey, what the hell are you doing?" a male voice called as the cellphone cameras began to appear everywhere. "We're calling the police," a female voice warned.

"You dumb fuck," Clark Kent barked at Wilde as he offered him the gun he had dropped. "You know you can't swim."

Brian sat down beside the dead man, drew up his knees and lowered his head. The sound of an electronic siren yelped in the distance.

The rain finally ended about eleven, but by then everyone was soaked. Investigating a murder outdoors was always a challenge. Investigating one on a rainy night was a special misery. The side of the court around Brian's apartment and the now covered body was cordoned off with yellow police line tape, and several uniformed officers stood guard keeping the crowd away from the scene.

Several television crews had arrived and were waiting with the crowd, shooting filler from those claiming to know what happened. Wilder and Clark Kent had been transported away from the scene. Both men were to spend most of their night with OIS, the Officer Involved Shooting team. Brian was more fortunate. He was interrogated in his own apartment. It was both good news and bad that again, the two detectives interviewing him were Collins and Baxter. As they talked, the cellphone Brian had borrowed from Wilder vibrated and danced on an end table. Brian looked at the caller ID. It was Pamela Moss calling. Brian decided not to answer. He didn't know what he could or would say. It was one-thirty when it ended.

Brian turned out all the lights after the two detectives left. He took the Bible from his nightstand and clutched it to his chest. He didn't know why; he just did it. He remembered taking off his wet clothes in the bathroom to put on jeans and a T-Shirt. He remembered some of the questions the detectives had asked but he couldn't remember his answers. It didn't matter, he didn't care. He was numb and beyond hurting. He glanced at an illuminated bedside clock. It was ten minutes to two AM. "Damnit, he was five hours from day watch roll call. The cellphone lay waiting beside the clock. He considered calling Pamela and decided against it. She had a trial waiting for her in the morning and he was still uncertain what he would say to her. He wondered what sane people were doing—sane people were in bed. Brian Culpepper was not.

He sat in the dark room, uncertain if he'd ever sleep again, fearful he'd see the man's rain-streaked, frightened face. He had been looking into the man's eyes when the bullets ripped through him. The last thing the man was to see in his life was Brian's face. He tried to force the thought from his mind. People ruled their own lives. The man's misery was his own choice. Brian tried convincing himself he was not an evil man. He'd always tried to do what was right. Someday. Somehow, he would. A siren wailed far in the distance. Brian listened. It faded. Brian wished he were at work. There he wasn't alone. There he wouldn't have to sleep or sit in the darkness holding a Bible.

41

4 YOU CAN RUN, BUT YOU
CAN'T HIDE

Deputy District Attorney Pamela Moss sat on a bar stool at the counter dividing the kitchen from the living room in her west LA condo. Dressed in a terrycloth robe she was dividing her attention between a bottle of nail polish, a trial transcript, and morning talk radio. It wasn't likely the jury would ever see her toenails, but it added to her overall sense of being well groomed. Grooming was an important factor in manipulating juror opinion. When Brian didn't call, she concluded that Wilder's visit had turned into late night bar hopping along the strip in Venice Beach. She knew he would call. She hoped it would be before she left for court.

Jury summation was all that remained in the three-week trial of the shaved head biker for forcible rape of a twelve-year-old. Now, with her closing argument ready she was being careful with her personal appearance. Beauty, as Pamela had found, brought privilege and attention, but in front of a jury there was a fine line between being a confident well-groomed prosecutor and a sexy overly ambitious know it all. Pamela was determined to be the former. Thus, she would wear a heavier bra than usual. Nipples, for reasons that escaped her, made jurors uncomfortable. Perhaps it was the formality of the courtroom where sex allegedly didn't exist.

Whatever, this day she would strive for a nipple-less

girl-next-door look. Skirt below the knee. Modest blouse with a jacket. Low heels. Moderate makeup, hair pulled back and just a hint of Chanel. When she was done, the jury would think they'd just bought a box of girl scout cookies.

Pamela's attention was fully on her toenails until the voice on the radio sitting on the counter mentioned late-night police shooting in Venice Beach. She paused, turned up the volume on the radio.

Reliable sources report the man shot to death by off-duty LAPD officers, at the Rock Mount apartments in Venice Beach, was in fact the father of the girl shot to death on Wilshire Boulevard yesterday afternoon. Police in Fresno are reporting the dead man's wife, the mother of the girl shot by Los Angeles police, hung herself just several hours after being informed of her husband's death. Police here in Los Angeles are refusing comment. In other news...

Pamela was stunned. She switched off the radio. Now she knew why Brian hadn't called. What could have happened? The father of the girl shot to death! Her mother found dead. My God, what hadn't he told her? A mix of disappointment and confusion flooded her mind. Her heart raced. Maybe Wilder was the answer. That would explain Brian not calling. She fought an urge to call him. Was he alright? No, the report on the radio had said nothing about officers being injured. Damnit, why wouldn't he call? Be patient, he'll call. There was good reason he hadn't. The price of dating a cop, Pamela concluded, screwing the cap on her nail polish. They had been dating seven months. Was it serious if you counted the months? The thought made her smile. It wasn't intense dating; neither of their schedules permitted that, but what their relationship lacked in quantity it seemed to have in quality. Although she had once vowed she'd never date a cop, Brian made her forget the promise. Ego, as it was with most cops, didn't seem a problem with Brian. She remembered what her mother often said, "Who, is much more important than what."

Perhaps Mom was right. Pamela had found a common bond with this man. It seemed they were kindred spirits on a similar path. She was comfortable with Brian Culpepper, relieved he wanted more than sex, although their sex had proven to be more satisfying than she anticipated. She dropped her polished toenails to the floor. It was time to dress. She wondered what color the men on the jury would prefer. She picked up her cellphone as she moved for her bedroom. Maybe he'd call.

Sleep was evasive, troubling, and Brian used it as an excuse to leave early for the station. He was relieved to find the decking outside his door and the pool water were now free of blood stains. The investigation into the shooting by RHD and OIS had gone on most of the night, followed by a cleanup crew using what sounded like high pressure hoses. His interview had lasted over two hours. He knew they would want more. Brian was glad to drive away from it. He wondered what his neighbors thought. Did they now know he was a cop? They did now? What would that mean? Might mean a new apartment. Could he, would he, ever be able to forget what had happened outside his door. The answer was no. Maybe it would be an excuse to move in with Pamela. They had traded sleepover nights. Was it time to consider something more? What would it mean to their relationship? Brian made himself a promise to call her after morning roll call.

The locker room was alive with half naked men as day watch made their transition from civilian clothes to uniform. Brian pushed through the door and made his way to his locker, unbuttoning his shirt as he walked. He expected an onslaught of questions, certain by now the shooting death of the girl's father would be common knowledge. Officer involved shootings usually swept through the department like a wildfire. The twenty plus cops in the locker room did know, and upon hearing of it they felt much the same anguish Brian and Wilder did. At least they imagined they did. But this shooting was different, not for locker room banter or jokes.

Wilder was half naked. His open locker was next to Brian's. Brian offered a nod as he unlocked his locker. He didn't know what to say. Wilder, seeming never at a loss for words, spoke in a soft tone as if others might hear. "Talked to JD downstairs. He said the lieutenant wants you, me, and Clark Kent down at RHD by oh-nine-hundred."

Brian was puzzled. "Downtown? Why aren't they coming here?"

Wilder looked around as he buttoned his uniform shirt, then to Brian. "'Cause the press is down in the lobby. CNN, Fox, and a shit load of others. Ever since word got out about the girl's mother hanging herself."

Brian was shocked, he stared at Wilder. "What? Who hung themselves?"

"Watch my lips," Wilder challenged, leaning toward Brian. "The mother of the girl you smoked yesterday. RHD had Fresno PD go out and inform her that her old man, like her kid, had been shot and killed by the police. This morning, not more than a fucking hour ago, they call back, a relative finds the woman hanging in her bathroom. Like the bitch was fucking punishing us."

Brian said nothing. He stared into his open locker. His neck muscles tightened as his breath quickened.

"So, I'm driving in," Wilder continued, strapping on his gun belt, "and this piece of shit on the radio says, police shootings result in the death of an entire family. The prick. You'd think we caused the whole fucking thing."

Brian shook his head, looked to Wilder. "It's not fair."

"Fair! What the fuck is that?" Wilder defended. "Has something to do with weather, doesn't it?" He finished buttoning his uniform shirt. "You still got my phone?"

Brian reached into a back pocket, gathered the cellphone, and placed it in Wilder's extended palm. "You didn't look at my collection of naked pictures, did you?"

"Yeah," Brian nodded, "your dick really is tiny."

Wilder smiled, patted Brian on the shoulder and walked away buckling his gun belt.

Brian stood staring into his open locker. He dreaded more talk with RHD. What the hell else could they ask that he hadn't already told them time and time again. His thoughts turned to the woman hanging in her bathroom. Was she old, young? Attractive, ugly? Strong, weak? Whatever she was, whoever she was, Brian hated her. She was trying to hurt him the only way she could. She was the second one, he told himself. The second woman whose life he stole, as much as if he had shot her too. It wasn't fair. He wondered if she knew his name. Her husband did. She may not have known his name, but she knew who he was. She found him and hurt him. Damn her. He meant her no harm.

It didn't come in a conscious rush. It was more an unwillingness to accept the rush of painful thoughts about what lay ahead. Brian had no idea where he would go but he knew he couldn't stay. The protective cloak of being a cop was a myth. He felt shame and weakness. He had killed more than a blonde girl with no name. He had set the deadly tsunami in motion and an entire family was dead. Brian was alone and he knew it. He knew the investigation would find him blameless, but the guilt he felt was smothering. He swung his locker shut with a bang and headed for the door.

Sergeant JD Kent and Lieutenant Storm were climbing the stairs to the station's second floor roll call room when Brian, still in his off-duty clothes, passed them going down. He avoided the eyes of both men. JD Kent glanced at Brian. The lieutenant looked to JD. "He alright?"

JD looked to Storm. "I hope so."

Brian felt an ominous gloom as he drove from the station parking lot. He knew the day watch roll call would now be under way and his absence would soon be discovered. Wilder was avoiding a look at the empty space beside him where Brian usually sat. The pit of his stomach was telling him what the others would soon know. Brian was missing.

Although Brian knew the consequence of his unauthorized absence would be grave, there was no alternative. He did not belong there; he was no longer one of them. For reasons Brian Culpepper couldn't fathom he felt singled out by fate to become death's messenger. He'd been used, treated like a whore, become a pawn in a deadly game and he was determined to break free from it. Brian raced his pickup up a freeway ramp and quickly pushed the speedometer past seventy miles an hour. He had no idea where he was going. He only knew he had to go.

JD Kent and Lieutenant Storm were at the head of the roll call room. They were ten minutes into the briefing and Culpepper still hadn't returned. Storm couldn't stall any longer. He silently damned Culpepper for being stupid. He looked to the Black sergeant beside him. "Sergeant Kent," Storm said, "the assignments."

JD Kent nodded and pulled his tablet in front of him. "Alright, listen up. We've got to do a little juggling because of last night's officer involved. We're down three bodies. That's a team and a half. So, here it is." JD went through the assignments for the A cars, the two-man patrol units, followed by the desk, equipment bay and parking lot security assignments, ending it all with, "Wilder, Clark Kent, and Culpepper. The three of you report to RHD at oh-nine-hundred."

When he finished, he looked to the lieutenant. If Storm gave a nod, JD would dismiss the men and send them to work. If he did not, he would stand and call for an inspection line-up. It was part of their daily routine. Storm looked from JD to the door at the rear of the room. He was hoping Culpepper would step through the door. "Where's Culpepper?" he asked in an irritable tone.

"He's here, Lieutenant," Wilder offered. "I saw him in the locker room."

"Find him," Storm ordered.

Wilder and Clark Kent searched all over the station before moving to the parking lot. They knew what Brian drove. They separated and walked up and down the rows of private cars. They met, knowing the absence of Brian's pickup was ominous.

Wilder walked to the chunky uniformed officer standing guard at the mouth of the parkin g lot. His nick name was Milk Shake. "You see Culpepper out here?" Wilder asked.

"Yeah," Milk Shake answered without hesitation. "He drove out. Black pickup. I waved. He didn't. I thought he was going down to RHD."

"Jesus Christ," Clark Kent said joining the two. He heard what Milk Shake had said. "What's he doing? Where's he going?"

Wilder looked at the quiet street beyond the mouth of the parking lot. He was worried. "I don't know."

———————

Palm Springs was now nearly an hour behind Brian as he sped his pickup further and faster into Southern California's high desert. He was now nearly two hundred miles from the City of Angels.

The sprawling desert swept by on both sides of the divided interstate. The rolling dry hills were dotted with Joshua trees and rocks. Even with the air conditioner on, the interior of the pickup was warm. Brian's tense trapped feeling had eased some. He still had no idea where he was going but he knew the impending doom he felt was now behind him. He had escaped. Not run from it, he would never do that, he just turned away. That made it alright. It was his choice. Now all he had to do was start over.

He was wondering how he would do that when the pick-up's engine lost power. Brian pumped the accelerator beneath his foot and the engine regained its pull. His eyes went to the instruments. The gas gauge needle hung below empty. The engine sputtered again and fell silent. The speedometer fell as the car slowed. Brian checked his rear-view mirrors, then looked ahead. Nothing. No service stations, no exits, just the sprawling desert. As the pickup slowed, Brian eased it onto the sandy shoulder, damning himself for being so reckless.

Brian steered the pickup to a stop on the shoulder. You

could run but the reality of an empty gas tank could not be ignored. The warning lights on the dash glowed red. The only sound was the air conditioner's fan. Brian twisted the ignition key to off. The silence that followed was heavy. The lights on the dash were more than a warning he was out of gas. They were a warning he was going in the wrong direction. Shit, he didn't even have a phone. He glanced at his watch. More than four hours of his day watch duties were gone. He had missed the 0900 follow-up interview at RHD. Shit, they were going to fire him. He grimaced and struck the center of the steering wheel. The pickup's horn honked as if in protest. Several cars flashed by followed by a noisy eighteen-wheeler. The pickup rocked in their wake. Brian covered his face with his hands. His agony and regret were soul deep. They would think he was a coward. He had run away. He raised his face and took a deep breath. The interior of the pickup was already getting warm. He didn't know what he was going to do, but he knew running wasn't an answer. Determined to do something to salvage the mess he had made he pulled the keys and opened a door. The desert's heat swarmed around him. He didn't know what the temperature was, but it was hot. The CHP would often come by, he hoped. Brian locked the pickup; said a prayer the interstate buzzards wouldn't rape his truck. He patted the door and walked away.

The heat was overwhelming. He squinted, walking on the soft shoulder taking a glance back at the pickup. He'd find a gas station somewhere, buy some gas and somehow get back here. One step at a time. He drew in a breath. The hot dry air reached into his mouth and lungs. He walked on, looking back, hoping for traffic. Several cars were closing fast from the distance. Brian paused, stuck out a thumb. The cars were closer now. He stuck his arm and thumb out even farther. The cars flashed by without slowing. "Damnit."

Seven cars and two trucks ignored Brian's protruding thumb. His pickup was now far behind him. He had to find a gas station somewhere. Buy some gas and find a way to get back here. That would solve the immediate problem and the way you moved a mountain was one bucket of dirt at a time. The Corps had taught him that. Hell, he'd be on the road again. He could be back in LA by sunset. He'd call Wilder, talk to him about how to put things back together again before he stood himself in front of Lieutenant Storm.

Absent from duty for one day, maybe they'd just suspend him. No, they would know, they had already decided, he was a coward, but he knew he wasn't. What other cop had caused the death of an entire family? He had only shot the girl, but he was looking into her father's eyes when Wilder shot him. Hell, he didn't even know the name of the girl he had shot and killed. Her mother knew. Her husband and her daughter had been shot and killed by the police. He tried not to imagine her hanging. Somehow, he was going back and prove he wasn't a coward. Why, God, why me? Brian forced the consequence of all of it from his mind, one step at a time, but first someone had to pick him up. He checked for traffic again. A van was coming his way. Fast. Brian paused again and stuck out his thumb. Damn it was hot. His feet were beginning to feel hot, and his shirt was sticking to his back. The van was almost to him. Brian stuck out his thumb. He glanced at his watch. He'd been walking almost an hour. He was taking his time. Exertion in the heat, he knew could be a killer. The Corps had taught him that. Slow and easy was the rule. Damn it was hot. He hoped the van would stop. He was clean, nicely dressed and obviously in trouble. No one walked out here because they wanted to.

The van was a gray primer color. A chevy Brian guessed. Lowered in front. The driver had a full beard and a sweat-band on his forehead. There was a girl in the middle and a heavier clean-shaven man on the passenger's side. The van was pulling a trailer with two motorcycles strapped on it. Brian felt elation as the van pulled onto the shoulder sending up billows of dust as it approached. Brian was surprised the van wasn't slowing. It was almost to him, speeding, sending up even more dust. They were headed straight for him, smiling, laughing. Brian dove, rolling in the grainy sand and brush. The van roared by. An empty wine bottle tumbled by his face and shattered, slamming into the rocks. The driver laid on the horn. A cloud of grimy dust engulfed Brian. He covered his mouth and pushed to his feet. There was sand in one of his shoes. He watched the van fade into the distance as the dust cleared. "You bastards," Brian snarled.

He knew them. Even though he'd never seen them, and likely he'd never see them again, he knew them. He knew in the van, thick with the smell of sweat there would be a lid of marijuana, zig zag papers, an open six pack, and guns. He knew them and obviously they knew him. He wiped at the grim on his neck and walked on. The heat was beginning to worry him.

Eight cars, a Greyhound bus and six trucks swept by during the next hour. All ignored Brian's plea for a ride. Another car flashed by at near eighty miles an hour. A woman on the passenger's side was drinking something. She looked away as Brian's eyes searched for hers. He walked another three miles. His throat was parched, and his neck was burning. He heard a heavy truck approaching but didn't bother to turn around. Many had already passed. Air brakes hissed and gears meshed as the big rig downshifted. Brian turned. The cab over tractor with its fifty-three-foot trailer swept by him and pulled onto the shoulder and stopped. Brian ran alongside the trailer to the cab of the truck. He climber up and opened the cab door. The driver was an older man wearing a time worn cowboy hat. "Get in here, boy. You're gonna let all the cold out."

Brian climbed up and into the cab of the truck. The instrument ladened cab was air conditioned and its cool temperature was a welcome relief. Brian slid onto the passenger's seat and pulled the door shut. "Thanks for stopping," Brian said with a sigh and a look to the driver. The cowboy released the air brakes and pushed the truck in gear. The engine labored loud as the big truck crawled forward. The driver shifted gears again, adjusted his hat. "That your pickup, couple miles back?"

"Yeah." Brian nodded. "Ran out of gas."

"Blythe is up ahead, twenty minutes or so. They got lots of garages and gas stations. Someone will give you a ride back for a couple bucks." The cowboy nodded as he pushed the truck into an even higher gear as the big rig regained momentum. "You always carry a gun out here in the desert?"

Brian instinctively reached to touch his off-duty gun on his right waistband. He offered a smile to comfort the man. "Got a badge to go with it. LAPD."

The cowboy offered a smile in return. "Saw it when you climbed up. You're driving away from LA you know? It's a good three hundred behind us."

Brian looked at the road ahead, then the driver. "Yeah, I made a wrong turn this morning." It was a near confession.

The cowboy understood Brian's candor. "Yeah, made a couple of those myself. You like being a cop?"

Brian adjusted the air conditioning vent on the dash to aim more of the cool air at his face. "You like driving a truck?"

"Alright." The cowboy nodded acknowledgement. "So, here we are, two happy souls doing what we love, but only one of us is going in the wrong direction?"

Brian looked to the driver. His attention returned to the road ahead as if allowing him time to answer. "I figured I was going in the wrong direction a couple hours ago," Brian offered candidly.

"Yep." The cowboy hat smiled. "Done that a couple times too. Listen, got some bottled water up there in the ice chest. While you're getting yours get me one too?"

Brian parted a curtain to find the ice chest. An aroma of aftershave engulfed him from a padded mattress in the cab's bunk area. He lifted the top of the ice chest and gathered two bottles of water. Twisting the caps off he handed one the driver. Brian took three heavy swallows nearly emptying the bottle. Lowering it he looked to the cowboy. "Do you by chance have a cellphone?"

The cowboy nodded and reached down in a side pocket

of his door. His hand came up with a cellphone. He offered it to Brian. "Tell her I said hello." He smiled.

Deputy District Attorney Pamela Moss was sitting at the prosecutor's desk in department 106 deep in the heart of the LA County's Criminal Courts Building. She had come to court prepared for her summary to the jury, but the bald biker rapist had surprised her again. After the judge sat down behind his bench and called the court in session, the biker's defense attorney stood up and told the judge his client was prepared to offer a guilty plea. Pamela was pleased. She suspected her threat of telling the biker she had recorded his obscene invitation had worked. Pamela felt smug. She would tell Brian about it later. He could be trusted. The cell phone in her jacket pocket vibrated. Pamela carefully raised it to glance at the number. Spam she concluded after not recognizing it. She clicked the phone silent and released it in her pocket.

The eighteen-wheel Daimler tractor trailer, with its load of automobile tires from China had regained its cruising speed of nearly seventy-five miles an hour. Brian lowered the cellphone from his ear. He looked to the cowboy. "She's a deputy district attorney," he explained offering the phone to the driver. "Probably in court and can't answer."

The cowboy took the cellphone and returned it to the pocket on the door. "She's not the reason you're out here driving east when you work in the west?"

"No," Brian answered thinking of Pam and his situation. "She's a good woman. She doesn't even know about my shooting." Brian grimaced at his inadvertent remark.

The cowboy saw his reaction. "So that's what got you out here running eastbound until you ran out of gas."

Brian looked to the road ahead as the asphalt raced

toward them, disappearing beneath the wheels of the truck. "Not something I can talk about," he defended.

"Understand," the cowboy answered. His tone was reassuring. "You know, I had this teacher in high school. English teacher. Mrs. Goss. Big breasts," he gestured. "She said every man lives three lives. His public life, like the man you'd see on the street. Second is a man's private life. What goes on after he goes home and closes the front door. That's private. And number three, was a man's secret life. Secrets we share with no one. Mrs. Goss said we all have them, and you know what, she was right."

Brian nodded agreement.

"Like I said, probably why you're out here in God's country," the cowboy continued. "Things get covered with all the noise when you're in the middle of it. Come out here and the picture usually gets a little clearer."

"You're not going to bill me for all this free advice, are you?" Brian teased as he downed the remainder of his water.

In the heart of downtown Los Angeles, Chief of Police James Peck, a fit fifty-four-year-old with a full head of gray hair, linked to his thirty-two years of service with the LAPD, sat alone at the head of the long oval table in a conference room adjacent to his office. He was studying a voluminous city budget, highlighting points with a yellow marker when Renna Lincoln, an attractive Black uniformed policewoman entered. She was the chief's aide. The chief paused from his reading. The policewoman rounded the table, pulled out a chair near the chief and sat down. "Press relations reached out. OIC says they've had twenty-six queries regarding our missing psycho cop. They want some advice on how you want this colored."

The chief laid his marker aside and closed the budget. He laid a hand atop it. "A cop in Minneapolis chokes a man to death and that results in LA's mayor ordering us to cut eight million dollars from our budget."

The aide said nothing.

The chief pushed the thick budget away. It slid toward the center of the table before coming to rest. "This missing cop, what's his name?"

"Culpepper. Brian Culpepper," the aide answered.

"So, he shoots an armed young woman who tried to kill him, and he's called a psycho, a lady killer. Her father comes to his apartment and tries to kill him, but it's Culpepper who's the psycho. Then the dead girl's mother hangs herself, but Culpepper is still the psycho cop who caused it all. How old is this officer?"

"Twenty-eight, I believe. Four years plus on the job," the aide answered.

"We have to hope Culpepper hasn't crawled into some hole somewhere and ate his gun," the chief said. "He's running. Hell, I feel like running some days too. He may not have been shot, but we're looking for a man with a wounded heart."

The aide's polished nails drummed the polished table-top. "I talked to his watch commander at Wilshire, a Lieu-tenant Storm. He told me Culpepper showed up, but when their roll call began, he was missing. An officer on station security reported Culpepper drove out of Wilshire station just as day watch roll call was starting."

"We need to find him," the chief continued. "We don't shoot our wounded. I want him found. You make sure every badge in this city gets that message." The chief straightened in his chair, flattening his hands on the smooth tabletop. "Here's what we tell the press. The cause of this tragedy is the man that put that nineteen-year-old in front of that bank with a gun in her hand. There's the psycho we need to find."

Sergeant JD Kent, Clark Kent, Wilder and Flemming were at a table in the first-floor coffee room at Wilshire Station. End of watch was behind them and they were dressed in casual street clothes. The table was dotted with paper cups and candy wrappers from the collection of vending machines at the end of the room. They were like moths fluttering around a flame, waiting, hoping for word on Culpepper.

"He's your partner, Wilder. Who's he dating?" JD asked. "He must have talked about someone. A name, a place they may have gone?"

"Yeah," Wilder granted looking up from his cup, "I know he likes girls. I talk about what Shirl and I got going. He's talked about a skirt named Pam, no, Pamela. Said they went out to the desert once, a concert at the Hollywood Bowl."

"Never a last name?" JD pressed.

Wilder shook his head and returned his look to his near empty cup.

Lieutenant Storm, still in uniform, came in carrying a computer printout. The group around the table fell quiet. Storm raised the paper to stress its importance. "Just got this from the CHP in Indio. They found Culpepper's pickup."

The group at the table bolted to their feet, spilling a paper cup. Coffee pooled and ran off the table. It was ignored. "Where...? Have they seen Brian? Was he in an accident? What happened?" Their voices came in a rush.

The lieutenant read from the printout. "Vehicle was found parked and locked on the east bound shoulder of interstate ten, thirty-eight miles east of Desert Center near mile marker forty-four. No evidence of tampering or damage. Vehicle was impounded. No one observed in the vicinity."

"Fucking CHP," Wilder growled, "have they ever heard of footprints? Last I heard the desert was sandy. Which way did he walk when he left his pickup?"

"Where the hell was he going?" Clark Kent said.

"What's out there?" Flemming asked.

"I called the CHP in Indio," the lieutenant continued. "Gave them a description of Culpepper. Told them it was important we find him. They said they'd give the Riverside Sheriffs a heads up."

"My partner disappeared at a mile marker in the middle of the fucking Mojave Desert. I'm going out there and find him."

"You're on the front desk tomorrow," Clark Kent said. "I know because I'm there with you thanks to our buddies at RHD."

"No," Storm said, "you're both off tomorrow."

"Lieutenant, I think Wilder's right," JD Kent said. "I'm the one that made up the schedule. They're both grounded until the shooting review board..."

"And I'm the watch commander," Storm said, cutting JD short with a sober look. "Now, like I said, they're both off. As a matter of fact, you are too, Sergeant. Get the picture?"

JD was embarrassed that he'd misunderstood. He was about to respond when Wilder slapped him on the shoulder. "Come on. We'll take my Jeep."

The three cops bolted for the door.

"Call me!" Storm yelled after them.

5 GIRLS JUST WANNA HAVE FUN!

The afternoon sun was sinking low on the western horizon when Brian Culpepper opened the passenger's side door of the big tractor. He looked down at the ground and then turned to the cowboy sitting behind the wheel of the idling truck. They had pulled off interstate 10 at the highway 95 exit, the last stop in California before the highway spanned the emerald green Colorado River to trace its way into Arizona. Brian smiled, leaned in, offering an open hand to the cowboy. "Ben Hanks, I'm not going to forget you."

The cowboy took Brian's hand, and they shook. "And it's not likely I'm gonna forget you, Joe Friday."

Brian dropped down to the ground, granted the cowboy a smile and swung the door shut on the idling tractor. The engine growled. Dark smoke jetted from the exhaust stacks and the big truck pulled away.

The 95-exit put Brian on the eastern end of Blythe, California. Blythe, with its population of just over ten thousand, was a collection of cheap motels, restaurants, beer bars and service stations that sprawled along the busy interstate, depending on it for its life's blood. It was a hot, seemingly barren place. Twilight was fading as a collection of neon and flood lamps blinked on. Brian took a final look at the lights on the cowboy's truck as it labored in the distance toward an interstate onramp and then turned his attention to a gas station across the street. A collection of cars, trucks and campers surrounded the station. There was a steak house behind the gas station. Brian looked at it as he crossed the street.

The sight of the restaurant made him realize he was hungry. Maybe after seeing if the gas station had a 5-gallon gas can he'd go have something to eat. Brian was nearing the curb when he spotted the van parked beside the station. It was the Chevy, primer gray with the motorcycle trailer hitched behind. His pulse quickened as he approached it. There was no doubt in his mind. It was the same van that had tried to run him down in the desert. The heat of anger grew on his ears and neck as he neared the van. He was certain he'd recognize the three.

The bearded driver with sweat band, the baby-faced girl, and the heavy-jowled man that threw the wine bottle. He'd see what kind of balls they had when they weren't driving by at sixty miles an hour. He was ready for the fight when he reached the van. Aching for the relief a brief intense physical struggle could bring Brian grabbed the passenger's door and jerked it open. The bittersweet smell of wine, sweat and marijuana teased at his nostrils. He expected to find them sprawled, asleep, perhaps even taking turns with the girl, but the van was empty.

"Shit," Brian said. He slammed the door. His eyes, desperate, searched the area and spotted them. The fat man was at the salad bar in the illuminated steak house. The bearded man and the girl sat in a booth with their backs to the tinted window. Thoughts of the confrontation flowed through Brian's angry mind. He briefly considered going in after them but the sight of a couple with two young children stopped him. Then he had a better idea.

A tall gaunt man in coveralls was working beneath a raised car in one of the gas station's illuminated service bays when Brian approached. The man glanced at him, "Can I help you?"

"Yeah," Brian said. "I'd like to borrow a screwdriver."

The man paused, sniffed, and pointed to a wall with the

wrench he held. Brian looked. A bold sign read NO TOOLS LOANED. The man resumed his work. His business with Brian was over. Brian dug out his wallet and pulled out a five-dollar bill. He stepped to the man and roughly jammed the bill into a breast pocket on his coveralls. "You just sold me a screwdriver," Brian said.

Brian rummaged in the clutter on the bench at the rear of the service bays until he found a long, narrow shanked screwdriver. The man in the coveralls was watching, but he said nothing. Brian's anger was obvious.

Returning to the van Brian looked to the wide windows of the restaurant. Now the fat man was sitting with the other two, pushing forkfuls of green salad into his mouth. Brian knelt beside the van, drew back his arm and plunged the screwdriver through the sidewall of the right front tire. He jerked it out and the hiss of escaping air made him smile. Rounding the insect-spotted front of the van Brian stabbed the other front tire. Once extracted, the tire sighed and sank toward the pavement. He moved to the rear tires and repeated the stabbing twice more. When he finished, he was sweating profusely. He was brushing sweat from his chin when he noticed the man in coveralls. He was standing at the mouth of the garage, watching. The van was now setting on four flat tires. The man looked at the van, then Brian. Brian walked to him. The man stiffened visibly. He adjusted his grip on the chromed adjustable wrench he held. Brian paused, smiled at the man, and then tossed him the screwdriver. "Thanks," he said and walked away.

A large illuminated red rooster formed from twisted neon tubing sat atop the roof of the beer bar. Beneath the rooster, a smaller sign, for illiterates, Brian decided, read, "The Red Rooster—Beer, wine, and no regrets". A collection of mud splattered dusty pickups and cars sat in front. Brian was still covered with sweat. The sun was gone, but the heat wasn't. The idea of a cold beer was inviting. Plus, the bar just might be holding the answer on how he would get back to his pickup. Some blue collar who would listen to his story of woe and for a couple bucks drive him back to his truck. He opened the door and went in.

There was no table service. Brian bought a cold bottle of beer from a muscular fifty-year-old with rolled up sleeves and tattoos covering his arms and neck. Most sat at the bar. Brian chose a table in a corner. Damn, the beer tasted good. He thought about his return to LA. He decided calling Pam or Wilder or anyone else could wait until he was home. It would be late when he got back but they could wait. And the department?

He'd learned early in his career that truth mattered. Lies, hunches, and suspicions didn't matter. Truth did. As a cop in LA, he had sworn an oath to protect the citizens of Los Angeles.

To Protect and Serve, was the motto inscribed on the side of every patrol car in the City of Angels. It was also imprinted on the mind, and spirit of every cop in LA. Had he violated his oath? Brian didn't like the thought that quickly came to mind. He bought a second beer. A juke box poured out a steady string of country music. The men and women lining the bar were older. They talked, laughed, smoked, and drank. Brian studied them. He wondered who they were. It seemed no one in Blythe ever had to think about killing a young woman, or someone's father grasping their bleeding chest just before falling into a pool. No, in Blyth you drank a beer with your friends and...Brian's thought suddenly vanished as the two men stepped through the door. The bearded man with the sweat band around his forehead was first. Close behind him was the fat man in a quilted vest. They paused, eyes searching the shadows in the bar.

Brian knew why they were there. He pushed his beer aside trying to decide which of the two would be first. He knew it would have to be quick. This wouldn't be a barroom brawl. This would be a fight to break bones and spirit. Revenge fights always meant blood, lots of it. The fat man spotted him and pointed. Brian sucked in a breath and held it as they moved toward him. He pushed out of his chair as the two men marched toward him. Several men at the bar turned to watch. Then the bartender looked, drying his hands on a towel. Conversation at the bar stopped as more heads turned. The two men stopped a few feet from Brian. They stood shoulder to shoulder; a mistake, Brian noted. He could reach both and if his reflexes were fast enough, he'd drop them before they were on him. The man with the beard had intense blue eyes. The fat man spoke but Brian's attention stayed on the thinner of the two. "Where's your screwdriver, motherfucker?"

"With your wine bottle, asshole," Brian answered with equal threat. His pulse pounded in his ears. He felt a trace of sweat as it traced down the hollow of his back.

The fat man seemed surprised. He looked to his thinner companion. The bearded man seemed to take it as a cue. He shot out an arm and grabbed Brian by the front of his shirt, surprising him. He punched him hard in the face. Blood spurted from Brian's nose. Brian knew he only had one chance. He kicked hard, landing a foot squarely in the bearded man's groin. It proved effective.

The bearded man's eyes went wide and rolled back as pain swept over him. He fell backwards heavily, without breaking his fall. Brian shielded a blow from the fat man with his arm. It nearly knocked him over. He stabbed the web between thumb and forefinger at the fat man's throat. The fat man surprised Brian with his speed. He ducked to avoid the blow. Brian's thrust grazed the man's jaw and ripped at his ear. The fat man dropped into a crouched position. Brian grabbed him by the front of his vest to pull him up when he realized what the man was doing. He was grabbing for a gun at his waistband. Brian slammed a fist hard into the man's face. Blood splattered from his mouth. Brian hit him a second time, quick and hard. The man sank onto his knees. He grabbed at Brian's legs. He was hurt.

The barroom was alive with a mixture of screams and shouts. Brian pulled away from the fat man's desperate grasp. He stepped back and was readying a kick when the muscular bar tender hit him from behind with a baseball bat. Brian collapsed in an awkward heap.

"That prick's an LA cop," Brian heard the angry shouting.

There was a smarting, burning, dull ache behind his right ear. He tried to reach for his neck and found his wrists were shacked behind his back. He blinked his eyes. The images and lights were fuzzy, but he realized he was sitting in the backseat of a patrol car. "Sonofabitch," Brian muttered, pulling at his wrists. Damn, the handcuffs were tight. The fat man and his bearded partner stood outside the patrol car arguing with two uniformed Riverside County Sheriff's deputies. "I don't give a shit if he is a cop. He tried to kill us." The fat man pointed at shackled Brian.

"Bartender said you two came in looking for a fight," the older of the two deputies said with a glance. His attention was on a blue steel automatic Beretta pistol he held. "Did you tell him you were Federal Agents?" he asked with a look at Brian in the back seat.

Brian was listening. His heart sank. Christ, they were feds. It made the pain in his neck even worse.

"When you're working undercover you don't shout, federal agents, in a crowded bar," the bearded man said.

"Listen, Jack," the fat man growled after a look of contempt at Brian. "As an agent with the DEA, I'm placing this piece of shit under arrest for assault and battery on a federal officer."

The deputy pushed the Beretta into the fat man's chest. His anger was obvious. The fat man grabbed awkwardly at the gun.

"The name's Webster, not Jack. And you two are going to get in my partner's car and follow me to the station. There we'll decide who's under arrest. You understand?"

The fat man jammed his pistol into his waistband. He glanced at his partner and the two turned toward the waiting patrol car.

63

The first light of day was spreading over the dusty streets of Blythe when the two LAPD staff cars pulled into the Riverside Sheriff's substation parking lot. It was five-forty AM and the blinking time and temp sign above the United California Bank read eighty-seven degrees. The substation's parking lot was jammed with cars. Sergeant JD Kent, Wilder, Clark Kent and Flemming were waiting in the reception area where Deputy Webster sat behind a counter, laboring with a report. JD and his trio looked tired and restless.

Brian lay on a bunk in a small back room. He was relieved he was not in a cell. The pain from the lump on the back of his head had subsided some. He had refused the deputies' suggestion they take him to a hospital to be examined. He lay watching light grow around a heavy green pull shade that covered the room's only window. The voice in the outer room awoke him. At first, they were just voices but now they were shouts, angry and loud, covering one another. Closing his eyes, he vaguely remembered someone being in the room, telling him he'd be going back to Los Angeles soon, to jail.

Agent David Manning, the fat man, told his story well. He and his partner, Bobby Dacosta, along with a female informant were enroute to Tucson to make a major undercover buy of heroin. They stopped in Blythe for gas and a bite to eat. When they entered the Red Rooster to buy a sandwich, with their informant waiting in the van, they were confronted by Culpepper, who, without provocation, assaulted them.

Deputy Chief Searcy and Commander Hays were first into the room to interview Brian. Brian sat on the edge of the bunk. "I have nothing to say." He was absent from duty. He now knew the two men he fought were federal agents from the DEA, the Drug Enforcement Agency. None the less, assholes, but still agents. His knew his police career was over, and he was going to jail. Saying anything to anybody would make little difference. They slammed the door when they left.

A few minutes later, Lieutenant Storm entered. Brian had never seen Storm out of uniform before. The lieutenant looked younger. Somehow it unnerved him. Brian offered a nod. "Lieutenant."

Storm acknowledged him with a sober look as he leaned an elbow atop a steel cabinet. He studied Brian. "Culpepper, you've got three friends sitting out there in the lobby. Wilder, Clark Kent, and Flemming. They drove nearly three hundred miles last night because they thought you needed help. Consider this, if it weren't for Wilder, you'd probably be a dead man. Telling us you don't want to talk is like pissing on our shoes."

Brian was listening. He shook his head, and his eyes went to the floor.

"I'm not here because I'm your buddy, Culpepper. I'm here because I'm your watch commander. Everything you do, on or off duty, is a reflection on my leadership. The important thing is not who you are, it's what you are. You're a Los Angeles police officer assigned to day watch patrol in Wilshire Area. When you drove away yesterday, no sign lit up the sky saying I quit! Even if you said that, we'd would still be here. Why? Because we're cops and we take care of one another."

Storm knew it was time to ask the question. "Bartender told the sheriffs the two feds started the fight. Is that right?"

An awkward silence followed. Storm could see emotion welling in Brian. Finally, he raised his eyes to the lieutenant. "I ran out of gas. I was hitchhiking. They tried to run me down, threw a wine bottle at me. When I got here, I saw their van. I was angry, I flattened their tires. I didn't know they were agents until after the fight."

Storm listened. He was certain Brian was telling the truth. Without hesitation he called Deputy Chief Searcy, Commander Hayes, and Captain Winslow back into the room. Storm retold Brian's story. When he finished there were questions. Brian willingly provided the answers. The four men talked for over 30 minutes. When they finished, they were all comfortable with the facts.

The hostility that had haunted them earlier was gone and in its place was a sense of us against them, a sense of brotherhood. Brian was surprised when there were no questions about his absence from duty, or where he was going. Brian was relieved. He wasn't about to bring it up.

"Okay," Deputy Chief Searcy said. "We're ready for them."

Brian was left to wait in the room, but he could hear the voices in the front room. They were not encouraging. The Sheriff's lieutenant in charge of the station, reading the level of tension between the LAPD and the DEA, called his boss as well as a Deputy from the Riverside County District Attorney's Office to help find a legal path through the maze of accusations being hurled by both sides. The two DEA agents had also called for help. Frank Buccini, a Field Operations Director had driven in from Phoenix bringing another agent with him as well as a female executive assistant. Battle lines had been drawn. The two agents from the altercation were insisting Culpepper started the fight after learning they were DEA Agents. They wanted him jailed for assault on a federal agent.

They gathered in the station's command office. The door was closed but the volume of disagreement told all it was not going well. JD Kent looked at the frosted glass on the office door as he listened to the voices on the other side.

He knew the struggle was no longer just Brian Culpepper and the two DEA agents. Now it was a power play as the two agencies fought for a position of advantage, and it meant Culpepper had little chance of surviving. JD listened as he heard calls being made to Chief Peck in LA, and another to the director of the DEA in Washington. Someone had to do something, and JD had an idea. The thought had come to him earlier when Lieutenant Storm gave them Brian's side of his confrontation with the two agents. He waited, hoping he'd have a chance to talk with the lieutenant, but Storm was now in the office with the others.

JD knew it had become a case of now or never. "Fuck

them." JD bolted to his feet. He slapped Wilder on the shoulder. "Come on."

Wilder, Clark Kent and Flemming all stood. "You two are staying," JD said to Clark Kent and Flemming. "Don't let them take Culpepper anywhere before we get back."

"And just how in the hell do we do that?" Clark Kent argued pointing at the frosted glass on the door. "There's a deputy chief, a commander from Internal Affairs and a captain in there. Plus, enough feds to rewrite the constitution."

JD led Wilder toward the door. "You'll think of something."

The motel office was small, neat, and cool, a welcome relief from the heat outside. A chime sounded as JD and Wilder stepped inside. A young busty redhead in glasses appeared from a backroom where a television played. She eyed the two men. "May I help you?"

"Hi," JD said cheerfully, reaching for his badge case. He flipped it open for the woman to glance at the oval silver and gold badge of the LAPD. JD quickly returned it to his pocket. The redhead opened her mouth to speak but JD took the chance from her. "We're with the DEA agents. They said they'd be here at the Travel Lodge." JD was lying. This was the fourth motel office he and Wilder had checked.

"Oh," the redhead said.

JD glanced at the glass door behind them, "That's their gray van out there. Could you tell us what room they're in?"

The redhead nodded moving to a computer screen on the reception desk separating them. She studied the screen for a moment then with a glance at JD. "Room One-sixteen."

"Thanks." JD smiled at the nipples pushing beneath the girl's blouse.

A rap on the motel room door startled the girl inside. She pushed up on an elbow and listened. The curtains were closed and the only light in the room came from the television set that flickered with the afternoon images of *General Hospital*. The hum of the air conditioner mixed with the voices on the TV. Maybe, she thought, it was someone at the room next door. David Manning had a key. He wouldn't knock. The rap sounded again. Now there was no doubt. She pushed off the bed, moved to the door, paused.

"David?" she asked reaching for the deadbolt lock.

"Come on," a voice urged from outside. "I forgot my key."

The girl ran a hand back through her hair. She wondered if David was still angry. When he dropped her at the motel, he was livid. Cursing and swearing, he was threatening to kill the cop that fought them. She silently wondered why they had a fight with a cop but didn't dare ask. She wanted nothing to interfere with the buy in Tucson. She was worried the fight would. They had to be there by four and she only had enough stuff for one more fix. Big Dog, the dealer she was set to betray to save her own ass wouldn't deal with her if she were hungry. Reaching for the deadbolt she hoped they were ready to go.

JD and Wilder exchanged a look as the lock snapped open. Wilder was glad they weren't going to have to kick the door in. In the searing heat, he wasn't sure they could. He was drenched in his own sweat. Even his socks felt damp. The door cracked open and as it did JD hit it solidly with a shoulder and shoved.

The girl saw the unfamiliar Black face, but it was too late. The door hit her arm, knee, and forehead sending her backward to fall awkwardly onto the bed. She was still high from an earlier fix and it all seemed dreamlike. The bedspread felt rough on her cheek and she had fuzz sticking to her lipstick. She was brushing it away when the hands grabbed her. JD jerked the girl to her feet and clamped a hand over her mouth as Wilder locked the door.

JD stared into the girl's eyes. Her pupils were dime sized. He knew what it meant. Two years working narcotics had taught him what junkies looked like. "You scream, girl," he

68

said to the gaunt frightened face, still covering her face with his hand, "and I'll hurt you. You understand me?"

Tears welled in the girl's pale-blue eyes and spilled down over the hand holding her face. Suddenly the hand was gone and then with the tooth jarring impact of an open hand slammed into her face. "I said do you understand me?"

"Jesus, JD," Wilder said. JD's tone and action had him worried. "Take it easy."

JD ignored Wilder. He gave the frightened face a final look and pushed her backward onto the bed. "She's not going to move. Let's see what we can find."

There were their suitcases in the room. Wilder began his search of one while JD dumped two others on the floor and kicked through the contents. A variety of men's T-Shirts, jeans, shorts, socks, a box of ammunition, shaving gear, and more was scattered about the floor. Nothing seemed of interest to JD. "I'll get the bathroom," he said and moved away.

Wilder rummaged through silk panties, bras, a bathing suit, a bottle of Windsong, a box of tampons. He wished he knew what JD was searching for but felt asking might make him look stupid. He was worried about being there. He was worried about how JD had treated the girl. He looked at her. She sat rigid; eyes clamped shut. Her skirt was pushed high on her narrow thighs. Her bare arms were thin.

Wilder could see the needle track marks on the inner elbows of both arms. This wasn't some thirty something girl; this was a hype. He pushed the suitcase aside and moved to a bedside dresser. In it he found a Bible. Wilder glanced at the Bible and then the girl. "You know who John the Baptist is?"

The girl cautiously opened her eyes as if she feared she was going to be slapped again. "Is he a dealer?"

"A dealer..." Wilder smiled. "Yeah, he's sort of a dealer."

JD emerged from the bathroom with a zip bag in hand. "Found her get down kit." Wilder watched as JD unzipped the bag and rummaged. He held up a blacked spoon, a hypodermic syringe, and a knotted nylon. Then, tossing the bag to the unmade bed he moved for the door. "Keep an eye on Miss America. I'll have a look in the van."

Not knowing what else to do, Wilder glanced at the girl. Her eyes were closed again. She was high. He knelt on the carpet and looked under the bed. In addition to dust, soiled tissues, and a man's sock he spotted a briefcase. Wilder reached, pulled it out and sat it on the bed behind the girl.

The briefcase was gray with a silver trim. It looked expensive. Wilder smirked, damned feds. He pushed the release button and the locks snapped open. Wilder lifted the lid. Several yellow tablets filled with notes, a Rand McNally map of the United States, a rubber band wrapped packet of mug shots, a handbook for the Recognition and Identification of Controlled Substances, and several packs of Marlboro cigarettes. Lifting a divider Wilder found a bundle of twenty-dollar bills wrapped tight with a wide rubber band. He thumbed through the bills—*one hundred, two hundred, three...damn.*

He tossed the money onto the bed behind the girl and continued his search. He found another packet of photos wrapped with a rubber band. He pulled the rubber band away. The first picture surprised him. He recognized the girl. In the picture she was sitting in a chair, coffee cup in hand, smiling, completely nude. Wilder leafed through more. Most showed the girl, nude, smiling, inviting on a bed, in the shower, in the van, toweling herself, but it was the last photo Wilder knew JD was searching for.

JD returned. "Nothing in the van. Half a bottle of Jack, couple hand-held flashlights."

"Look what I got," Wilder said holding up the pictures.

JD moved to him.

Wilder offered the pictures and JD eagerly thumbed through them.

"Hot damn," he said.

In the photograph, the fat man, David Manning, was slumped in a comfortable chair, his head back, mouth open with his pants pushed down below his knees. Kneeling in front of him the girl, nude, was leaning into his crotch with his erection in her mouth.

"Fat son of a bitch just couldn't fight it," JD said.

JD stuck the pictures into a back pocket and moved to kneel in front of the girl on the edge of the bed.

"Hey, open your eyes. We're not going to hurt you." His tone was different now, almost apologetic. The girl didn't respond. JD moved a finger to her chin, raised it. Wilder was surprised at the sharp contrast between JD's black finger and the girl's white flesh. He seldom thought of JD as a Black man, but now with him kneeling in front of the girl he was thinking it.

The girl sniffed and opened her eyes. They were red and rimmed with tears. She wiped at her nose with the back of a hand. She avoided JD's dark eyes.

"I'm going to ask you a few questions and if you tell us the truth, the absolute truth, we'll be finished, and you can leave. Do you understand?"

The girl nodded as a tear spilled and traced down her cheek. Wilder hoped she would brush it away. She didn't.

"The pictures of you. Who took them?"

She sniffed again. Her drugs were beginning to fade. She was growing uncomfortable. "David did. He took most of them."

"Who's David?"

"You know the big dude. David Manning. One of the feds."

"Did you know they were feds?"

"Yeah, I knew."

"Did he pay you to take the pictures?"

The girl was slow to answer.

"Did he pay you?"

"Not money."

"Then what?"

"I...was. I needed something you know?"

"Something? You mean H? He gave you heroin for taking the pictures?"

The girl nodded and lowered her head. JD wanted more from her. He wanted her to say it.

"He gave you dope to pose for the pictures and go down on him? Say it if it's true."

A chill swept over the girl. It made her shudder. "He said all I had to do was take my clothes off to see if I had tracks."

"And then?"

The girl dug at a fingernail. "Then he made me pose. Said I wasn't going to get anything if I didn't. So, I did. Wasn't like I'm a virgin or anything. He got all turned on, like horny." She shrugged as if it weren't important. "So, then he pulls his pants down and says, do me. So, DaCosta took the picture."

"And after you did him, they gave you dope?"

"Yeah, but that wasn't here. This was a couple days ago in LA."

JD pushed to his feet, looked to Wilder, then the girl. "You have any money?"

"Three dollars," the girl said. "A dollar of it in quarters."

Wilder reached to the bed and picked up the wrapped packet of hundred-dollar bills. He tossed it to JD who smiled and pushed the money into the girl's hands. "Think of this as a graduation present."

"I can't, I can't take the money."

"Yes, you can. You're done with the feds. The heat's on and your only hope is to get your ass out of Dodge. That pot of gold you're chasing isn't out there. This is big league shit and all you're gonna get is hurt."

The girl fingered the roll of money carefully and then she looked first to JD and then Wilder. "Are you guys cops?"

6 THE BROTHERHOOD OF THE BADGE

Commander Hays from Internal Affairs was making a final plea to the collective group in the substations command office. Buccini, the DOE from the DEA in Phoenix office and his staff sat on one side while Deputy Chief Searcy, Captain Winslow and Lieutenant Storm sat across from them. It was as if a battle line had been drawn and the two groups had chosen sides. In fact, they had. The graying commander deliberately paced back and forth between the two groups staring at the floor. It was a tactic to make those listening eager to hear what he would say. Clasping his hands behind his back, Hays paused and looked to the feds. He had nothing but contempt for them and talking to them as if they were professionals was difficult for him. "We're all the same brotherhood, we all carry badges and we're all peace officers. All of us are in this business because we believe in law and order." He looked to the faces. None of the federal agents granted him a response.

The commander continued, "As veteran peace officers we're all men of experience. We've seen it all. Battered wives, battered kids, bloodied bodies, stinking bodies, overdosed bodies, runaway juveniles, runaway adults, homosexuals, tri-sexuals, bi-sexuals, fakes, the famous, the heroes, the cowards, the best, but mostly the worst. We've seen the pretty, sometimes the beautiful, but mainly the ugly. There's little in the human experience that at least one of us hasn't seen. In short, we've got a lot in common. We need each other. The only thing that stands between us and eighteen cents' of lead is the knowledge that if you hurt one of us, you're not going to find a place to hide."

The commander continued his slow pace, hands clasped behind his back, reading faces. "The law breakers don't give a shit if we're city cops, county cops, or feds. They don't care if our uniforms are blue, green, khaki, or no uniform at all. To them we're all the same—cops. So, to us, you, me, every man in this room, it should be the same because," the commander pointed a finger at the window, "that's the way it is out there, and that's how it's got to be in here. We must stand together. We're family. We're one. We go washing our dirty laundry in public, you'll find a lot of people don't like us. There're the ones who think every time we strap on a gun, we get an erection. There are people who think we like putting men in jail. There are people, good people who just don't like us. They believe we're drunk half the time and chasing skirts the other half. These good, well intentioned, people will sometimes take something like this misunderstanding and turn it into mayhem and attempted murder."

The commander paused and looked directly at the federal agents. "In short, gentlemen, if we don't handle this ourselves, we're going to regret it. We gain nothing with the filing of criminal charges. I assure you we will deal with Officer Culpepper. If you insist a criminal complaint be filed, the matter is then beyond my reach...and yours. Thank you."

Lieutenant Storm was proud of the commander. He had delivered a sermon. He had touched Storm and looking across the room at the collection of federal agents Storm knew they had been touched, too. This was police business and by God it needed to be handled by the police themselves. Storm's muscles were tight with pride. He had little doubt the feds were going to agree.

Frank Buccini was glad the commander had finished. He glanced at his staff, suspecting many of them were silently agreeing with the graying police commander. Agreeing, he thought, because they opposed every decision he made. Two of them wanted his job and were awaiting the chance to push him into a mistake. He silently wished there were time for him to call his father-in-law, the federal judge in Atlanta, and seek his advice. The silence had hung heavy in the room. He knew they were waiting for him to speak. His heart was pounding in his ears. He wished he'd never come to Blythe. Had he known this mess was waiting he wouldn't have.

Early word was that one of his men was hurt and he envisioned himself standing bedside at the hospital, laying a hand on the man's shoulder, and telling him they'd get the bastard that put him there. He knew word would spread quickly through the rank and file that Frank Buccini cared about his men. It was important to him that he have their respect.

He had no way of knowing that the rank and file of the DEA thought of him as just another passing appointee. Most would never know his name and those who did could have cared how Frank Buccini felt about anything. Theirs was a thankless, tiring, dirty job, not made easier by the revolving door at the top of the organization, bringing them new political leadership every couple years.

To those who knew him, Frank Buccini was known as the *Judge's Boy*, and the many jokes were made about the numerous cellphone calls to Atlanta. As Frank Buccini pushed to his feet, he tried to imagine how the judge would handle this situation. He cleared his throat. He had often seen the judge do that. "Well," Buccini began, "let's look at the facts...just the facts. Fact is two of my men were assaulted."

Lieutenant Storm felt the heat of anger spread across the back of his hairline and ears. He knew Commander Hays's plea was lost and he hated the political Frank Buccini.

Sergeant JD Kent paced in the substation's outer office. Wilder sat with Clark Kent and Flemming. There was no conversation. They were all listening to the muffled voice of

Frank Buccini coming from behind the frosted glass. Finally, it ended, and Lieutenant Storm came out. His face was a mask of anger and frustration. He avoided a look at any of the waiting men and crossed directly to the door and stepped outside. JD Kent followed him.

Standing in the glare of the afternoon sun, Storm took in a deep breath and let it out slowly. JD stood beside him in silence, waiting. Finally, Storm looked to him. "We lost," he said flatly. "They want Culpepper locked up."

"Then I suggest plan B," JD said and pulled the six pictures from a rear pocket and offered them to Storm.

Storm thumbed through the pictures. After he scanned all of them, he looked to JD. "Where did you get these?"

"From the girl," JD answered.

"How?" Storm pressed.

JD drew in a breath. "Don't ask.

Commander Hays, Captain Winslow and Deputy Chief Searcy went to the substation's bunk room to tell Brian of the decision. The feds were insisting on filing a complaint and the deputy district attorney agreed. Brian would be transported to the Riverside County Jail where he would be booked for assault and battery on a federal officer.

Brian only half listened as Deputy Chief Searcy explained how arrangements would be made to isolate him from the other prisoners in the county jail. Commander Hays added that Jim Sanchez from the Police Protective League had called and that he was already working on hiring an attorney and planning for bail.

Brian was thinking of what Lieutenant Storm said. They weren't doing this for him. He wasn't important. What made him important was the fact that he was a police officer. If that were true, he asked himself, why didn't he feel like one of them? Why did he feel so alone?

Lieutenant Storm stepped into the room to speak briefly with the Deputy Chief Searcy listened intently then took Commander Hays by the arm. "Let's step out," he said.

Brian glanced at the three as they left the room. He was glad to be alone again.

The three men stood in the rear office where they examined the pictures. Commander Hays, after looking at them a second time, stabbed the pictures at Lieutenant Storm. "Get rid of them. We're not blackmailers."

"Blackmail!" Storm almost shouted. "These pictures aren't blackmail. They're evidence. If you want to destroy evidence, Commander, you get rid of them."

"Don't play word games with me, Storm," the commander warned. "I know what you're suggesting, and the answer is, no."

Storm looked to Captain Winslow and Deputy Chief Searcy. It was a silent plea.

"Seems to me," Searcy said, taking the pictures from Storm, "the lieutenant has a point, Commander. A federal agent involved in the act of oral copulation with an informant. An informant he rewarded with heroin. Are those facts you, as the commander of Internal Affairs, should ignore?"

"No, it is not. Not in itself." The commander's stance stiffened. "But you know what Storm's trying to do. He's trying to use one crime to cover another, and as a police officer I find that reprehensible."

Storm lost his temper. Hunger, fatigue, all contributed to his outburst, but mainly he was just fed up. "Reprehensible my ass. You're talking like this was some Goddamned game. It's not. It's Culpepper's life, his career. He didn't shoot a nineteen-year-old girl for the thrill of it. We paid him to do it, and now that he's upset over blowing a hole through her neck, he's a problem for us? An embarrassment? Let's throw him to the wolves. He's in trouble, so fuck him, right? Trying to protect him from those asshole feds is blackmail?"

Frank Buccini and his staff gathered in the station's front lobby to await Culpepper being escorted out. The heavy-set agent David Manning and his bearded partner were with them. They were laughing, joking, they were the victors.

Manning was telling the others how he had dropped Culpepper with a single punch after he tried to tear his ear off. Manning was still wearing a gauze patch on his ear.

JD, Wilder, Clark Kent, and Flemming stood in a tight cluster across from the feds. They were not smiling. JD elbowed Wilder when Deputy Chief Searcy emerged from the back hallway with Commander Hays and Captain Winslow. He saw the photos in Searcy's hand.

Searcy walked directly to the group of feds. Their conversation died as the deputy chief reached them. Not wasting words, Searcy raised the photos, sticking them directly in Manning's face. "Is this how the DEA trains an informant?"

Manning's face flushed red. The other agents there jockeyed their positions trying to see.

There were muttered exclamations...

"Holy shit."

"Oh. Fuck."

"Manning, you son of a bitch," Buccini cursed when he saw the picture.

Without warning Manning reached and grabbed the photos from Searcy's hand, "You prick."

Searcy resisted and the pictures fell scattering onto the floor. Searcy pushed Manning aside and reached for the scattered pictures. Manning grabbed Searcy by the front of his shirt pulled him up and slammed a fist hard into the Deputy Chief's face.

Blood sprang from Searcy's lip. He staggered backwards and fell. Manning moved after the fallen Searcy raising a foot to stomp him, but JD stepped into his path, taking a martial arts stance he shouted and drove a clenched fist into Manning's stomach followed by another quick chop to his neck. Manning fell like a tree. Captain Winslow got into a pushing contest with an agent trying to pick up the photos. He grabbed the man around the neck and they both went crashing to the floor.

"You asshole," another of the agents growled and tackled JD. They went crashing to the floor. Wilder, Clark Kent, and

Flemming were quickly across the room and into the mayhem. Frank Buccini was headed for a door when Wilder kicked him in the ass.

Another of the DEA agents, a tall quiet man, another trained in martial arts quickly dispensed of Clark Kent and Flemming just before Wilder hit him with a fire extinguisher he'd torn from the wall.

Sheriffs' Lieutenant Mark Pereda put an end to the fight when he stepped into the lobby, looked at the melee, drew his pistol and fired two shots into the ceiling. The action stopped as if they were all frozen. Bits of plaster fluttered down from the ceiling mixing with acid smell of gunpowder. "Anybody says or does another fucking thing, you're all going to jail."

The injured were treated at the Blythe Community hospital. Among the injuries was a split lip, a broken finger, a bruised neck, two cracked ribs, a sprained ankle, and a swollen black eye. Nobody disclosed how they were injured.

Lieutenant Pereda called for reinforcements, and by late afternoon he had ten deputies on hand. Deputy Chief Searcy, his lip swollen, along with Commander Hays, Captain Winslow, and Lieutenant Storm were held under house arrest at the substation with five deputies standing by.

Frank Buccini, having been treated for contusions to his tailbone and buttocks was, along with all the other DEA personnel, being detained in the room at the Travel Lodge guarded by another five deputies.

Fred Rogers, the Deputy District Attorney was frantic. Conflict between competing law enforce agencies was nothing new and early on he was dealing with the sensitive issue of one officer assaulting another. The melee had changed all that. There were now eight charges of assault and battery on a police officer, disorderly conduct, destruction of evidence, causing bodily injury to a federal officer, obstruction of an investigation, illegal possession of a controlled substance, sexual relations with an informant and conduct unbecoming an officer—knowingly conducting police investigations and identifying oneself as a police officer outside assigned jurisdictions.

The telephone conferences concluded with a grudging agreement between the LAPD and the DEA after the District Attorney from Riverside County concluded there was no winner. Truth was the DA wanted nothing to do with such a political mud fest.

Word of the melee which included an LAPD deputy chief, the commander of Internal Affairs, and an area captain, a police sergeant, and three officers on one side, while on the other a DEA director of field operations for the Western United States, his female assistant, a case manager, two case analysis officers, and four field officers were all given a choice between criminal charges or sworn silence. Once agreement was made the DA had the final word, "Now, get the fuck out of Riverside county."

Eighteen minutes later, two LAPD staff cars followed by Wilder's Jeep, which now carried JD, Clark Kent, Flemming, and Culpepper, swung on to Interstate 10. A roadside sign read, *Los Angeles 234 miles*. "Get comfortable," Wilder urged. "I'll have you there in three hours...or so."

Comfort was elusive with five of them jammed in the Jeep, but none had wanted to ride in one of the staff cars.

The staff cars quickly outpaced Wilder's Jeep and disappeared into the distance on the freeway. There was a mix of relief, humor, and kinship in the Jeep. They talked about the girl in the motel, the fight, and the fact they were witness to the commander of Internal Affairs, the Satan of the LAPD, involved in a fight with DEA agents.

"I heard one of the calls the deputy district attorney made after the fight was to Jesus," Clark Kent said. They laughed. Culpepper among them. His feeling of desperation and dread was lifting. He was riding with men who had risked all for his undeserving ass. He was one of them.

Sheriff's Deputy Pereda had returned Culpepper's badge and gun and patted him on the shoulder just before they left. The deputy hadn't said anything. He didn't have to; his smile had said it all. Culpepper was once again a cop. A cop on his way home. A cop who still had a job. A cop who would call Pamela Moss just as soon as he got home. A cop who now knew how painful it would be to lose his badge. A cop who vowed never to get that close to the edge again.

An hour and a half of nothing but the dark of the desert night and a seemingly endless train of speeding noisy trucks carried them to the Indio sub-station of the California Highway Patrol to find Culpepper's impounded pickup. An attractive uniformed female CHP officer was a little unnerved by the five until JD produced his badge and advised they were all LAPD cops. The relieved deputy went to a desktop monitor and keyboard. "What were you doing way out here to have your truck impounded?" she asked Culpepper as she typed.

"Took the wrong onramp in LA," Culpepper answered.

"You know," Clark Kent said, pushing Culpepper aside to talk with the attractive officer. "in LA you'd be earning about six thousand dollars more than the CHP is paying you."

"I hear there's violence in LA."

"Come on in, I'll take you for a ride. Show you around our town," Clark Kent proposed. "That is if your husband doesn't object."

"No, husband." The officer smiled. Then with a look to Culpepper she read from the screen. "Three hundred and sixty-eight dollars and you drive away in your pickup."

Culpepper argued for a police discount, but the officer defended the impound lot was run by an independent who took nothing but cash, all of it. Culpepper wasn't pleased but the impound lot had an ATM. They had to wake up the driver on duty. JD offered to ride home with Culpepper, but Brian begged off.

"If you don't mind, Sarge, I want to buy some gas, put the windows down and turn the music up."

JD understood. "Alright, but don't get stopped by the CHP, and if you're going directly to Pam you need to know we talked with her last night."

"You what!" Culpepper was shocked.

"Hey, we're cops. You got no private life. Plus, she called us."

Chief of Police James Peck was waiting in his car in front of the Towering Royal Oaks condominiums when the headlights of the unmarked staff car driven by Deputy Chief Searcy turned onto the block. Peck watched as the car disappeared into the subterranean garage before he climbed out. The chief found the two men on the sixteenth floor at the door to Searcy's condo. Searcy paused when he saw Peck. The chief smiled as he looked at the deputy chief. Searcy wore a white bandage across his bruised nose. Both his eyes were shadowed with bruising. Commander Hays wore a bandage on his right hand. He had a broken finger.

"Don't say a God damned word," Searcy said as he unlocked the door.

Inside Chief Peck and Commander Hays sat while Searcy found a bottle of Jack Daniel's and three glasses. They sat and drank until the bottle was nearly empty. There was talk about Blythe, the fight with DEA, but the discussion never turned serious as the chief thought it would. No matter how it was told, and they tried every conceivable way, the incident came off as humorous. It was Commander Hays, with a little help from Jack Daniel's, who labeled the entire event, "Bad Blood at Blythe."

Chief Peck decided it was time to turn serious. "Okay, I agreed with the Riverside DA's order that we keep all of this quiet. DEA agreed to the same, but then there's Culpepper. What do we do with him?"

Searcy exchanged a look with Commander Hays then downed the remainder of his drink before answering, "I haven't seen the OIS's report on Culpepper, but Hays says it's in policy. Tragic, but clean." He paused to allow the commander time to nod of agreement. "Same with Wilder and the girl's father. In policy. What makes this all so tragic is the fact it has resulted in the death of an entire family. Daughter, father, and mother are dead as the result a single police action. That's big news."

"It's even bigger news when you factor in one of our officers goes psycho and disappears," Peck said.

"Let's take the DEA out of this for a moment," Commander Hays proposed. "Every shrink in the city would say, Culpepper ran because his spirit was wounded, and he was in the grip of emotional pain. We added to his pain by not being sympathetic. We're experienced professionals. We're LAPD strong. We can take it. Bullshit! We should have seen what was happening to him. Everyone else did. Hell, every time I tell the story it gives me a chill. Culpepper should have had time off after the shooting. Did we give him that? No! We interviewed him for three hours after he shot a girl who tried to kill him. Plus, even before his interview he sees the scene of the shooting turn into a disturbance that took us five hours to put down. Then he goes home to have the girls' father knock on his door and threaten to kill him. Wilder steps in and shoots the man. What do we do? We're so fucking professional we interview Culpepper all over again, for another three hours. It all ends at about three AM. What do we expect of Culpepper and Wilder and the others? We expect them to show up for roll call at eight AM where they're told there're going to RHD for one more fucking interview."

The three sat quietly for a moment after Hays finished, then Chief Peck spoke. "Seems you'd like to see our Officer Involved Shooting policies changed," Chief Peck added soberly.

"Our Officer Involved Shooting policies have changed, Jim." Hays answered.

Searcy adjusted the bandage on his nose and poured another round for all three of them. "Okay, we contributed to Culpepper's dilemma. That's our problem. His problem is to get back in line. Either he gets over this or he's out."

"All Culpepper is guilty of is a failure to report for his

assigned duties," Hays added. "Now he's back. The question has become, what do we do with him?"

"I say we put him somewhere out of public view. Worse case would be Sixty Minutes or Hannity finding him for an in-depth interview," the chief said.

"I'm hearing two issues coming our way," Deputy Chief Searcy offered. "Culpepper's wellbeing and the department's reaction to the death of this family." He looked to the chief. "We've got to be wide open with this, admit we're as shocked and dismayed as the public is, admit we've got to do something for the wellbeing of our officers, then what can be said? We go transparent. Truth doesn't have any shadows. Truth wins."

"Except for the shit fest in Blythe we're covering up," Peck said.

"Yeah, but I think we can justify that because the publics not involved. No one got shot. We can come up with a dozen reasons for being out there. Now, what Searcy is suggesting sounds right," Commander Hays added almost enthusiastically. "We call a press conference in the morning. You open it, Chief. Talk candidly about what happened. What a tragedy it is. Then I'll follow with talk about our current policy and practices. I'll invite the two OIS teams. Hell, we'll give the press more than what they came for. Shit they've never heard before. We'll give them so much they won't need to talk with Culpepper or Wilder. Plus, the fact we're insulating the two officers demonstrates we care about them. Truth works."

The chief nodded agreement. "I like it, but, Searcy, you're staying away. No pun, but we don't want your nose in this."

Their talk was to go on for another hour. It stopped after the bottle of Jack was empty. When Chief Peck and Commander Hays finally left, Searcy was asleep in a recliner. His shoes were off, and a cat named Killer was asleep in his lap. The two men walked together to the sidewalk in front of the complex. "How's Culpepper, Bill?"

"Better than the two of us. He was in a bunk room in the back of the station when the fight broke out."

"What do we do with him?" the chief pressed.

Hays shrugged. "I'll think of something. He was apologetic, remorseful over his failure to report for duty. The press will go after him. They already have. He suffered a wound few cops ever do."

"Find a place to bury him. This will pass."

Hays nodded agreement. "I'll let you know what we do."

The chief patted the commander on the shoulder and walked away into the shadows.

Culpepper didn't roll his windows down or play loud music. He drove with caution in mind, obeying the speed limit, yielding to other cars. He was taking no chances. He had, he concluded, had his chance. He wasn't sure who to thank so he repeatedly thanked God, time and time again. He was a cop. He wasn't prepared to be anything else. He wasn't even certain he could be anything else. The department he loved had been what he hoped it would be. It was more than a surprise; it was a thrill. A thrill he could never really talk about. A thrill that belonged more to Wilder, Clark Kent, and Flemming and others than to him. They were the ones in the fight. He wondered if they really understood what they were fighting for. An illuminated freeway sign put an end to his thoughts, *Lankershim Blvd—Right Lane Only*. He was only blocks from Pamela's apartment.

Culpepper rang the doorbell with no idea what to say to her. JD had told him she had called so she knew something. He wished he had asked what they told her, if anything. Pamela surprised him by opening the door quickly. It was as if she had been waiting and, she was. Dressed in a terry cloth robe and barefoot Pamela threw her arms around Brian's neck and pulled him to her. Brian returned the hug. Her hair covered his face. It smelled fresh and clean. He kissed her neck and shoulder where the robe pushed aside. "I was going to call," he whispered into the hair.

"Be quiet," Pamela said, pulling him inside to push the

door shut with a foot. She took him by the hand and led him into her bedroom. "Take your shoes off," she said as she unbuttoned his shirt.

"I'm sorry it's so late, but..."

She quieted him with a finger to his mouth. "Be quiet," Pamela urged moving from him to turn off a bedside lamp. Returning to Brian, Pamela pushed her robe off her shoulders. It fell to the floor. She was nude. She reached and unbuckled his belt. "Take them off," she ordered.

Brian quickly undressed and followed Pamela into the bed. It was warm and soft. She pulled him into her arms. "You're going to sleep now. Hear me? Sleep. We can talk in the morning."

"It is morning," he whispered into her hair pushing his erection between her legs.

"Brian," she smiled in the shadows as she moved her body from his, "sleep."

Brian reluctantly agreed. He massaged her back. It was warm and smooth. "I love you, Pamela," he whispered.

He waited for an answer, hoped for it, held his breath.

"And I love you, Brian. Now, shut up," she answered softly in his ear.

Culpepper searched for sleep. He did his best to ignore the naked sensual warm body next to his. He forced thoughts, images, wondering if Wilder was home. Was he with his wife? Did they talk? And Clark Kent trying to hustle a CHP officer. Did she accept? His mind was a maze of questions and emotions and then the gentle massage at the base of his neck won. He was asleep.

He awoke to the sounds of Mighty six-ninety talk radio and a warning of a tie-up on the southbound Hollywood Freeway. He didn't know what time it was, but he knew he was late. Pamela was already up, dressed in a bra and panties, she brought a cup of coffee as Brian emerged from the bathroom. He looked at his image in the mirror. He was not pleased with what he saw. It had been two days since he shaved and showered, and he was not at home.

"Yeah," Pamela said kissing him on the cheek, "it's late.

We overslept." She picked up a brush and went to work on her hair in front of the wide mirror behind the bathroom counter. Brian sampled his coffee. "Let's save our talk for tonight," Pamela said. "I'm in one-oh-six again. Judge Frey is a real dick about punctuality."

Brian ran a hand back through his bed head. "We don't want you dealing with a real dick." He shaved with a pink razor he found on the edge of her bathtub and then brushed his teeth with a finger and Colgate Extra Whitener. Pamela was dressed and ready to go while Brian still searched for one of his socks.

"See you back here tonight," she said, kissing him on the cheek. Her professional persona and beauty were intimidating him as he looked at his unkempt image in the mirror.

If the Marine Corps had taught Brian Culpepper anything it was how to make a bunk. After Pamela was gone, he put his best effort into making Pamela's queen-sized bed. The soft billowy spread and fluffy pillows made the task challenging and finally knowing time was an issue, Brian gave up and headed for the door.

It was on the freeway, moving with the flow of morning traffic, that Brian let the first few thoughts of yesterday into his mind. Carefully at first, a few quick reflections, like a child taking their first look at a cut finger. If he didn't see it, if he didn't look at it, the pain wouldn't be nearly as bad. Slowly he thought of each event, not really dwelling on any, nudging them around in his mind, like a thousand scattered pieces. Examining, fitting, reshuffling, studying the partial images that appeared as the pieces molded together until he could see it clearly, and then he felt foolish. Although alone in his car he flushed warm with a smarting embarrassment he'd not know since his aunt caught him masturbating on his fourteenth birthday.

What Brian needed was to clear his mind's eye. He needed to get back to the streets. There you could leave it all behind. There you weren't some guy bringing his problems to work. On the street, carrying a badge and a gun, you were the man, you were in charge, you were the law. Going back to the street would prove he wasn't weak. What he did, he told himself, was rooted in emotional poor judgement, not cowardice.

Brian liked that thought. He promised himself he'd use it when he talked to Lieutenant Storm. He deliberately turned his thoughts to the days ahead.

Things were going to be alright. He was back where he belonged, doing what he should be doing. He was a cop and things were going to work out. He held that thought as he eased his pickup toward the Sixth Street off ramp. No one wanted to remember yesterday, he was sure of that.

Lieutenant Storm was in uniform at the desk in the watch commander's office. He knew Culpepper had arrived and when he was certain Brian had enough time to change into uniform, he sent a desk officer to summon him. Storm, Captain Winslow, and Commander Hays from Internal Affairs had joined in a teleconference earlier. The decision on what to do with Culpepper had been decided and Storm was the one picked to deliver the news. Storm knew the management problem the department had with Officer Brian Culpepper been resolved. It was now overshadowed by the clash with the DEA in Blythe. When Blythe was discussed, and with a deputy chief punched in the face he knew it would be, it wouldn't be Culpepper that would be remembered, it would be Deputy Chief Searcy. The thought made Storm smile.

Although department brass, in their typical humble fashion, had resolved the problem it was Lieutenant Storm who now had to make it work. Storm knew if they did nothing, the Culpepper incident could become a morale problem. The men and women assigned to his watch knew he was a disciplinarian and doing nothing set a dangerous precedent for future conduct. Ironically, those with knowledge of the incident also knew there was no official recognition that the incident ever occurred, but an example had to be made, a price had to be paid. No matter how he felt personally Storm kept coming to the same conclusion. Culpepper had to go.

Storm deliberately waited until Culpepper would be in uniform, knowing if a man looked like a policeman, odds were, he'd act like one. It was psychological role playing but it worked. Storm knew Culpepper was walking a wire. He was worth saving but he was just one man. Storm had seen other good men lost. That decision, Storm told himself was not his, it was Culpepper's.

"You wanted to see me, Lieutenant," Brian said, stepping into the watch commander's office.

"Close the door," Storm said soberly as he straightened himself in his chair. Brian slid the windowed door shut.

Storm studied Brian, allowing the circumstances to work as he sat behind his desk with a uniformed subordinate waiting. If Culpepper was on the edge, he was doing a good job hiding it Storm concluded. Dressed in his tailored blue uniform with his gold and silver LAPD badge pinned on his chest, gun belt strapped around his mid-section, boots polished, Storm decided Brian looked much like a poster for the LAPD.

"This is not a subject we will discuss or argue," Storm said flattening his palms on his desktop. "Nor is it punishment, but it is a necessary action as a result of what happened yesterday."

Brian stood silent. A muscle on the back of his right leg twitched with tension. His heart was racing.

"You've been transferred," Lieutenant Storm continued. "As of oh-eight hundred this morning you've been transferred to Management Services Division."

Brian stood silent, wooden. There were no words. He knew what Management Services was. It was a bunch of neutered non-combatants, a collection of cop-clerks that worked silently behind doors deep in Police headquarters. They were paper pushing pussies, eight to four bankers, climbers, those who used the department for graduate study. Supposed cops who concerned themselves with the big picture, the abstract theories of modern urban policing, management techniques and budget. They were everything Brian Culpepper wasn't. For a fleeting moment he considered asking the lieutenant why they came to Blythe to get him but then the answer came to him. He wasn't important. It was not who he was, it was what he was, and seemingly now that Blythe was history, so was he. They were finished with him. Brian turned and walked from the office.

7 LANDING IN THE BRIAR PATCH

The transfer to Management Services was humiliating for Brian. He no longer felt like a cop. Now he was a clerk. The closeness and camaraderie he had known in Wilshire Area was gone. LAPD headquarters seemed like a rabbit warren. Brian felt, acted, and was treated like a stranger. The other clerks and cops knew why he was there and few if any expected him to stay. He was a fuck-up, banished from the street, sentenced to Management Services to serve out his term or resign. Bets were he would resign.

Life upside down was compounded when Brian moved from his apartment in Venice Beach. Staying there was like life in a crime scene. Images of the girl's bloody father falling into the pool were too painful. He found a second-floor apartment in Marina Del Ray. In comparison to Venice the apartment and the streets around it were quiet. He called Pamela late on the evening of his transfer. He didn't mention the transfer. He had finally replaced his cell-phone. He gave her his new number along with excuses about why he was moving. "Just too noisy living next to a pool, my drive to work will be shorter, and there was too much stomping from the apartment above." It sounded lame.

Pamela was surprised. "Would you like some help?"

"Thanks but moving is a guy thing. You know lots of lifting and stuff."

Pamela had already sensed the chill. Was it because she had blunted his advances in bed? They had made love before. He had no reason to think they wouldn't make love again. She was puzzled, worried. Was it the shooting? She was bright enough to have connected the dots.

Pamela knew Brian shot the girl. She also knew Wilder was the one who shot and killed her father when he showed up at Brian's apartment with a gun. She hadn't asked Brian about any of it. She knew he would talk about it when he was ready. Was she wrong? Did he think her silence was simply a lack of caring? Pamela was worried. She loved this man and somehow the relationship she thought she had finally found was somehow now slipping away. "I like to see it after you're moved in," she said to hold on to what seemed to be a fading dream.

"Sure, I'll give you a call," Brian answered, but he didn't.

The sergeant in charge at Management Services loaded Brian down with a series of monotonous and painstaking tasks that kept him constantly at his desk. Deadlines were set that were impossible to meet without overtime, but no overtime was authorized. Brian sat his desk, alone, working into the late hours of the night. He did not complain.

The more pressure his bosses applied; the greater Brian's determination became to overcome it. Without knowing it they became his reason for staying. Soon they tired of finding work for him and the pressure began to ease. Brian Culpepper was never to be welcomed or accepted but he would be tolerated.

Wilder and Clark Kent visited regularly, for a while. Clark Kent was now dating Janet Williams, the CHP officer from Indio. JD Kent came by once. He didn't stay long, but Brian was pleased to find the Black sergeant remembered him. They sat, drank beer, joked, and told and retold the Blythe story. The story changed as time went by but none of them seemed to care. Brian found himself listening instead of talking. He had no new stories and there was nothing at

Management Services that was even vaguely humorous. As expected, Wilder called on a Thursday night. A bunch of guys were going over to Chinatown on a whore hunt and Brian was invited. He declined and the final string was cut.

Time passed and things did change. There were more police shootings. More demonstrations and protests, more political crises, and the world moved on. Brian Culpepper slowly realized no matter what he thought or did, tomorrow was going to be a new day. What he did with each day was a matter of personal choice.

Without cognizant recognition Brian's sense of well-being was returning. The days passed and the death of the girl, the incident in Blythe, like his memories of Iraq, faded deeper and deeper into the recesses of his mind. He covered them with daily workouts at the old LAPD academy near Dodger Stadium. His workouts there were capped with solitary runs that snaked through the hills of Elysian Park. He was finding his mental health was linked to his physical health. The truth was his spirit was healing and he was finding he was once again hungry for life.

It was true, the name lady killer, shouted by some unseen face in a crowd was right. He had shot and killed a lady, but what he learned was the shooting was only one dimension of his life. A dimension that was further and further behind him every day.

Without realizing it, Brian had locked everyone out of his life. It was as if he was trying to sweep everything and everybody away to start anew. His friends at Wilshire Area were gone. Pamela Moss was gone. He hadn't dated in nearly a year. He hadn't talked with his brother in Ohio in months and his once loved pickup sat dirty and neglected in need of tires. Truth was finding its way back into his life. His spirit was healing. Without a firm date and time or even a conscious recognition of a decision Brian Culpepper returned to Los Angeles, the city he had never left.

Brian had to grudgingly admit the assignment to Management Services did one thing. It gave him the opportunity to study the paper police department. Now he knew how the bureaucratic giant operated. The LAPD was a government within the larger government of the City of Angels, and it was a dictatorship run by the chief of police. Reading and studying the seemingly endless flow of paper not only going to but coming from the office of the chief of police, Brian began to understand the awesome responsibility the man in that office carried. He had even once wondered if the chief of police knew of the incident in Blythe. He supposed not.

Nothing happened in the LAPD without it first being written down on paper, lots of paper, and if it was on paper it came from, or it was going to Management Services. It was paper that planted the seed for Brian Culpepper's escape. An announcement for the department-wide written examination for the position of LAPD detective sergeant caught his attention. The thought excited him. He had found a way out, and the way out was up.

Now, at his desk in Management Services when Brian wasn't working, he was studying. Patrol tactics, line supervision, personnel management, the department's eight-inch Bible, and a wealth of training bulletins and special orders. He studied them all, time and time again. He became a brown bagger and spent his lunch break at his desk studying, and when end of watch came, he would pack up the material, take it home and study more. It became a disciplined routine and Brian never let up.

The countdown for the exam was now only three weeks away. Brian intensified his efforts and began getting up at four a.m. so he would have an additional two hours of study time before his monotonous workday began in Management Services. It was the third morning of his new routine when he arrived at the Management Services office complex to find all the office chairs inverted and set atop the desks. A Black janitor was running a noisy buffer over the bare floor. Spotting Brian, the custodian switched off the electric buffer. He gave Brian a puzzled look. "They got you working Saturdays, huh?"

94

Brian flushed with embarrassment. Lost in his passion to study he'd simply forgotten what day it was.

The day for the sergeants' exam finally arrived. Brian was surprised. He was only one of three hundred and sixty-eight men and women taking the exam. A representative from the Civil Service Commission explained the nuance of the testing procedure. "There will be no talking. You are not allowed to use any reference or research materials. You will be on closed circuit television. If you object you will be excused. In the event you need a comfort break you please inform the monitor in your area. The monitor will escort you to the restroom on this level. It has been reserved for our use. You will have two hours to complete your exam. In the event you finish earlier bring your test packet to me at the head of the room. Make sure you have put your full name, serial number, and current assignment on the cover page of the test packet. Any questions?" There were none. "You may begin."

Brian opened the test packet and read question number one. "You are a patrol sergeant assigned to an a.m. Watch. A broadcast from communications announces, One-Adam-nine, see the woman, a prowler there now, at fourteen-oh-six west Hancock. One-Adam-nine, your call is code two. One-Adam-fourteen, a 484 suspect there now, Golden Dragon liquor, twenty-six-twelve West Monroe. Use caution, manager reports he is armed. One-Adam-Fourteen your call is code two." The question brought a smile to Brian's face. It was if he were reading one of the many training bulletins published by Management Services. He was to finish the test in less than ninety minutes. When done he waited, not wanting to be first to turn in the test pamphlet. After three men and two women turned in their pamphlets, Brian pushed out of his chair. He was confident he had done well on the exam. The question remaining was how well?

The morning after the test, Brian returned to his desk to find a pink telephone message note pushed into the corner of his desk calendar. Brian read it as he sat down at his desk.

The message was short, concise. Dep DA Pamela Moss called. 956-5667. Brian studied the message. Pamela Moss was part a life he had left behind. In his mind he had consciously promised himself not to look back, only ahead, but she called and now he was uncomfortable with the mix of emotions and memories that flooded in. His concentration had been fixed. His goal set and everything else had been locked out, but now Pamela Moss had broken through. They had dated before he shot the girl, before he became the lady killer. Pamela was his safe place to fall when he drove home from Blythe, but since his transfer into Management Services she had been shelved along with the others he avoided. Avoided because it was easier not to talk to them, easier not to explain the grip of emotions that had him crying in the middle of the night, easier not to talk about a future filled with anxiety.

Pamela's message brought an avalanche of memories and images. Their relationship before the shooting could only be described as serious. They hadn't announced or cemented anything but they both knew; both had confessed a shared love. They had made love, exchanged keys, slept over and shared just about anything that could be shared, but that was then, and everything after that had changed. How it changed, and what changed was like a heavy wet curtain standing between then and now. He had once loved this woman, but now, he would have to explain what happened, explain how it felt to kill a woman. He wasn't sure he could do that. If you loved someone, could you stop loving them? Especially if the loved one had done nothing wrong. Could love start and stop? Could it be put on hold? Was it possible this woman was calling him to profess her love for him? Not likely. And did her call mean she now knew where he worked? The answers came in a rush. Brian was uncertain with them all, especially when they concerned Pamela Moss.

Pamela Moss was a contemporary woman, bright, attractive, and educated, but she had another dimension that drew him to her. Although being a deputy district attorney in Los Angeles announced her personal success, she was also an anachronism, a throwback to hard work and a fading morality. As a single cop Brian had his share of what they called "camp followers", but Pamela was different. She wasn't husband hunting. The fact she accepted his put off after the shooting spoke of her character. Their relationship had just stopped, but now she had called. What was next? Brian didn't have an answer. All he had was a message that Pamela Moss had called.

Before her call to Brian Culpepper, Deputy District Attorney Pamela Moss had been mapping out a strategy on yet another rape case. Somehow, she had become Ms. sex crime. The district attorney had been blunt when she complained to him about being assigned to what appeared to be a succession of rape cases. "If you want to convict a rapist you make sure your prosecutor is a beautiful woman. Why? Because the jury will look at you and think about sex. Not a pretty picture, but an accurate one. And you're the beautiful woman who's been sending rapist to prison."

There was a weak point in the people's case and Pamela Moss had found it. The two arresting officers claimed their probable cause to arrest the defendant was based on "The profile of a rapist", an LAPD inter-departmental training bulletin originating in the department's Management Services Division. The six-page training bulletin profiled a composite rapist and its author seemed to know the defendant because it described his personality, his physical appearance, and his age, as well as the neighborhood where his crimes were usually committed and the approximate age of his victim. The problem for Pamela was to prove to the court that The Profile of a Rapist was a valid police tool. The fact it had proven itself valid seemed somehow not relevant to the court. Until it stood the test of the law at the bar it was mere speculation and Pamela was worried. Worried that any testimony, or supposed evidence, that labeled the accused a criminal type, was likely to fall short of probable cause for a lawful arrest. Without a lawful arrest all the other evidence was tainted. Fruit of the poison tree, as judges often said.

Pamela first called the District Attorney's research department. They suggested she save herself time and call LAPD Management Services. She first spoke with Sergeant Trader, the OIC of the statistical unit. Trader listened briefly and then suggested she talk to officer Culpepper, the author of the training bulletin. The name made Pamela take a deep breath. Her heart raced as the telephone clicked to hold. Shifting the receiver on her ear she straightened in her chair as the rush of memories flooded in. How long had it been? She last heard Brian had transferred to the Valley. She was surprised to find herself excited. Her breath quickened, she covered the mouthpiece, cleared her throat, and made a conscious effort to calm down.

After what she considered their serious relationship, Brian had never called again. After learning he was the shooter of the girl at the bank, she understood his need for time, even used it as an excuse for him not calling. Maybe she'd come on too strong. Perhaps it was true, cops and prosecutors don't mix. The police distrust of attorneys, deputy district attorney or not, was legendary. Maybe that was it. She regretted the loss of the relationship, but the choice was his.

He was the first cop she had ever dated. She expected him to be all hands and beer. Brian was neither. She had to admit she loved him and never stopped thinking of him. Now faced with having to talk to him she felt insecure and wary. The telephone clicked in her ear and Pamela tensed. "This is Officer Culpepper," the voice said in her ear and she knew it was him.

"Brian, it's Pamela. Pamela Moss."

"Pamela...how have you been?" Brian asked awkwardly.

"Well, thank you. I'm calling to ask your help," she said, and immediately regretted it.

"How can I help?" Now his voice was cooler, professional.

"I need a copy of the training bulletin called, The Profile of a Rapist," Pamela answered. "I'm told you put it together."

"That's easy. I'll email a copy to you."

"I'm preparing a case for trial," she explained, "Could you get me the data you used in building the profile?"

"Yeah, may take a while, but I'll find it."

"I'm three days from trial," Pamela explained. "The sooner the better."

"Tomorrow...late afternoon. Say three."

"Could you bring it over?" she said as the thought entered her mind. She wanted to see him. It was just curiosity she told herself, knowing it was a lie. "I'm in seven-seventeen, the criminal courts building."

"Seven-seventeen," the voice in her ear repeated. She pictured him making notes with a pencil and perhaps jotting Pamela underneath it. She waited for him to say something...she wanted him to...and when he didn't, she did. "Thanks, Brian." Her fear was gone now, and her voice was sincere. It's been nice talking with you again. I've often wondered where you were, how you were and believe it or not, many times I worried about you, and I'm really looking forward to seeing you tomorrow. She thought it, she felt it, but she said none of it.

"Around three," Brian said in her ear.

"Three it is," she heard herself say. "Goodbye."

Pamela put extra effort into her makeup and wardrobe the following morning. She made a conscious effort to make sure her office was neat and clean. The morning dragged by and she tried not to clock watch but finally morning yielded to afternoon. Three o'clock came and Brian Culpepper did not. She waited thirty minutes before deciding to call. Damn him! He may choose to ignore her personally but failure to keep a business appointment with a deputy district attorney was another matter. That she could do something about. Her anger swelled as she dialed the number. Brian Culpepper, along with the entire police department could all go to hell.

The officer answering the telephone in Management Services was polite. Pamela demanded to talk to Brian. She was put on hold. She drummed polished nails on her desktop while she waited. Finally, the officer came back on the line and told her Brian was out of the office. Pamela asked when he was expected back. "This late in day, Ma'am, I would guess tomorrow," the officer answered. "Is there something I can help you with?"

Pamela slammed the receiver down in anger. Pushing to her feet she began jamming law books, briefs, and notes into her briefcase. Tomorrow, she told herself, she'd call the commander of Management Services and file a complaint against him. He had no right to do this. She'd waited nearly an hour, it was an insult, and she wasn't going to take it. The bastard, he must have a live in. She hoped whoever it was was fat with hairy legs and bad breath.

"Pamela," a voice said. She knew it was Brian. He stood in the open door of her office. He was in uniform. He looked taller than she remembered. She hadn't seen him in uniform that much before. The silver and gold badge of the LAPD on his chest. The gun belt. The name tags. It all combined to present a persona of authority. She knew cops called it command presence.

"Where have you been?" she demanded. "It's almost four." Her anger was still showing.

"I thought of some material that might be helpful. I stopped by our library." Brian offered a manila packet. She took it.

"Sorry, it's been a long day," she almost stammered in reply.

"Sorry to make you wait. I should have called. When's the trial?" he asked.

"Thursday," she answered, wishing she could end the rush of thoughts that raced through her mind keeping her from saying anything right. Pamela studied him for a moment. She was regaining her composure. "Why didn't you call, Brian?"

"I didn't think I was going to be that late. I'm sorry."

"I'm not talking about the training bulletin," Pamela's court room demeanor was creeping in. She wanted answers. "I'm talking about us. You do remember us, don't you?"

Brian straightened his stance. He looked uncomfortable as he searched for an answer. "Yeah, I remember us, but one of us changed. Life got difficult. I thought you'd be better off without me and my problems."

"I called you yesterday and asked for your help. Were you willing to help me?"

"Yes," Brian answered, understanding her point. He looked to the floor for a moment and then raised his eyes to hers. "I learned I can't change much that I've done. All I can do is offer a sincere apology and ask for your under-standing."

Pamela nodded. She wished she could hug him. She realized she was holding her breath. Not knowing what to say she stuffed the packet Brian brought into her open tote bag.

"I see you're leaving." Brian glanced at her open bag. "I won't keep you."

"For the trial," Pamela said, stabbing the packet even deeper inside her bag. She wanted to tell him she wasn't in a hurry and invite him to sit down. She was about to speak but Brian spoke first.

"I hope the material helps. If you have any questions, give me a call."

It sounded so final. All she could think of was, "I will."

He nodded, smiled. "Goodbye, Pam."

"Thanks, Brian," she called after him as he stepped out the doorway and was gone.

Brian thought about Pamela Moss as he drove home. Damn, she was attractive. He didn't remember her being so busty. Was it the blouse? The bra? Whatever it was it added to her allure. He remembered their dates and savored the memory of her perfume and her warmth.

I have to get back to life, Brian thought. It was as if he'd been benched, sitting on the sidelines watching life go by. He hadn't been looking forward or back—he'd been stagnant. It was time to live again. Life was a journey, he told himself, and it was time for him to move on. It was time for a new beginning.

He was on his way to become a sergeant. The Civil Service system guaranteed him a chance even if the LAPD wouldn't. Maybe Pamela Moss could become part of his new beginning? Just the thought of it brought him a sense of excitement and anticipation that he hadn't known in a long time. A sharp warning from a car horn brought Brian out of his daydream. He was sitting through a green light, much like my life, Brian mused. He stomped on the gas and drove on.

8 A NATION WYDE SEARCH

Veronica Washington was Black, attractive, twenty-four years old, and thirteen minutes from her death. She sat in the kitchen of her dim, three-room apartment on South Hoover with a cocked .32 caliber automatic pistol laying heavy in her lap. Water dripped steadily from a tarnished faucet onto a collection of dirty plates in the nearby sink. Several large flies buzzed around feeding on food scraps. In the cluttered bedroom behind Veronica two children played on stained sheets. Angela, the youngest was eleven months old. Her diaper was soiled. There were no clean ones. Lovell was older at two. Neither shared the same father. A small television atop a dresser, a few feet from the bed, illuminated the room with its picture and sound of Sesame Street.

Veronica was a desperate woman. She had once again trusted, and once again been betrayed. Nathaniel Wyde, better known on the street as Nation Wyde, the man with whom she'd lived for more months than she could remember, had taken her last money and disappeared. He had promised to return with milk, diapers, and baby food. That was last night! Veronica knew he'd return, empty handed. She had believed him. They had met at her cousin's birthday party. Nation was a handsome man, a smooth talker. He told her he knew an agent who produced television commercials and she had a look that would sell. He collected three hundred dollars for the pictures he took. Every agent needed pictures, and then the nude pictures followed. Nation was sure he could sell them. Hell, there were plenty of magazines buying nude pictures, and she was beautiful. That cost her another two hundred dollars. And now he was talking shit about someone he knew that was producing a movie. He was certain she could be a star, but it was all a lie. The money was gone and so was he. There was no money, no hope, and no tomorrow. Nation Wyde was a lying piece of shit. The last time she complained about his lies he beat her. He would not beat her again.

Nation Wyde, as he would say, had his shit together when he reached the door to Veronica Washington's second-story apartment. He'd spent the money Veronica gave him on beer, eight ball and a late-night dinner of Popeyes Chicken. She'd be hot, but he knew how to calm her down. By midnight they'd all be eating steaks. As soon as he got his thirty-two automatic, he and Bubba Rodgers were gonna take off a liquor store. It was a "sweetheart" deal. The manager of the liquor store would get a cut and give the police a phony description. Easy pickings for maybe as much as a thousand. Nation smiled as he bounded up the stairs.

"Hey, woman," Nation Wyde called pushing open the door. Then he saw her and stopped short.

Veronica sat in a wooden chair just a few feet from the door. Tears traced down her. She held the gun outstretched in two shaking hands aimed at Nation Wyde's torso.

Nation stretched a hand toward her, extending his long fingers, as if to ward off the deadly lead which he was certain would tear through him any second. His eyes were wide, his mouth open. He tried to speak and found his breath had left him.

"Why? Why?" Veronica screamed hysterically. Her fingers were wrapped tight around the trigger. "You shouldn't have done this to me."

"Da Da," a small voice came from the bedroom.

Nation stared at the shaking gun. "Please, please, Baby, don't," he pleaded with a failing voice.

It happened fast. Veronica opened her mouth, turned the gun, and jammed it deep into her throat. Nation Wyde grimaced. She jerked the trigger. The muffled shot was mixed with the children's screams and the sound of Veronica's chair smashing against the floor as it fell backwards onto the floor. Bits of plaster, flesh, hair, and blood spewed from a gaping hole the lead tore in the soft kitchen wall. Veronica's legs kicked in a quick spasmodic fashion and then were still. Both children cried loudly. Nation turned, scrambled down the stairs, nearly falling. At the bottom he collided with a heavy-set Black woman who lived in the apartment across the hall from Veronica, nearly knocking her down, scattering the mail she had just collected.

"Ignorant no-good, unemployed bum," Mrs. Long muttered as she picked up the scattered envelopes. She could hear the two children crying from the hall at the top of the stairs. That was not unusual.

Nation Wyde ran south on Hoover for three blocks before he stopped and threw-up in front of a drug store. Mrs. Long had just reached the top of the stairs. Through the open door of Veronica's apartment, she saw the lifeless form on the floor and the sobbing child sitting beside it in the widening pool of blood. She gagged, covered her mouth, and staggered toward her apartment.

The officer on the complaint board in communications rocked forward and depressed a winking light on the control panel. He had been on duty for one hour and ten minutes. This was his seventeenth call. Of the seventeen he remembered only the woman who wanted help with her husband's ghost. "Police Emergency, may I help you?"

"Oh...oh...oh," the heavy voice gasped in the officer's headset.

The officer straightened in his chair, readied a pen, and waited.

"She's dead. My God she's dead," the headset cried.

"Where is she?" the officer asked coolly, ignoring the hysteria.

"In her apartment!" the voice screamed. "And she's dead. He shot her."

"What's the address?"

"Forty-two-oh-seven South Hoover." The officer's pen made notes. "I saw him run outta the house." The headset continued loud and fast. "He ran right into me. He musta' just did it."

SOUTHWEST UNITS IN THE VICINITY AND THREE-ADAM-NINETY-EIGHT. A POSSIBLE ONE-EIGHTY-SEVEN JUST OCCURRED AT FORTY-TWO-OH-SEVEN, SOUTH HOOVER. SUSPECT DESCRIBED AS A MALE BLACK. LAST SEEN RUNNING FROM THE LOCATION. NO FURTHER. THREE-ADAM-NINETY-EIGHT, YOUR CALL IS CODE THREE.

Uniformed Sergeant Thompson turned his black and white south onto Hoover from Santa Barbara. He was only two blocks from the address when he heard the call. Thompson stepped on the gas. He knew he'd be on the scene in a few seconds. He flashed by a bus, drove fast for a block, and then wheeled his black and white to the curb in front of the two-story apartment house. Picking up the radio mike Thompson keyed it, "Three-L-Twenty is Code Six at Forty-two-oh-seven South Hoover."

"Roger, Three-L-Twenty," a male voice on the radio answered.

The sergeant climbed out. Several Black kids played across the street. A few doors away several older men stood talking casually. Traffic passed routinely. If a murder had occurred nearby, no one knew, or perhaps, no one cared. The sergeant headed for the door.

At the top of the stairs, Sergeant Thompson spotted the open door and heard the crying babies. Unsnapping his holster and gripping his Glock he inched to the door and peered inside. He grimaced, drawing in heavy breaths through his nose. Taking a deep breath, he held it, and stepped through the door.

The younger of the two children was still on the bed, laying on its side crying. The other sat beside its sprawled, lifeless, bloodied mother on the kitchen floor. The baby's hands, face and arms were covered with sticky, crimson blood. The bloodied two-year-old raised a stainless tablespoon, offered an innocent smile, and said, "Poon."

Sergeant Thompson's eyes scanned the room. A few inches from the dead woman's outstretched hand lay a thirty-two automatic. The child pushed to its feet, slipped in the sticky blood, nearly fell, and then stood. The child raised the spoon proudly and stepped toward the uniformed sergeant. "*Poon.*"

Sergeant Thompson stepped around the child, reached down, picked up the thirty-two automatic and tossed it to the cluttered kitchen sink.

The blood-smeared child took another step toward the sergeant. He reached, gathered the child, crossed to the other younger child on the bed, gathered it under his other arm and moved for the door. The theme from *Sesame Street* played in the background.

Little changed in the City of Los Angeles with the death of Veronica Washington. It didn't make the evening news, although an overturned truckload of carrots, jamming the southbound Santa Ana Freeway did. Two homicide detectives, Boone, and Ketch, from Southwest Area worked three and a half hours documenting the case. A van from the Coroner's office arrived and took the body away, and at twenty-thirty hours PST a teletype was sent to every law enforcement agency in the Southwestern United States. Nathaniel Wyde, aka Nation Wyde, was wanted for 187 PC —Murder.

9 THE AUGUST MOON

Officer Brian Culpepper was six days from his sergeant's oral board interview, and it seemed to him the pressure in Management Services had eased some. He didn't really care why but he thought about it anyway as he rode the elevator in the Criminal Courts Building toward the seventeenth floor. As soon as he picked up a packet of blank felony complaint forms from the DA's office he was finished for the day. If he stopped on the way home and bought a sandwich, he would have at least four hours of study time.

The elevator slid to a smooth stop on the sixth floor. Brian was the car's only occupant and he stood against the back wall. For good reason, when in uniform, he never stood in front of people. The elevator's doors parted to reveal Pamela Moss waiting. Brian stood in the open elevator, looking at her. It wasn't a stare. His look did not make Pamela uncomfortable as she stood outside the car, case folder in hand, waiting. The elevator's chime sounded, and the rubber cushioned doors began to close. Brian moved and stabbed the hold button. The door stopped and then parted. Brian offered Pamela a smile. "Do you know what the odds are on us seeing one another in one week?"

"Obviously," Pamela smiled in return, stepping into the elevator, "the odds are two to one."

The elevator doors closed and then resumed its smooth

climb. They stood facing one another a few feet apart. The faint smell of Pamela's perfume reached Brian and teased at his nostrils.

"Your rape trial started today, didn't it?" Brian asked.

"Started and nearly ended," Pamela answered.

"That bad, huh?"

Pamela nodded. "Victim is a recent divorcee, lives alone, invited the defendant in to repair her TV, told him he was handsome."

The elevator halted and the doors parted.

"Nice seeing you again," Pamela said as Brian held the door. She didn't want him to go, and it was as if he had read her mind.

"Listen, if you've got time, I'd like to look at the case file," Brian said.

"Why?" Pamela asked.

"Because I know rapists," Brian said. "Not from experience," he smiled, "but I researched over a thousand arrestees for the profile, and the one thing I learned is that even though they're creatures of habit, they all have unique peculiarities, many times that's their Achilles heel."

"Let's go to my office," Pam said.

Brian sat behind Pamela's desk thumbing through the wealth of reports, papers, and notes in the thick case folder, while she waited. She sat across the desk from him enjoying his presence. Brian paused, glanced up at her. "I won't be long."

"Take your time."

Finally, Brian seemed to find something. He studied it for a moment and then looked to Pamela again. "Let me show you something."

Pamela pushed up and moved around the desk to look over Brian's shoulder. She was leaning close. Brian felt the pressure of her breast on his shoulder. He wondered if she knew she was doing that?

She knew.

Brian had a finger on a thin 5.10 arrest disposition report. Pamela leaned closer. Their faces were only inches apart. Pamela studied the grain of his hair, his jawline, the blue hint of beard on his cheek. The musk smell of his nearness reached her. "Here under person to notify in the event of an emergency," Brian said, looking at the line on the report, "your man, Marsh, gave the jailor the name Mary Barley, 246-6804."

"Yes," Pamela said. She hadn't really been listening. Brian turned his face to Pamela's. He could see flecks of green inside the pale blue halo of her eyes.

"When Marsh was arrested," Brian explained, "and booked into jail they asked him the routine question of who to contact in the event of an emergency. He gave the name of a female. It's not his mother so odds are it was someone he was close to. A lover. If that's the case, she might know how your man acts in the bedroom."

Pamela was surprised. His suggestion was so simple. "It's so basic."

"Basic, but still a long shot."

Brian pushed from the desk and moved for the door.

Pamela didn't want him to leave. "I'll keep you in the loop."

"You do that," he said with a smile and was gone.

Pamela sank into her office chair. She was angry at Brian, angry at herself. A second chance had come and gone. They had been so close, her lips only inches from his. What was wrong with him? She was attractive. Other men proved that. She was pursued. Was he blind? Wasn't he attracted, at least by her physical being? The answer that came was a disappointing one. She silently hoped she'd never see him again, but then had to admit that was a lie.

Brian's insight to the accused rapist proved invaluable. The next day Pamela located his former lover who, with a little prodding, proved willing to testify that her one-time boyfriend liked kinky sex. Games of rape and bondage were common and brutal. "That's why we broke up. He hurt me, and I knew eventually he'd hurt someone else."

The defendant promptly changed his plea of innocence to guilty and the trial was over. It was a significant win for

Pamela, and it drew a note of congratulations from the district attorney himself.

Walking to the elevators Pamela enjoyed the congratulations she collected from the more senior trial deputies. She was riding an emotional high when she stepped off the elevator There was little in life she wanted that had eluded her. And, now that the most recent pursuit was hers, she was savoring its taste. She had become a seasoned successful trial lawyer. Then the thought of the other fleeting want crept into her mind and tainted her victory. Brian Culpepper.

She reached her office. She stepped in and closed the door. Her mind was now fixed on him. She looked across her desk to the empty chair where he had sat. Damn him, she thought, he gave her the victory, showed her the way but then he tarnished it. She wished she could hate him, forget him, love him. Her eyes went to the telephone, then to her watch. It was three-fifty; he'd still be in his office. She wanted to call and hear his voice so much it was becoming an ache but damned herself for wanting it at the same time. Pride stopped her. She was District Attorney Pamela Moss. She had just defeated one of the most respected criminal defense attorneys in California; she didn't have to call anyone. Let me know how it turns out, she remembered Brian asking. Ha! Never. Me call you. Ha! I don't have to. I could have any man in the Criminal Courts Building, including the judges. But, she reasoned, calling Brian just to let him know how the case turned out was a legitimate professional courtesy, and she was a professional. She glanced at her watch again. Damn! It was four o'clock now. She hoped he would still be there as she stabbed at the telephone with a polished nail.

A busy signal buzzed in Pamela's ear. She damned the telephone and hung up in a fit of frustration. She pushed out her chair and paced, damning herself for her girlish behavior but promptly excused it. After all calling him was only a courtesy. She would have kept it short, business like. Hello, Brian, this is Pamela Moss. I just called and tell you the defendant changed his plea to guilt. On behalf of the district attorney's office, I'd like to thank you for your valuable assistance.

The telephone on Pamela's desk rang.

"Hello."

"Pamela?"

"Brian, I won!" She was excited.

"I heard. Congratulation."

"Thank you for helping. I would have never thought of that woman. She was a prosecutor's dream."

"That's what friends are for."

"Well, friend, if you ever need help with anything..."

"As a matter of fact, that's why I'm calling," Brian answered.

Here it comes, Pamela thought. Reality. Her heart sank. The real reason for his call. It would be a request to review a will prepared by a parent, an insurance policy he needed interpreted, maybe a problem with a landlord, or anything else that could save him a buck on attorney's fees. It was one of the hazards of being an attorney, and he had helped her.

"What is it?" She was disappointed and wanted it over with.

"I know it's late," he began, and she thought, damn, he not only wants free advice, but he wants me to work late too. No, she told herself. Not this night. This night was going to be one of celebration. Maybe John Howard from major crimes would be interested in joining her. He was always hitting on her.

"And it's Friday," Brian continued, "but would you consider allowing a cop to buy you dinner? I'm sorry for not calling, and hooray you won the case."

"Yes," Pamela answered without hesitation.

"Yes, you'll consider it, or yes, you accept?" the voice in her ear asked.

"Yes, I accept."

"Great," he sounded relieved. "How's eight o'clock?"

"Fine."

"And you're still on Stone Court Drive?"

"Yes."

"I'll be the cop at your door at eight."

Pamela had to smile when Brian proved he was punctual and still drove a black pickup truck with oversized mud tires. No one on the freeway they passed driving into the hills of Glendale north of Los Angeles would have made them as an LAPD cop and a deputy district attorney. Pamela was beginning to understand the allure the truck held for Brian. In his pickup the cop with his ton of baggage could quickly become just another face in the City of Angels.

The restaurant stood hidden behind a stand of towering pines and its lights glowed through the sweeps of the evergreens. "It's been a while since I've been here," Brian explained as they pulled into the parking lot. Low Chinese lanterns spilled light on a path that twisted through the pines. The air was cool and crisp; stirring the pines it filled the darkness with a sweet scent. Pamela took the arm Brian offered. The muscles beneath his jacket were hard against her touch as she followed him along the pine needle cushioned path.

They were greeted by a Chinese man in his thirties. He had jet black hair and horn-rimmed glasses to match. He was dressed in a white shirt and a red jacket. Brian called him Henry and the man smiled and shook Brian's hand. It was obvious they were friends. Henry looked to Pamela. He smiled approvingly and offered a slight bow. "So, this is the beautiful woman you have spoke about?"

"Thanks, Henry, I need all the help I can get."

Henry escorted them to a quiet corner in the wide candle-lit dining room. A waiter poured tea and then Brian ordered dinner. Pamela noticed he did not use the menu. It was obvious he knew it. When the waiter moved away Brian raised his teacup. "To friendship."

Pamela raised her cup until it clinked against his. "To friendship."

113

The tea was mild and warm, and Pamela enjoyed its taste. While they waited, Brian told her about Henry. The two men had worked together at a Walmart in the Valley while Brian awaited his academy class to start.

Henry worked in produce and Brian was a stock boy. Brian had helped Henry, an immigrant who had fled China seven years earlier, build the "August Moon".

Henry had called on every blood relative he had in southern California to help with the task, but it still had taken five years. Brian was proud to be the only non-Chinese invited to help. Brian labored on his days off and many nights with the crew of eighteen Chinese. The August Moon was finally completed three years after Brian became a policeman. He was the only non-Chinese invited when a Chinese priest was brought in to bless the restaurant before it opened.

"Come on," Brian said, taking Pamela's hand. He led her across the room to where water cascaded down over smooth polished rocks to pool in a fountain of crystal water. The collection of wet rocks and clear water was dotted with a collection of silver coins. Thrown on impulse by hundreds of customers giving in to the allure of a wishing well. Brian's eyes showed pride as he told her of collecting the rocks on the nearby mountain side and pushing them into the wet grainy cement as they built the fountain.

Brian was still holding Pamela's hand. He looked to her. "Henry promised he's going to let the coins collect until I get married. Then I get them as a wedding gift."

"Stay here, I'll be right back." Pamela left Brian standing at the fountain as she returned to their table to dig in her purse. She returned to Brian with several coins in hand. Reaching Brian, she closed her eyes. "I'm making a wish."

"Penny for your thoughts?" Brian said with a smile.

Pamela opened her eyes and shook her head. "If you tell it doesn't come true." She tossed the coins. They tumbled and fell into the water with a distinct plop.

"Thanks for the wedding gift," Brian said.

After dinner, Henry arrived at their table with a dark clay bottle and two small cups. He made a great ceremony of pouring each a finger cupful and then skillfully set each aflame with a concealed match.

The blue alcohol flame licked around the edge of the two small cups for a second and then Henry smothered it. Then he bowed, said something in Chinese and moved away.

Pamela looked to Brian. She spoke in a near whisper, "What is this?"

Brian picked up his small cup and sniffed it. "I asked Henry once. He said something about fermenting rice and potatoes. I told him I didn't want to know any more."

Pamela picked up her cup. "How do you drink it?"

"The Chinese down it with a gulp. I don't recommend that. Try sipping it."

Pamela followed Brian's lead as he sipped his cup. The liquor was warm like the tea, but sharp and bitter. Its warmth traced down Pamela's throat and warmed her stomach. Her eye's glazed with tears.

"It's..." she couldn't finish, but with the Chinese liquor dulling the edge of her anxiety Pamela led the way into the gulf of time that had separated them. Now it stood dark, awkward, and ominous between them and Pamela wanted it removed. She wanted to know this man, and she wanted him to know her. She took another drink from her cup. Heavier this time. It was hot in her mouth. She swallowed and felt it spread, adding to the glow already burning inside. "Brian," she said, finding his eyes and taking his hand in hers, "why didn't you call me? What happened?"

Brian answered, but he was deliberately vague. He released her hand and picked his words carefully. He didn't allow himself to focus on the girl he had shot. It was as if his memory came from a newspaper account he had read. He was no longer the man that pulled the trigger. Time had dulled and mellowed until all of it, the girl, her father, her mother, and the incident in Blythe ran together like wet paint, mixed to become a gray almost forgotten memory.

Pamela saw it was painful but began to understand Brian

was trying to focus on what lay ahead and ignore what was past. She hoped she could be part of his future.

The red jacketed Henry arrived at their table. Neither realized how long they had been talking. "I'm sorry. You must go home now. We are closing."

On the freeway, with the pickup's interior warm and the engine purring, Brian broke the comfortable quiet. "I enjoyed tonight," he said, taking her hand. It was warm and soft. Their fingers interlaced.

"Me too," Pamela said.

They didn't speak again and with the hour late and traffic thin the drive went quickly. Pamela's pulse quickened when Brian finally swung the pickup onto Stone Court Drive. They parked in front and walked inside to Pamela's apartment. At the door Pamela dug in her purse for a key. They still hadn't spoken. Pamela unlocked the door and stepped inside. Her heart was pounding in her ears. She looked to Brian, opened the door wider. He understood and stepped inside.

Pamela closed and locked the door. The metallic click of the lock was loud in the quiet. She sat her purse down and turned to him. Their eyes meet and held; he stepped to her. She raised her face and they kissed. Her arms went around his neck. Their kiss was hungry and passionate, unfinished business from the past. Pamela pressed into him and held him as their mouths and tongues mingled and explored. When the embrace ended, Brian held her and drank in the scent of her hair as he stroked her shoulders and neck with open hands.

Pamela's head was buried between his neck and shoulder. Brian's smell of musk and aftershave teased at her nostrils. She surrendered to an impulse and bit lightly into his neck. The barb of his whiskers pressed against her lips. A hand moved to her face and lifted as his mouth covered hers. She moaned and pushed even tighter against him, while her tongue teased at his. He was warm and hard against her and she could feel the heat through her slacks and panties. Pamela pushed up on her toes and moved the ache of passion between her thighs to him. Brian pressed against her and moved his hands down over her back to the curve of her buttocks.

Pamela gasped when their kiss ended. She was trembling. She looked into Brian's eyes. There was a question there and she understood it. She took him by the hand and led him toward the bedroom, dropping her shawl, on the way.

The bedroom was dark. The only light was spilling in from the living room. Pamela squeezed Brian's hand. "I don't want you to leave."

Brian raised a finger to her lips to quiet her. He moved his finger away and his mouth found hers. Locked in an embrace they sank to the bed.

10 A FEW GOOD MEN

Brian Culpepper saw it as his final chance to rebuild his career with the LAPD and it was now just four days away. His initial application, the two-hour written exam and now an oral interview, scheduled for one o'clock Thursday afternoon in City Hall would decide whether or not he was fit to become a detective sergeant. He would be facing three of them. A police commander, a captain and impartial representative from the Civil Service Board. Three men would decide who among the four hundred and three police applicants would wear the badge of an LAPD detective sergeant.

Brian's strategy was simple. Monday, Tuesday, and Wednesday nights were to be devoted entirely to uninterrupted study and review, but the plan had been formulated before Pamela. Now with her filling his every waking thought the interview, once all important, was now slipping into a distant second. On Monday, with Brian in the Management Services office at Parker Center office, and Pamela three blocks away in the Criminal Courts building they gave in to their impulses. Brian called Pamela twice and she called him three times. Pamela wanted to help, Brian accepted her offer. They would meet after work, pick up dinner, and spend the evening reviewing the study material.

The fried chicken Brian brought home with him was

never eaten. As soon as Pamela stepped into his apartment, they were in each other's arms and shortly thereafter in bed. Pamela left at eleven. Brian promised himself he would study twice as much Tuesday night.

They agreed on the telephone Tuesday that the oral interview was, for now, the most important thing and their lovemaking could wait until Thursday night. They both pledged to exercise self-discipline when they met at Brian's apartment that evening.

Tuesday night was different. They, at least, ate the fish and chips dinner Pamela brought before they made love on the living room floor. The study material surrounded them and that was as close as they got to studying.

Brian reluctantly said goodnight to Pamela at midnight.

Pamela, with great restraint, refused to call Brian on Wednesday. He called her three times before she finally gave in and took his fourth call. He wanted her help on the final night of studying. Pamela told him no. It hadn't worked. Neither of them had the ability or desire to say no, and the oral interview was less than twenty-four hours away. Brian pleaded, promising he would study with her help, while arguing that he'd get nothing done without her. Pamela reluctantly gave in.

Brian bought chicken again and this time they reviewed the study material while they ate. Brian paced as Pamela, thumbed through three-by-five cards, asking random questions. Brian answered all with confident accuracy and never a moment's hesitation. At eleven o'clock, after five hours of review, they stopped. Pamela helped him select a shirt and matching tie and then sat with him while he polished his shoes. At eleven thirty Brian was finished and nervous. Pamela, gathering her purse, suggested he take a hot shower and go to bed early. Brian argued that if she left him now, he'd have to take a cold shower. Pamela wished him luck, broke off the goodnight kiss, when he tried to make it more, and said goodnight.

After Pamela left, Brian gathered the study material scattered around the living room. The scent of her perfume still hung in the air. A glass displayed a faint red lip imprint on its rim and a note in Pamela's concise handwriting, held in place by a small magnet on the face of the refrigerator, announced: "Dare to Dream". Brian ran a finger around the note and whispered, "I am," before heading to the bedroom. Not only was he dreaming, but Brian also allowed himself to admit, he was "hoping". Pamela Moss brought him sensual physical pleasure when he hungered for, yet she was so much more. For the first time in a long time, he had hope…he was filled with it. He believed in it, and he was, as Pamela urged, daring to dream.

After showering, Brian lay in the darkness of his bedroom waiting on sleep. His thoughts were focused on the oral interview. He knew he would be facing a panel of three. A captain and a commander along with a Civil Service rep. They would be selected from a pool, at random. He would not know who they were until he was escorted into the room. And likewise, the three men would not know who the prospective candidate was until twenty minutes before the interview began, when a representative of the Civil Service Commission would carry the man's manila bound personnel file into the room for their review.

Brian was confident the paper officer, Brian D. Culpepper, serial number 33982, bound in a bland manila folder would stand the toughest of scrutiny. The recorded history of his police work was impressive. The collection of Personnel Rating Reports showed the paper officer, Brian D. Culpepper, rated consistently as an "outstanding" officer, but Brian knew the board would be considering other influences. The paper told only part of the story and Brian, like the men he would be facing, knew that. On the rating reports there were small boxes to be checked for personal characteristics, loyalty, diplomacy, presence of mind, duty performance, initiative, reliability, perseverance, and a variety of others, both desirable and undesirable, but only so much of a man could be captured on paper. The rest was reputation.

There was no official documentation of the incident in

Blyth, or the events that led to it, but the story was known. How it was known, how it was understood, depended on who was telling the story and why? Was it a group of cops, putting their asses on the line to save a fellow cop? Or was it a coward jeopardizing other's career? Was it bad judgement, good judgment, or lack-of-judgement? They knew about Blythe. They knew, and they already had an opinion. Brian knew his fate was set. He was just one of the few that didn't know what it was. Soon, he told himself, he'd know too and as Brian surrendered to sleep, he was covered with a light chilling sweat.

The interviews were held on the ground floor of the city Personnel Offices. The office complex had a wide reception waiting room with three interview rooms in an adjoining wing. Brian arrived twenty minutes early. He'd been awake since five-thirty, spending thirty minutes on his tie-knot alone. He was ready and eager. Now the waiting was just a grating annoyance. The interviews began daily at eight-thirty and ran continuously throughout the day. There were three interview boards and each devoted approximately thirty minutes to the prospective candidates assigned to them by a Civil Service Board representative. Two-hundred-and-eighty-eight policemen were scheduled for interviews.

Brian, dressed in his best suit and tie, checked in with the receptionist, an attractive Black woman with white even teeth that remined him of JD Kent. The woman asked to see Brian's I.D. card. She examined the card, comparing the picture on it to Brian. Then she ran a polished nail down a roster of names to place a red check by a name Brian assumed was his. Returning the I.D. card, the woman smiled. "Please be seated. We'll call your name. If you must leave the room, please check out with me."

"Thank you."

There were three other candidates waiting, two men and a woman. Selecting a chair, Brian guessed the three, like he, were waiting for interviews. One of the three was a broad-shouldered man in his early thirties. His short hair was combed perfectly, and a thick neck gave him a muscular fit look that his suit could not hide. To Brian the man looked like he should be a sergeant. He had an aura of confidence about him, and that Brian envied. One of the other two was overweight and Brian suspected that would eliminate his chances of promotion. The Los Angeles Police Department hated fat. Fat was lazy. Fat was no self-discipline. Fat was a bad image, and image above all else, was important to those who ran the L.A.P.D.

Brian settled to wait with a glance at the wall clock. In an hour, his oral interview would be over. All the months of study and preparation were being drawn toward the magic hour. The worry and anxiety he felt earlier was easing some. Being a police sergeant was no longer the most important thing in his life. He fought a smile the thought provoked.

He'd been smiling a lot lately. Why? I'm happy, he told himself. He couldn't remember ever being so happy. Even the hours in Management Services Division over the past week hadn't been bad. The reason was simple, her name was Pamela. She brought him happiness. That was important. Loving her, having her love him, that was happiness. That was important. Only with Pamela's love could anything else take on any importance. Becoming a sergeant was no longer just a ticket out of Management Services Division. Now it was important because Pamela would be proud of him. That made it worthwhile.

Being a police sergeant or detective and having Pamela Moss; what more could life offer? He had turned a corner in his life. A significant one. The turbulent disturbing years just past were fading and the future was bright. Nothing more was chance. Now he was in command. The decisions were his and he had a wealth of experience on which to draw. He was confident he would make a good police sergeant. He was ready. He promised himself to make that point to the three men he would soon be facing.

At ten minutes to the hour an attractive shapely woman in her forties came out of one of the interview rooms and walked to a file cabinet in the waiting area. There she gathered a personnel file, glanced at the identifying name. It read, Culpepper, Brian D. Serial # 33982.

Brian watched as the woman crossed the room, moved down the hallway and disappeared into an interview room. When she stepped inside, Brian's interest in her ended. The odds were one in three it was his file, or was it, two to one, he wasn't sure. The thought seemed silly, and he could never figure odds. He glanced at his watch. He had ten minutes yet. That didn't need odds. That was a fact. Facts were much easier than odds.

His mind was a rush of random thoughts and he wished he could hold onto a single idea. Concentration had always been an escape for him, but now as the seconds ticked away it was eluding him. How to control anxiety. Breathe deeply, focus on what you were afraid of, who's waiting in that room? He didn't know and that worried him. More than worry it unnerved him. Once he saw them, shook their hands, his anxiety would be gone. He hoped. He looked at his watch again. Eight minutes to go. Damn, his throat was dry.

In interview room C the gray-haired Captain Hays sat at the table, leafing through Culpepper's personnel file. There were four chairs in the small room. Three for the board members on one side of the table and one for the candidate on the other side. Commander Hays, the OIC of Internal Affairs was pacing, arms folded, he looked troubled. "I don't know how the hell we get around this, Captain. It's not what's in Culpepper's file that we must deal with. It's what isn't in there."

"Gentlemen," the female representative from the Civil Service Board said from where she sat beside Captain Winslow. "I must caution you we are limited to judging this candidate on what's in his personnel file and his answers to our questions. Not hearsay that may bias the interview."

Commander Hays paused and gave the Civil Service rep a go to hell look. "Don't kick our asses yet. We're just talking."

"Well," Captain Winslow said, flipping the personnel file closed. "Culpepper looks good on paper. Good mix of patrol assignments. Seventy-seventh, Southwest, Wilshire, tour in Vice, and currently Management Services."

"Ratings?" Commander Hays pressed.

"Straight upper tens. Several commendations. One shooting. In policy," the captain said, "only one negative, a failure to report for duty without a call off."

Commander Hays nodded and returned his attention to the woman. "This may merit you getting us a waiver on this interview?"

"Based on what, Commander?" the woman asked, putting on her glasses. "Waivers require cause. If you're prepared to go on record?"

The commander sat down beside Captain Winslow and drummed his fingers on the tabletop. "Where did he place on the written?"

The captain checked a list in front of him. "Nineteenth out of three hundred and four."

"Maybe we should pass on him. Send him to another board." Hays was being indecisive.

"Why don't we quit beating around the bush and talk about what happened?" the captain offered.

"You mean Blythe?" the commander asked.

"You and I were there, Commander. We pass on Culpepper; he'll have to deal with someone who will judge him on the rumors they've heard."

The commander took in a breath and let it out slowly before looking to the other two. "Okay, we go with it," he said with a look at the Civil Service rep. "Call him in."

Brian was on the edge of his chair in the waiting room; he had checked his watch, and the wall clock, both showed ten minutes past the hour. The other candidates who had been waiting had been called in promptly on the hour and now three others had arrived.

Brian knew there was a problem. He knew why he was being singled out. Why? He had put it behind him. He was still a good cop. Bullshit! Because of it, he was a better cop.

Because of it he would be a better sergeant. Why were they looking back? He was looking ahead. Hadn't he proved that? What did the department want from him? He had done his best. Many thought his best was shooting a nineteen-year-old girl who tried to kill him. Brian knew his best was regretting the killing. He had done his duty with regret. Those who could kill without regret were mentally unstable. The days when cop shootings were celebrated as a mark of courage were long gone, or at least that's what he believed. A deep-rooted dark emotion was settling over him. Brian looked at his hands as if expecting to find the girls' blood there.

"Officer Culpepper," a female voice called. It was the Civil Service representative.

Brian pushed to his feet. The woman stood at the mouth of the hallway leading to the interview rooms. Brian button his jacket and followed her. Ironic, Brian thought. They had sent a woman to summon him.

"My name is Candice Marshal," the woman said pausing at the door to the interview room, she offered a hand to Brian. "I'm the Civil Service representative that will be sitting in on your interview today. There will be a recording. Now, allow me to introduce you to the chairman of your board, Commander Hays."

Brian stiffened. The woman opened the door, held it. The two men at the table pushed to their feet. The stocky Commander Hays was at the center of the table. Captain Winslow was to his right. Brian stared at the two in silence. He was shocked. The last time he had seen either man was in Blythe, California.

The woman opened the door wider, gesturing Brian inside. Brian stepped in on wooden legs. "Officer Culpepper this is Commander Hays," the civil service rep continued.

The commander extended a hand. Brian stepped forward and took the commander's hand. It was strong and firm. The commander glanced to Winslow. "This is Captain Winslow. I believe you served with him at Wilshire."

Winslow offered a hand and a nod. Brian took the hand.

It felt stiff. Awkward. "Hello, Brian." The captain smiled. The woman closed the door behind them and joined the two men facing Brian.

"Please sit down, Officer," the commander said.

Brian sat facing the three. He could feel sweat beading on his neck. He prayed he'd be able to speak. Commander Hays leaned his elbows on the table. "We've been selected by the chief of police and the Civil Service Board to evaluate you as a candidate for promotion to the rank of sergeant. In addition to asking you questions on which we will base our evaluation we'd like to provide you with an opportunity to tell us why you think you should be considered. Would you care to make an opening statement?"

"Yes, sir, I would," Brian answered mechanically.

The commander nodded approval. "Very well. Go ahead."

Brian had made the speech a hundred times to his bathroom mirror. He had once bragged to Pamela that he knew it so well he could say it backwards, but now sitting in front of the three who were to decide his fate he couldn't remember a single word. There was an awkward heavy silence as they awaited him to speak. Brian's heart pounded in his ears.

"Please, go ahead, Officer," Commander Hays said with a hand gesture. "We're waiting."

Brian's eyes searched their faces. They were sober, waiting.

Brian realized he wasn't going to give his opening remarks. His anxiety was fading. It was as if he suddenly realized the three in front of him were not responsible for his life, his happiness, or his wellbeing. He respected them but he wasn't about to surrender his future to them. The ripples from the shooting of the nineteen-year-old were continuing, like waves hammering a beach. He knew they were feeling it too, perhaps more than he. He knew what he had done was just. He regretted it, but the peace he found came from the realization he may have shot the girl, but whoever put her in front of that bank with a gun in her hands was the real lady killer. Brian sensed a decision had already been made. He could see it on their faces. His fate had been decided before he walked through the door. They weren't judging him on his qualifications or the shooting. They were judging him because of what happened in Blythe.

Brian drew in a breath to steady himself before he spoke. He noticed the Civil Service rep push a button on a small tape recorder setting in front of her.

"While I waited, I wondered who would be behind these doors. I know the LAPD goes to great length to ensure these interviews are impartial. So, I can only conclude that fate played a role in deciding who I would meet today. Gentlemen, it's good to see you again."

"Pardon me, Officer," the female Civil Service rep said raising a hand.

"Am I to understand you know these men?"

Both the commander and the captain sat sober and silent.

"Yes, we know one another."

"Then it's your right, Officer. Under Civil Service rules, you may request another board."

Brian looked to the commander and the captain. They both looked stone sober.

"No need for another board," Brian said. "Things happen that never appear in a personnel file. Things happen beyond the reach of the LAPD, but they can still be important. Very important."

Neither the commander nor the captain reacted. The commander sat with his hands folded on the table. His Internal Affairs persona was showing.

Brian leaned forward in his chair. "You two are the reason I'm here today. Thank you for what you did. You put your careers on the line far from any authority the LAPD grants you. I'm still a cop because of what you did. You didn't know me. All you knew was that I was an LA cop and I needed help. Thank you."

The commander and the captain seemed surprised, they tried to hide it by exchanging a glance.

"My service, my personnel file and my test scores show I am a viable candidate for sergeant." Brian pointed at the file on the table in front of the commander. "But nowhere in my personnel file does it show I regret shooting a nineteen-year-old girl?"

The Civil Service rep straightened in her chair.

"I'm over it," Brian assured in a confident tone exchanging a look with all three across the table. "Why, because the LAPD became my safe place to fall. My shooting was justified, but justified or not, I regret it. Taking a human life is traumatic, but I'm confident experiencing it will make me a better sergeant." Brian pushed back in his chair. Power in the room had shifted. He had taken it away from the two powerful LAPD figures, two figures who anticipated they would decide whether or not Brian Culpepper became a sergeant.

"I want to be a sergeant. I studied, I stayed up nights, I did mock interviews, I gave up watching the Lakers," Brian continued, "all to get ready for today, but I wasn't prepared to see you."

"And seeing the two of us has made you feel what?" Commander Hays asked.

"It made me feel this may be the real test. Every cop's career is built on the shoulders of other cops. You helped me and I learned from it. I didn't ask for your help, but you gave it. That's a lesson I will remember and it's a lesson that will make me a better sergeant."

Commander Hays looked to Captain Winslow. "Captain, do you have a question?"

"Yes, Officer Culpepper," the captain said, leaning his elbows on the table. "Tell us what happened in Blythe?"

The commander raised a hand in protest. "Captain, I'm not sure we should go there."

"Commander," the Civil Service rep said, "the officer didn't bring this subject up. He has a right to answer."

The commander was annoyed. He gave the rep an angry look but accepted her ruling.

"Officer," the rep said with a look at Culpepper, "would you like to comment?"

Culpepper nodded appreciation, looked to the two men. "What happened in Blythe," he mused. "A lot happened."

Commander Hays was visibly worried.

"Let's consider why we're here," Culpepper continued. "What happened to me in Blythe is the question. I'm still seeking answers but what happened demonstrated the importance of leadership. There is the letter of the law and the spirit of the law. It took leadership to choose the right path. My career was on the line. I am proud to be a Los Angeles police. I can't imagine being anything else, but at that place and at that time I needed leadership." He looked directly at the two men. "You provided that. That's what happened in Blythe."

The commander and the captain exchanged a look. Culpepper pushed out of his chair. "Gentlemen," he said, extending a hand, first to the commander who pushed to his feet, and then Captain Winslow who also stood.

It appeared Culpepper was in charge. "My career was once in your hands." He forced a smile. "It seems again today my career is in your hands." He offered a nod of appreciation to the Civil Service rep and turned to the door.

As the door closed, the commander and the captain sank to their chairs.

"Well, I'll be a son-of-a-bitch," Commander Hays mumbled.

11 FOR THE GOOD OF ALL

In room six-eighteen of the LAPD's headquarters building on West First Street a hastily called meeting was taking place. Crowded around one end of the long, polished conference table sat Deputy Chief Searcy, Commander Hays, and Captain Winslow. The three were silent as they listened to a tape recorder sitting on the table playing Brian Culpepper's voice from the earlier interview.

"Let's consider why we're here. What happened to me in Blythe is the question. I'm still seeking answers but what happened demonstrated the importance of leadership. There is the letter of the law and the spirit of the law. It took leadership to choose the right path. My career was on the line. I am proud to be a Los Angeles police. I can't imagine being anything else, but at that place and at that time I needed help. You provided that. That's what happened in Blythe. Gentlemen, my career was once in your hands. Again, today my career is in your hands."

Commander Hays switched off the tape recorder. He looked to Deputy Chief Searcy. "So, that's it. Blythe is now out of the box."

"But I heard no mention of the melee with the DEA," Deputy Chief Searcy said with a look at the two men. "No, talk about who all was there or what happened."

"I think that's his ace," Hays said. "He doesn't make sergeant with his top twenty written exam he blames us. He appeals and then we have the Civil Service Board investigating."

"And their first question is going to be, tell us about Blythe," Captain Winslow offered.

Deputy Chief Searcy got up out of his chair and walked to a window to look out at the surrounding buildings and the traffic passing below. The commander and the captain waited. Finally, Searcy turned to them. "So, you think Culpepper is blackmailing his way to sergeant."

"What else could it be?" Hays answered.

"What if he was sincere?" Searcy asked.

"You want to bet becoming chief of police in two years on that?"

Searcy returned to the table, but he didn't sit down. He leaned on the back of his chair and looked at the tape recorder. "Let's say we didn't have the tape. What would you do with him? Recommend for promotion or not?"

The commander and Captain Winslow exchanged a look. "But we do have the tape and he brought up Blythe. We didn't," Hays said.

"But he thanked you for being there," Searcy said. "Answer my question."

Again, the commander and captain exchanged a look. Captain Winslow reached and tapped the recorder. "If the tape wasn't part of this, Culpepper would have my vote. He was a good troop when worked Wilshire. He's had lots of time to talk about Blythe and he hasn't."

"Valid point," Searcy agreed. "It doesn't matter what's on the tape. It only matters if someone wants to make it an issue. And no one involved gains anything by talking about it."

"Unless the someone who's involved doesn't make sergeant. You think he wouldn't want a piece of our asses then," Commander Hays said.

The door to the room opened and Chief of Police Peck entered. The commander and the captain pushed up out of their chairs. The chief motioned the two to remain seated.

"Taylor," the chief said with a look at Deputy Chief

Searcy. "We've got Councilman Hahn and his staff arriving for their tour in twenty minutes. You ready for them?"

"Ready as one can be for a councilman who wants to be mayor."

The chief looked at Commander Hays and Captain Winslow and the tape recorder on the table. He read the sober faces. "You want to tell me what's going on or do I just call Culpepper and get the story from him?"

The three men smiled and exchanged looks, relying on the deputy chief to answer. Searcy nodded acknowledgement to the chief's statement.

"Seems your sources are as good as ours."

"Maybe," the chief granted as he sat down at the conference table. "So how did he do on his oral?"

Searcy looked to Commander Hays, urging him to answer.

The commander straightened in his chair. "He surprised us. He thanked us for going out to Blythe."

Now it was the chief who smiled. "So, you're going to promote him?"

"He's the one that brought up Blythe," Hays said.

The chief leaned an elbow on the table. "But you were there, weren't you?"

"Yes, we were there," Hays answered soberly.

"So, he's not afraid to talk about it," the chief said.

"Could result in the story getting out," Captain Winslow added.

"I've heard the story," the chief said. "Much like the two cops from Venice Area who drove to Vegas and back during AM watch. Nothing happened to them. Except they had to buy their own gas. When I heard the Blythe story, it was about a knock down drag out between a trio of LA cops and a dozen DEA agents. Not many believe the story," he paused and looked at Searcy. "Then there's the one about a deputy chief getting punched in the face by a DEA agent." He paused, tapping a finger on the polished table. "Play the tape for me?"

Pamela made fried shrimp and a salad for her and Brian. He was evasive about how he thought his interview had gone. "We'll know in a couple weeks when they publish the list."

Pamela understood. He was uncertain. She knew eventually he would talk about it.

After the table was cleared, she invited Brian to go for a walk. It was a warm California evening and they both welcomed getting outside.

Stone Court Drive twisted for three blocks west before it came to an end at the sprawling Westwood campus of UCLA. Arm in arm, Brian and Pamela strolled there. At the campus they walked in among the towering, gnarled trees and sat on the grass. It was quiet and peaceful and except for occasional joggers and ten-speed bikes they were alone.

They sat for a long time listening to the distant city. Eventually a black and white patrol car came into view, casually skirting the campus and then disappearing. "Wondering where they're going," Pamela said.

"You know, until today, I wondered where I was going," Brian began. "It was as if somehow I made sergeant, then everything else would be forgotten."

Pamela took his hand in hers.

"I learned in Iraq that shit happens. You can't dwell on it," Brian said.

Pamela massaged his hand, wondering how this gentle man had ever hurt anyone. Brian's voice tightened when he spoke of the girl's father and the rainy night he came to his apartment. Pamela could feel the anguish flowing from his hand to hers. He'd never spoken of this before.

Brian unknowingly tightened his grip on Pamela's hand when he told of hearing the girls' mother had hung herself. An entire family was dead, and no matter how it was told he had set it in motion. He ran, not knowing where, he just ran. And in running from one problem, he created another. He told her about Blythe, about the fight with the DEA agents, about JD,

Wilder, Clark Kent, and the others who came, unasked, to his aid, and how the problem was resolved with his banishment to Management Services. He ended it by telling her the problem was solved by love. Her love. Somehow the love he felt for her was now greater than before. "You lifted me out of my darkness," he said, raising her hand to kiss it.

Brian spent the night with Pamela. After making love, they slept soundly, wrapped in each other's arms.

It was business as usual in Management Services. Brian was ignored. That was routine. Four weeks after the oral examinations for sergeant began, they ended. The Civil Service Board spent another two weeks computing the scores, hearing protests that challenged both written and oral questions, combining the written and oral scores, until finally a list was compiled. It was as if Moses were returning from the mountain. The two hundred and eighty-seven names on the original list granting candidates an oral examination had in its final form been reduced to one hundred and six names.

Hump day found Brian arriving at his desk at 0730. He went through his usual morning routine. Unlocked his desk, checked the incoming departmental mail, checked the assignment board, got a cup of coffee, and returned to his desk. He was at his desk scanning pages he'd written the day before. His current assignment was to increase vehicle parking space at the department's geographic areas while decreasing the actual space used. He wondered why he wore a gun to do all this. It was his third attempt on the project.

Two other plans he had completed were promptly rejected. Both were stamped unacceptable. Undaunted, Brian started anew. In seven hours, his workday would be over, and he'd have his evening with Pamela. What he did until then was their business, not his, and if they wanted a third parking plan, he'd spend another two weeks formulating one. He was sure the citizens of Los Angeles would sleep sounder at night once he came up with a plan that put more police vehicles in fewer square feet at each of their police stations. It seemed to Brian the cars should be on the street instead of parked at the station. A solution Brian considered putting in his report but then decided against it. He was no longer a rebel. He didn't want any problems. He wanted them to forget who he was.

Brian was trying to compute the number of square feet in Hollywood Area's parking lot when Lieutenant Trader, a forty something policewoman, the OIC of Management Services walked by. "Congratulations," she said in passing.

Brian paused and glanced up from his work. The lieutenant was posting a list on a bulletin board. Five others from the office crowded around. They eagerly searched the list for their names. Brian knew it was the sergeants' list. He'd almost forgotten about it. He wondered how many names were on it and how far he was from the bottom. Perhaps not even on it he concluded, thinking the lieutenant intended her remark as sarcasm. He wasn't about to go look while the others were there. Screw them. He went back to work, pretending he didn't care about becoming a sergeant or getting out of Management Services. Although he did allow a fleeting dream of a night of celebration at the August Moon with Pamela.

Pamela called midmorning and they chatted briefly. She'd been assigned another trial. Two-eleven P.C., robbery. She was excited and eager, and Brian was happy for her. She promised to bring home the case file so he could read it. Their conversation ended with the smack of a telephonic kiss.

Brian worked, as one by one, everyone in the office trekked to the bulletin board to examine the newly posted sergeants' list. Occasionally two or more would gather there, talk in hushed tones, take covert glances at Brian. He ignored them. Taking pleasure in the fact the list was not important to him. He'd taken that away from them.

At noon, the office emptied and left alone, Brian lifted out his brown bag. He was opening a bologna and cheese sandwich made by Pamela when he remembered the list. He looked to it. It hung silent, waiting on the bulletin board. If he didn't look at it, Brian said, it couldn't hurt him. But it was only a list he reasoned. His curiosity was baiting him, either look and learn or someone else will tell you. He didn't want someone else's word. He wanted to see. It was not going to be a surprise, he assured himself, as he pushed out of his chair. He walked to the bulletin board.

Brian ran a finger down the long list as he read.

Morris, Dennis L. ....Serial 34706

O'Conner, Franklin, m ....Serial 30317

Evans, Paul W ....Serial 23772

Bartlett, John, N........................Serial 32262

Nelson, Stanley A .... Serial 32916

Walker, Fred A ....Serial 31931

Smithson, Donald P ....Serial 35716

Lovell, Charles D .... Serial 32205

Culpepper, Brian D....................Serial 33982

Time stopped. Brian's finger was frozen at the name. His eyes were fixed on it. He read down the list a second time. His name was still there. It was real. It was true. It was a fact. He was afraid to breathe.

Lieutenant Storm had become the OIC, the Officer in Charge, of Southwest Homicide. As often happened among police ranks Storm followed Captain Winslow who was broadening his experience by becoming the captain of Southwest detectives. Storm as always was energetic and devoted to his job. The men in his unit were quick to tag him *J.C.* Although never to his face. There was also the ongoing joke of his spike scars on his hands and feet. Lieutenant Storm pursued each new homicide as if each victim were an immediate member of his family. Storm's marathon efforts of around the clock until a murder was solved led to the unit being called the "Storm Troopers". A name Captain Wells discouraged but names and jokes aside, the unit, and the lieutenant, enjoyed a city-wide reputation for their ability to get the job done.

Storm was in his homicide office laboring with paperwork. He was twenty-seven minutes from seeing the lifeless form of Sara Lee Jefferson. He had never seen her before and he would never see her again. To Lieutenant Storm, Sara Lee Jefferson would be homicide number forty-two for the calendar year in the eleven square miles of LA's ghetto that comprised Southwest Area. Sara Lee's death would be the only time her name ever appeared anywhere other than on a birth certificate in Georgia and a welfare roll in Los

Angeles. Her county check would continue to arrive at her apartment on the fifteenth of each month for eight months after her death. Winston Ducks, the new tenant and his common law, Polly Shilling, would promptly cash each one.

The door to Storms' office opened, Storm ignored it. Captain Winslow stepped in and sat down. "Let's talk," Winslow said.

Storm paused from his work and pushed back in his chair. "I assume you want to talk about Ketch."

"You gotta do something with him," the captain said. "I got a call from SID. They said he smelled like alcohol and he was fumbling his words when he was on the scene with them the other night."

"Formal complaint?" Storm asked.

"No, just a heads up, but it's just a matter of time," Winslow said. "He was a classmate of mine. I pity the poor bastard, but he's got to stop drinking."

Storm nodded agreement. "Lasski tells me it's gotten a lot worse. I'll call him for a conference and..." A rap sounded on the door cutting him short. "Yeah, what is it?"

Brian Culpepper opened the door carefully. He looked at the two men. "Sorry, I didn't mean to interrupt."

"Okay, Culpepper, take a seat out there, I'll be with you in a minute," Storm said.

Culpepper nodded and closed the door on the two men. Captain Winslow looked to Storm. "What does he want?"

"He called this morning," Storm explained. "Said he wanted to talk. Think he's looking for a job."

"You got nothing, and I got nothing open out in the bureau either. Too bad," Winslow said with a look at the closed door.

Brian sat in the waiting room of the homicide office. He'd decided earlier all Lieutenant Storm could say was no. An answer Brian had heard before. He had nothing to lose by asking. Being among the top ten on the sergeants' list gave him an edge. It was an unwritten LAPD tradition that the top ten got what they wanted. A reward for the effort that put them there. That combined with the fact Captain

Winslow sat on his oral board, and Lieutenant Storm knew him, helped. Brian had a chance. He hoped.

Southwest Area was no stranger to Brian. After graduation from the Police Academy, it became his first patrol assignment. He remained there for two years. A policeman's first area was like his first woman, never forgotten. Brian grew to know the streets, the alleys, the hangouts, better than he did his own neighborhood. He learned to love the Black ghetto. It had become his professional home. When he transferred out it was a painful parting. He hoped someday to return. Brian would never admit it but in his opinion one of the things attracting him to Southwest Area was the fact it was predominantly Black.

Perhaps, he thought, because he was white, better educated than most in the ghetto and he was "the man", carrying a badge and a gun. Ironically, although more cops were killed and injured in the ghetto, nevertheless, there cops were respected more than elsewhere in the City of Angels. Brian Culpepper was glad to be home. He hoped he could stay. He had his sales pitch all prepared and he was certain...well, hopeful, he could convince Lieutenant Storm to provide him an assignment.

The door from the hallway opened and a uniformed lieutenant entered. It was the PM patrol watch commander. He looked at Brian in his jacket and tie. "You work Homicide?"

"Not yet," Brian answered.

"Storm in there?" the lieutenant asked.

"Yeah."

The watch commander moved to the closed door of Storm's office. He rapped on the door, "Storm, got one for you."

A chair moved. The door opened. It was Storm. Brian straightened in his chair to listen. "Where?" Storm asked with a look at the watch commander.

"Twenty-seven South Denker," the watch commander answered. "Three-Adam-ninety-eight and Sergeant Taylor are on the scene. Deceased female. Lots of blood. It's all yours."

Storm nodded acceptance. The watch commander had done his part. It now belonged to Homicide. He turned, moved to the door and was gone.

Storm, standing in the open door of his office looked to Brian. "What is it you wanted, Culpepper?" He was blunt.

Brian stood. "I wanted to talk to you about my qualifications to become part of your unit."

"You want to work Homicide?"

Captain Winslow appeared beside Storm. He looked to Culpepper. "Hello, Sergeant."

It was the first time Brian had been called *sergeant*. It brought a smile to his face but given the circumstance the smile was short-lived. The captain looked to Storm. "Let me know what you find down there. I'll be in my office for another hour or so."

Storm answered him with a nod. The captain moved by him, crossed to the hall door and exited. Brian remained standing. He felt awkward, embarrassed, silently damning his timing.

"We just had one go down," Storm advised. "I'm going out to the scene. It may be a while."

"I'll wait," Brian answered without hesitation.

"Alright," Storm answered reaching for his jacket. "In my office you'll find a sworn personnel file. Get in it and find Lasski and Ketch. They're on standby. Give 'em a call. Tell them the address and that I'll be at the scene."

"Got it," Brian said, hoping he could remember the names of the two detectives and the street address.

"After you get them, call SID, photos, and prints. Get a P number from photos, and tell prints we don't have a DR yet, but we want them at the scene."

"Yes, sir." Brian was faking it, hoping his voice wasn't showing the lack of confidence he was feeling in his gut.

Storm moved for the door. "Get an ETA from both and then call the Coroner's office. We won't need them for an hour or so, but I want them standing by, and get the individual's name, time and Coroner's case number."

"Case number, right."

"I'll give you a land line from the scene if there is one." Storm was out the door and gone.

"Son-of-a-bitch," Brian said to the empty office. He remembered only one of the detective's names. Lasski. He searched through the name file in the lieutenant's office, found the three by five card with Lasski's name on it. Sitting down in the lieutenant's chair he dialed the number. He tensed as the telephone rang again and again. Storm hadn't told him what to do if he got no answer and he couldn't remember the other detective's name. That was it. His chance to work Southwest Homicide was down the drain. All because some prick on stand-by wouldn't answer his phone.

"Yeah," a male voice barked in his ear.

"Lasski," Brian blurted into the phone.

"You called my number. Who the hell did you think was going to answer?"

"I, ah…this is…there's been a murder," Brian stammered.

"Come on, damn it. I just got home."

"I'm sorry," Brian said, "Lieutenant Storm advised me to call you and…"

"Where is it?" Lasski interrupted.

Brian looked at the note he had made of the address. "Female victim. Twenty-seven South Denker."

"Alright, I'm on my way."

"Lasski," Brian called. "Wait a minute. Do you know your partner's name?"

"Hell, yes, I know his name," Lasski said and hung up.

"Smart bastard," Brian mumbled, and hung up.

141

13 TILL DEATH DOTH PART

A LAFD paramedic ambulance with its lights flashing made the address on South Denker easy for Lieutenant Storm to find. He parked his unmarked car behind the ambulance and climbed out. A uniformed officer was standing at the door.

"Who's up there?" Storm asked as he reached the officer. He could see stairs leading to second floor apartments.

The officer was adding the lieutenant's name to log he was maintaining. "My partner, Hutton. Sergeant Taylor and the ambulance crew."

Storm offered a nod. "Nobody else comes up until my team gets here."

"Yes, sir."

Storm started up the stairs. Sergeant Taylor, a Black man with muscular arms stood in the open doorway of the apartment at the top of the stairs. Reaching him Storm noted there were three other apartments. "A J, how are you?" He recognized the sergeant.

"We have to stop meeting like this, Lieutenant." The Black sergeant smiled.

"Who got here first?" Storm asked as he looked at the stairway and the other apartment doors.

"I was."

"Anybody else home up here?"

"Haven't checked yet."

Storm looked down the stairs again. "Looks like only one way out. Knock on the doors. See if anyone heard anything."

"Will do."

Storm stepped inside the open apartment. There were two LAFD paramedics, a Hispanic officer, and the dead woman. He looked to the three, offered the officer a nod.

One of the paramedics, a Black man with a shaved head, worked at filling out a medical form. Theirs would be the first official declaration of death and the first of a myriad of documents, papers and reports that would document the woman's murder. If Sara Lee Jackson's life went unnoticed, her death would not.

Watching his step, Storm went to where the woman laid. She was a heavy woman, with folds of flabby flesh on her thick knee-less legs. Storm guessed her as a thirty-year-old. The shapeless, light, flowered dress she wore was pushed high revealing she wore no pants. A dark triangle of pubic hair showed at the base of a bulging stomach. Both of her pudgy hands were clutching a kitchen butcher knife protruding from the base of her neck just above the rib cage.

Blood pooled around her neck and onto the floor. Blood splattered about the kitchen spoke of a struggle before she fell. A deep gash on her right shoulder, where the sleeveless dress hung, stood gaping open, revealing blood and dotted layers of yellow fatty tissue. Storm made a mental note of it. Defensive wound he concluded. The woman's eyes and mouth were open. Her dark eyes were beginning to dry as they stood open and tearless staring up at Storm. The tip of her tongue protruded from her mouth, forced out by the knife plunged into her throat. "May God rest your soul," Storm whispered to the body. The woman did not answer.

Forty-two-year-old detective Fred Ketch had been in his one bedroom when the telephone rang. Arriving home, he ate a stale doughnut, two handfuls of dry roasted peanuts, drank a can of cold beer, and chased it with two, okay, maybe three shots of Scotch. It helped with his neuropathy. He sat and took his shoes off and realized he had none clean. He knew he would have to trek to the laundry room on the first floor and do a few loads. To Ketch it seemed all he did since leaving his wife of eighteen years was wash clothes. Vickie, the records clerk he had left his wife for helped him for the first couple of weeks, but then decided she was more in love with a motor cop from Central Area. *Dumped for a fucking Harley Davidson pilot.*

After his new love abandoned him, Ketch had called his wife to see if he could return home. "I made a mistake, baby. I'm still in love with you," he had pled.

"Fuck you," was the brief answer he got from his estranged wife.

Beth, Ketch's daughter was in her second year at UC Santa Barbara. She no longer took his calls. David, his fourteen-year-old son had called once to ask for help. His mother had grounded him for a month after he was detained for possession at school. It was his third offense. He longer called either. Other than that, everything was fine, except for the indigestion. The burning knot that hung high in his chest and robbed him of breath. Ice cream helped. He ate a lot of it.

Ketch was laying on the couch, watching the Ellen Show when the telephone rang. Maybe he hoped, no, prayed it was Ellen to say come home. It wasn't. It was Lasski, his partner. They were the on-call team for the week. They had already been called out two other nights. Monday's was an all nightery. A gang killing. Wednesday's came at three in the morning, a liquor store robbery. Ketch had told Lasski if science could eliminate night and darkness, there would be less murder. He was right. Murder was a crime of darkness. Ketch was tired and fatigued. He hadn't had a good night's sleep in over a week, but choice was not part of the program.

"I'll meet you at the scene," he told Lasski. Ketch washed

his face, hoping the cold water would erase the tiredness. It did not. He chewed two Tums, ate some more peanuts, and strapped on his Glock. After slipping on his suit jacket, he took two Tylenols and downed them with the remainder of his beer.

Being the Homicide stand-by team, both Lasski and Ketch had driven unmarked detective cars home. Ketch was driving eighty-three miles an hour when the CHP stopped him on the south bound Harbor Freeway. As soon as the motor officer walked up on the drivers' side of his car, Ketch flashed his badge and drove away.

Lasski arrived at the scene on South Denker fifty-two minutes after being called. Ketch arrived ten minutes later.

The murder of Sara Lee Jackson was a simple case, so the on-scene investigation only lasted a little over two hours. Fifty-six digital pictures and two videos were taken, the apartment was measured, a scale drawing was made, an officer from SID latent prints dusted for prints and the other tenants were interviewed. It was Marsha Crosley in apartment twelve who heard the loud argument—one she had heard many times before. Sara Lee and her common-law, Manfred Davis getting at each other. There was shouting and screams. Not unusual, so Marsha did not call the police. They would never know who did. Marsha gave Detective Lasski a description of Manfred Davis, and five minutes later, a city wide BOLO broadcast was made. Manfred Davis was wanted for murder.

The Coroner's deputy arrived, a final liver temperature was taken from the body on the floor and then she was lifted onto a wheeled stretcher and covered with a heavy plastic sheet. The task was performed by Ketch and the small Black female deputy. "Why can't people die on the ground floor?" the deputy mused as she wheeled the heavy cart toward the door.

"I'll give you a hand," Ketch said. He was already sweating heavily with his jacket off.

Lasski and Lieutenant Storm were in the bedroom, rummaging through a collection of mail, personal papers and address books, trying to find a name or an address that led them to Manfred Davis. Ketch glanced at them, considered calling Lasski to help, then decided against it. "Let me get the front," he said following the cCoroner's deputy into the hallway.

In death Sara Lee Jackson weighed two hundred and sixty-one pounds. Ketch positioned himself in front of the wheeled stretcher. When they got to the top of the stairs, he strained, picked up the weight and started down. They worked their way bumping, straining, groaning slowly down the steps. It was dead weight in every sense. The small female deputy gripped the metal frame with all her might. She tried to hold back the weight; Ketch was red faced, covered with sweat. The first pain was sharp, and it was high on the inside of his left arm. Ketch grimaced and looked at it, straining to hold the weight he carried.

The deputy saw his look. "You okay?" she asked.

The pain was like a bolt of hot electricity and it shot through Ketch's chest. His eyes went wide and then closed tight as his heart seized and stopped. He was dead, but still on his feet.

"What's wrong?" the deputy shouted. "Help! Help!'

Ketch's knees buckled and he fell, backwards, crashing down the stairs. The deputy tried to hold the stretcher, but the weight was too great. The stainless tube frame slipped from her grasp and the body and frame bounced down the stairs, end over end, to slam into the fallen Ketch at the bottom. The stairway was filled with a shrill scream from the deputy.

Except for a trip to the men's room Brian Culpepper waited in the homicide office. It was now nearly nine o'clock. He had called Pam at seven, told her go ahead and eat. She wished him luck. At seven-thirty he decided he'd wait until eight. At eight he changed it to eight-thirty and then at eight-thirty he told himself he waited too long to leave without talking to Lieutenant Storm. Either Storm was going to think him stupid or determined. Glancing at his watch, Brian silently decided nine-fifteen was the limit.

Five minutes later, two uniformed officers walked into the office with the handcuffed Manfred Davis. Manfred was a meek looking forty-two year old Black man. In handcuffs he looked frightened and worried. His eyes were rimmed with tears.

"You work homicide?" one of the uniformed officers asked.

"No, I'm waiting to see the lieutenant," Brian admitted for a second time.

"Crap," the officer complained.

"Something I could help with," Brian offered.

"Yeah," the officer answered. "This is Manfred Davis. He's the one-eight-seven suspect from South Denker. My partner and I were on our way to SBI with a skirt arrested for four-eighty-four when we spot Manfred coming out of the rest room at the Standard station on looking at blood stains on his jacket. He was in there trying to wash it out."

"We had just heard the broadcast on him," the other officer added.

"Problem is we still got the skirt hooked up in the back of our car. We wait any longer to book her we're going to be at SBI all night."

"You want me to babysit him?" Brian asked.

"Would you?"

"Sure."

The two officers gave Brian their names, serial numbers, unit number as well as the time and circumstances of Manfred's arrest. Brian would brief the Homicide detectives when they arrived. They then took off their handcuffs and Brian put his on the man. The older of the two officers smiled at Manfred and said, "You have a nice day, sir."

Manfred not realizing the officer's remark was sarcasm answered him, "You too, Officer."

The officers smiled, gave Brian a look and stepped out the door.

147

Brian sat Manfred down on a bench and then sat down himself not far from him. Manfred's eyes roamed the room. He looked frightened. Finally, he found the courage to look at Brian. "Am I going to prison?"

"I can't answer that," Brian said candidly.

"Can I ask you something else?"

"Sure."

"What's that one-eighty-seven them officers said I was arrested for?"

"Murder," Brian said.

Manfred's eyes went to the tile floor. He sniffed. Tears spilled and ran down his face. "Figured she was dead."

"Manfred," Brian said, "I'm a police officer and you're under arrest. Keep in mind anything you say can be used against you."

Manfred held Brian's look. "It's alright. I ain't denying it. I kilt her."

Brian nodded. "Alright, Manfred, before you say anything else let me tell you your rights. You have the right to remain silent. You don't have to talk to me or anyone else, but if you do, whatever you say can be used against you in court. You have a right to speak with an attorney and have him with you when you are questioned. Even if you can't afford an attorney, one will be provided before you're questioned if that's what you want?"

Manfred was listening.

"Do you understand your rights?"

"I just wanna tell the truth and see how it plays. I killed a woman. You got any idea how that feels?"

Brian chose not to answer. He understood. He tried to mask the reaction he felt to the man's words.

"I'm sorry it happened. Real sorry." Manfred sniffled.

"Listen to me," Brian said, "I'm a police officer but I don't work homicide. You should wait until they arrive."

"I'm talking to you man to man," Manfred countered.

Brian nodded. He understood. He hadn't seen it for some time. It was the emotional swell of guilt that wanted to spill out. The compelling need to explain, to right the wrong, to seek understanding, approval. "You're right, Manfred. Say whatever you want."

"First," Manfred said, trying to make his shackled wrists comfortable behind him, "I wish to God it never happened."

Brian stiffened; His teeth tightened together.

"There comes a time," Manfred continued, "when a man just can't be pushed no further. I just couldn't take no more. I snapped. I've been living with Sara Lee for almost three years. I get a pension from the VA. Got a leg blown off in Iraq back in ninety-three." He raised a leg. "Uncle Sam gave me a nice plastic leg along with seven hundred and sixty-eight dollars every month. For three years I give my check to Sara Lee and said, cash it, buy groceries, collect a little rent from me and put fifty dollars in savings. Three years I expect I got me better part of two thousand dollars. I got a brother back in Pittsburgh. He's old and I wanted to go see him, so I say, Sara Lee show me my savings book."

Brian nodded. He knew there would be more.

"So, she gets all uppity and says, 'why, don't you trust me.' I said I'll trust you more when you give me my savings book. She finally confesses there ain't no savings. She gave it all to her mother. She lives over on the east side. Keeps two of Sara Lee's grown sisters. Ain't none of 'em worth a piss. All I wanted was to go see my brother. You know?"

Again, Brian nodded. Murderers talk, not always to the police, but they talk, to cell mates, loved ones, friends, priests, whores and sometimes even strangers. Brian had learned as a cop, sometimes all you had to do was listen.

"I couldn't believe she gave my money away. I asked Sara Lee why? She says you don't need it. You're just a man with no leg and no dick. Goddamned mine blew my dick off too. VA built me a new one." He smiled. "Took the skin off my good leg and patched it up. Course it doesn't get up or nothing. Just a drain. And then she throws a plate at me and says get out. I refused and she got a kitchen knife and said, you don't get out I'm gonna cut you. We fought over the knife and...well, you know...it just happened."

It was quiet between the two men for a moment then

149

Brian spoke. "Manfred, this isn't something you can solve without help. You need an attorney. I know you don't have any cash, and that's okay. When you appear in court, they'll appoint an attorney for you. No charge. You be sure to tell the attorney Sara Lee came at you with a knife."

Manfred nodded agreement, "Thank you, Officer. What's your name?"

"Brian."

"Thank you, Officer Brian."

Another thirty minutes dragged by and Brian knew he had to do something. He knew what to do. His twenty months in Management Services and cramming for the sergeant exam was still with him. He knew policy and procedures for a homicide. He knew what to do and how to do it. The question was what would Lieutenant Storm think of his laying hands on? Would he be thanked or damned? He decided the risk was worth a chance.

Brian uncuffed Manfred Davis and took him into one of the Homicide cubicles where there was a computer. "We're going to go over your story again. I'll type it in your own words," Brian explained. "It will be your statement. I'll let you read it and sign it."

"Am I going to jail?" Manfred asked.

"Yes."

"For killing Sara Lee?"

"Yes."

"Thought so," Manfred said, massaging his wrists where the handcuffs left impressions. "Okay if I have one of my smokes?"

They went over the story again and again as Brian typed. When it was complete Brian printed out the three pages and went over it with Manfred. When they finished, Manfred looked at Brian. "That's the truth. All of it."

Brian walked Manfred to the watch commander's office, got booking approval, and then escorted Manfred into the area jail. Once done, Brian returned to the Homicide Office where he sat down at the computer again to do the required arrest report and evidence report. He made them brief and concise as he knew they should be. Manfred's blood-stained sweater was placed in an analyzed evidence envelope. Matching the blood stain on the jacket with the victim's blood would be powerful evidence. He had just finished when Lieutenant Storm returned. He looked haggard and tired. "You're still here?"

"Manfred Davis, your one-eighty-seven suspect. Three-Adam-nine made an observation arrest, but they had a female that had to go SBI. I handled the booking. Here's the arrest and evidence report. There's also a voluntary statement." Brian offered the reports. He watched for a reaction on Storm's face as he skimmed the reports. He found none. Storm quickly skimmed the reports and then looked to Brian. "Where's the statement?"

Brian gathered the three-page statement from the desk and handed it to Storm. He watched as the lieutenant's dark eyes raced over the lines. Storm turned to the second page and then the third. When he finished, he looked to Brian. " Who told you to do this?"

"No one," Brian said. "Suspect was here. He wanted to talk. Maybe he would have talked later, maybe he wouldn't."

"So, you made the decision?"

Brian tensed. "Yes, sir."

Storm studied Brian. It was a sober chilling evaluation. "You still want a job here?"

"Yes, sir."

"You'll be on the next transfer. Two weeks." Storm headed for his office.

"Thank you, Lieutenant," Brian called after him. He was having a difficult time containing himself.

"Get out of here. I've got work to do."

"Yes, Sir! And thank you."

"I'm going to remind you about saying that six months from now," Storm warned from his open office. "Now get out of here."

"Yes, sir," Brian said, and then he was out the door.

14 THE WALKING DEAD

Brian's twenty-five-minute drive from the ghetto into west LA went quickly. It was late, dark, and traffic was light. He sang and whistled most of the way. He felt worthy. He felt like a real cop again. He was a ghetto homicide detective in LA. One of the storm troopers. If that wasn't a men's, there wasn't one.

He exited the freeway at Robertson's Boulevard. At the intersection of Robertson and Wilshire Boulevard, he slowed and stopped for a red traffic light. As he waited, a black and white LAPD patrol car slid to a stop beside him. A Wilshire Area car Brian guessed. The uniformed officer in the front passenger's seat gave him a look. Brian noticed and ran his window down. His mood and elation had him all smiles. He felt a real kinship with the two officers in the patrol car. "Hey, you guys are doing a great job," he called to the passenger officer, who had an arm resting in an open window.

The officer gave Brian a look of suspicion and then said something to his partner before they both returned their attention to Brian. "Be safe tonight," Brian added, but the traffic light changed, and the patrol car roared away.

Unlocking the front door of Pamela's condo, Brian found a single light on in the living room. Pamela's bedroom was dark. He sat down on the edge of the bed beside her. Pamela stirred and reached to pull him down beside her. She was warm and nude in bed. "I got it, babe. I got the job," he said, burying his face in her hair.

Lieutenant JC Storm's night was far different. He was still in his office at Southwest Area. He would be there most of the night working on the extensive fifteen-seven report he was writing on the accidental on-duty death of Detective Ketch.

Brian Culpepper would not hear the story until the next day and he, like most others, would never know the details. The details were private. They would remain the secret memories of Storm and Lasski forever. It was no one's business that Lasski gave Ketch resuscitation in the back of the Coroner's gray van as it careened through the streets on its way to the hospital. It was no one's business that Storm applied a steady desperate heart massage. It was no one's business that Ketch's bowels spilled and added to the already heavy stench in the back of the Coroner's van. It was no one's business that Lasski threatened to shoot the young ER doctor who pronounced Ketch dead without much effort to save him. It was no one's business that Ketch's new widow was having dinner with another man when Storm arrived to inform her of her husband's death. It was no one's business that Lasski cried uncontrollably after they left the hospital. It was no one's business that a woman who shed no tears for her dead husband would receive his pension as well as a quarter million-dollar accidental death payment from a city trying to avoid a lawsuit. The only important thing was Detective Frederick C. Ketch, serial 20693, with sixteen years of service, was dead.

The official cause of death would be given as a massive coronary thrombosis, a heart attack. But those who knew him, knew Ketch's killer went by the name of Jack Daniel's. Several of the storm troopers blamed JC Storm for Ketch's death. The long hours, the constant pressure. The demand for results. Storm heard their mutterings, but if they produced, if he had their grudging respect, he didn't care how they felt. He knew familiarity bred contempt and deliberately kept distant. It was all part of good leadership, in Storm's mind, and that was what he was getting paid for. That was what counted.

Excited and unable to sleep Brian laid awake at Pamela's side, staring at the dark ceiling, thinking of the path that led to homicide. It was death that took him to Management Services, and it was death that opened the door for him to leave. Now he was to become an investigator of death. It was to become his assignment. Death, he reasoned, would remain the great mystery. They would not investigate death. They would instead, investigate what caused death.

Death would remain the great mystery. The great unknown. Death, the event every living thing would eventually experience, but was to be avoided at all costs. Death, Brian was learning, was not only a question, sometimes it was the answer.

Lasski, badly shaken by Ketch's death, took a two-week vacation. He had tried coming back to work after the funeral, but Storm read the signs of grief and depression and sent him home. "Come back when we find you a new partner."

Brian tried not to count days or hours, or how many minutes were in an hour as he waited for the next transfer. He had also decided some time off before his new assignment was appropriate.

Reality was he was eager and grateful to be free from being a paper tiger in Management Services. Departmental transfers took place at the end of every deployment period. Again, his time in Management Services was providing answers.

Pamela helped. She took him shopping for new shoes, a jacket and two shirts. He bought her a transparent blue night gown he saw in a window at Fredrick's. She tactfully declined trying it on in the store. Brian washed his truck and Pamela's Toyota, cleaned the windows in her condo, went to the pistol range at the academy on the hill for his monthly qualification, spent several hours cleaning his Glock and awaited sunset. Every day.

The transfer finally became official, and Brian showed up at Southwest Area. He had just parked his truck in the employee lot when he spotted Sergeant JD Kent parking his car. It was a warm reunion. JD congratulated Brian and pumped his hand. "Welcome to the Storm Troopers, Dude."

JD led the way toward the Sworn Personnel Entrance. "Lasski is going to be your partner. He's taking a few days off. You know why?"

"Yeah, I heard."

They first met Fran Cox, an attractive Black woman in her early thirties, who served as the receptionist and support clerk for the Homicide Unit. "Welcome to the Storm Troopers," she said, smiling at Brian.

There were four men waiting at three desks in the Homicide complex. JD made the introductions. There was Justin Boone and his Black partner Gilbert Howser. They were a handsome, professional-looking team. Next came Neil Roberts and his partner Juan Delgado. They all shook hands with Brian and welcomed him to the unit. It was obvious to Brian that in addition to being introduced he was being evaluated.

"Must been hell down there in Management Service," Detective Roberts said, "Sitting at a desk all day. No call outs. No autopsies. Home for dinner every night."

"Yeah," Brian said granting him a brief smile. "It was intense."

"We heard you're shacking with a deputy DA. Is that true?" Detective Boone asked.

The small office became quiet. Brian studied Boone for a moment. It was meant as a challenge to the new guy and Brian understood that. He knew he had to be careful with his answer, but not too careful.

"You married?" Brian finally responded equally sober.

"Yeah."

"To a woman?"

The other men all laughed. Boone knew he had to yield.

"Alright," Boone countered. "Tell Pamela we all said hello."

JD put an end to the exchange by showing Brian the desk he would be sharing with Lasski. He pulled a stack of folders from a file cabinet and dropped them onto the desk in front of Brian. "I want you reading the unsolved cases. We call them whodunits. Study how they're written. Who did what and why? Until Lasski comes back you and I are the *Shit Detail*."

"Shit Detail?" Brian asked.

"Special Homicide Investigative Team," JD answered. "You and I will handle the naturals, the ODs, the suicides. All the petty stuff, so these guys can keep up with the heavy stuff."

Brian spent the day reading. For the most part he was alone. The other detectives were in the field on follow-ups. Fran Cox seemed to be on the telephone a lot. There were lots of telephone calls, but none for Brian. Even Pamela did not call. She had promised Brian she wouldn't.

JD Kent, serving as the Homicide coordinator, was across the hall in an office he shared with Lieutenant Storm. Brian saw the lieutenant when he came in, but the extent of their conversation was, "Good morning, Lieutenant."

"Good morning, Sergeant."

Brian read and reread and studied everything he could find on the desk. He read crime reports, follow-up reports, arrest reports, progress reports, evidence reports, medical examiner reports, logbooks, and case histories. Brian was learning a homicide detective made a written record of everything he saw, heard, thought, suspected, or guessed.

The other detectives came and went, made important phone calls, talked about ballistics, polygraph runs, scientific analysis of blood, sperm, hair, graphs, composite drawings, and suspects. Brian listened and read and waited his turn. He was intimidated and worried, hoping his skill set would fit with what seemed to be the significant demands of the unit. Late in the day his first test came.

JD Kent stepped into the office. "Come on, Culpepper, we got one."

Brian was quickly out of his chair grabbing for his jacket. "Homicide?"

"No, suicide," JD answered.

They drove west on Martin Luther King Avenue into Leimert Park. It was a quiet residential neighborhood lined with wide grassy traffic islands and shade trees. The rows of apartment buildings, two story splashes of stucco and tile, with their graceful Spanish architecture looked like anything but ghetto to Brian. He silently wondered how it looked to the Black JD Kent. Finally, JD wheeled their unmarked car onto Gartwait Avenue and pulled to the curb behind a black and white patrol car.

Two uniformed officers stood with an aging Black woman in front of the apartment house. JD and Brian climbed out and walked to them.

"Sergeant Kent," the taller of the two officers said. "This is Mrs. Fowler. She's the manager here. His eyes were masked behind sunglasses. "She called us after Mr. Paulson, upstairs, didn't respond to her knock on his door or answer his phone. She usually sees him a couple times every day."

"His wife died recently," Mrs. Fowler said. Her voice was trembling. "He's been upset, so I...well, I was worried. He's lived here twelve years. I knew something was wrong."

"We got the call," Sunglasses explained. "We knocked. Got no response. Mrs. Fowler gave us a key."

"The door was locked?" JD asked.

"Yeah," the officer said. "Safety chain was in place. Door opened far enough for us to see his shoes. So, we kicked it in."

JD turned his attention to the woman. "Mrs. Fowler, we may have some questions later, but that's all for now. Why don't you go back into your apartment and sit down. You've had a shock."

"I knew something was wrong. I just knew it."

The two officers led JD and Brian to the top of the stairs. The apartment was to their right. Its splintered door ajar.

"We'll have a look. If it's clean, we'll send you on your way," JD said to the two officers.

The officers waited at the door as JD and Brian stepped inside.

Winston Paulson had been a tall man. Hanging in an archway, dividing the living room from the kitchen, with a belt around his neck, the toes of his black shoes were only an inch off the floor. The leather belt holding him had been nailed into the wooden frame of the archway above his balding head. His frail arms hung slack at his side. The tip of his tongue was pinched between clamped teeth. There was an overturned chair on the floor behind him. The apartment was clean and tastefully decorated if your prime was in the seventies. The only sound was from an air pump on a small aquarium in the living room.

Brian could hear his own breathing. Death was quiet. JD was studying the room. Brian didn't know what he was looking at, but he did the same.

JD walked to the man hanging and looked at him, then beyond into the kitchen. He glanced at Brian. "Check the bedrooms. No touch."

"Got it," Brian said. He crossed the living room, staying away from the hanging man. The door to the bedroom was slightly open. Brian pushed it the wider. The double bed was made neatly, although the spread was faded and thread-bare. There was a framed faded picture of a smiling young Black couple atop a dresser. Another of a gaunt Black man in an army uniform on a wall. Brian moved a second door, eased it open. The scent of soap and aftershave reached him. The bathroom was neat and clean.

After the initial assessment of the scene, JD talked to the two officers. He jotted down their names, serial numbers, unit number, the time they got the call, the time they arrived, who they talked with. When he had it all, he thanked them and sent them on their way.

"What's next?" Brian asked.

"Photos and the Coroner," JD said, raising his cell phone.

His call to SID Photo Unit was answered, but unhelpful. One photo tech was in the field at the scene of a homicide in Rampart Area. Another was at the scene of a bank robbery with an OIS, and the third, an accidental death of an employee at the airport. The first one clear would be sent to them.

The girl at the Coroner's Office said much the same. They had three units out on BPUs—Body Pick Ups. As soon as one was clear...JD disconnected with a hard stab of his thumb. "Why do cops on TV never have to wait for anything. They all get instant service."

"So, what do we do?" Brian asked, careful of JD's obvious frustration.

"Welcome to my world," JD said. "We wait."

JD closed the front door and sat down in a comfortable living room chair.

Brian glanced at the body. It had turned slightly. It unnerved him. He glanced at JD. "I think the body moved..."

JD looked, shook his head. "He didn't *move*. He *turned*. Hanging like that, all his body fluids—blood, water, stomach contents—they're all draining down due to gravity and sinking into his legs and feet. He'll be shifting and turning till we cut 'im down."

"I never saw a hanging before," Brian confessed.

"They're neat compared to most," JD said in a matter-of-fact tone. "Hangers and ODs are no problem. It's the cutters that get messy. You know how many pints of blood a body holds?"

They waited for an hour and, when no one showed up, JD turned on the television. They watched the six o'clock news and then *House Hunters*.

The dead man hung silent behind them. Brian wished he could call Pamela. He sensed it was going to be much longer.

At seven-thirty, JD made a second call. Photos was tied up on a second murder in 77th Area. He didn't bother calling the Coroner's Office. He knew where they would be.

"This is exciting, big city detective stuff, isn't it?" JD said.

Brian didn't answer, knowing the question was rhetorical.

When it got dark, JD turned on several lights and sat down again to continue the wait.

"I'm fuckin' starved," JD said twenty minutes later. They flipped a coin to see who would go to the corner market. Brian won the toss. He was pleased. It would give him a chance to call Pamela.

"I want orange juice and two beef sticks," JD told Brian, who was out the door and gone.

JD settled in a chair in front of the television. Waiting was in his skill set. He'd had lots of practice. He surfed the channels for something of interest, finally settling on an old Boris Karloff film on *Turner Classic Movies*. JD had always been a horror film buff and in a few minutes, he was tensing and biting a lip as two archaeologists inched through the dark corridors of an ancient tomb with only a flickering candle to light their way. Out of the shadows, behind the two, came a towering, tattered mummy, silently stalking, moving closer and closer. JD's eyes were glued to the screen.

The nail Winston Paulson had driven through the leather belt, into the wooden frame of the arch in his living room earlier that morning was approximately three inches long. After puncturing the leather and wood it protruded two and one sixteenth of an inch into the plaster of the wall. When Winston kicked over the chair on which he stood, his one-hundred-and-sixty-three pounds dropped. His weight was transferred to the nail which was an eighth of an inch in diameter. The shaft of the nail first bent under the stress and then, over the hours, as his weight continued its steady pull, it began to withdraw.

On the television screen the laboring wrapped mummy was somehow keeping up with the two fleeing archaeologists. No matter how fast they ran, or where they hid, the mummy found them. JD Kent was grimacing, offering silent advice. The mummy cornered one of the men. "Run, damn it, run," JD urged.

Behind JD, because of his shouting and foot stamping, the nail moved the final fraction of an inch and sprang free. Sixty-three-year-old Winston Paulson, now dead for seven hours and stiff with full rigor mortis, thumped to the floor.

The noise startled the already tense JD. He sprang to his feet and turned. His dark eyes went wide, and his mouth dropped open. Winston Paulson, his head cocked to one side, the leather belt now hanging slack around his creased neck, stood facing JD. The dead man's arms were stiff in a penguin like stance. JD stood frozen with shock. The stiffened body teetered forward, like a heavy tree felled by an axe—*timber!*—and fell toward the floor in JD's direction. JD screamed and bolted for the door. The body slammed into the floor. The impact knocked a picture from the wall adding to the noise. JD was gone, out the door, scrambling noisily down the stairs.

———

Pamela was waiting when Brian called. They had planned on having dinner out. Nothing special, just a break in the his-and-hers cooking routine. She was hoping they could still go, but Brian erased her hope. It was almost eight and he didn't know when he'd be getting off. Pamela was disappointed, but she hid it. Brian promised if they finished by ten, he'd come by. If not, he'd see her tomorrow night.

After they'd hung up, Pamela felt lonely. Soaking in the tub later, she decided she was jealous of Brian's assignment. This was the second night it had stolen him from her. She knew there would be more. Maybe, Pamela thought, she would ask him to move in? It was a pleasant thought. Brian spent most of his nights with her anyway. Maybe, she allowed, as her thoughts grew bolder, he would take the hint and ask her to marry him. The idea warmed her empty evening.

———

161

Brian was to see a lot of death in the days that followed. Along with JD, he handled two other suicides and four naturals. Two of the naturals were *stinkers* and Brian learned the meaning of the term the hard way. The first was an elderly woman who lived alone on South Budlong. Her only friends were her two cats, and the mailman.

When the mail went uncollected from her box for four days, the mailman called the police. The uniformed officers smelled the unmistakable odor of decaying flesh at the backdoor of the small house and called Homicide. JD and Brian kicked in the kitchen door and the stinging, nauseating odor boiled out to engulf them. "Now you know why I smoke cigars," JD said, puffing on one.

The woman's swelled face was teaming with maggots, which filled her empty eye sockets. The kitchen was alive with a swarm of black files buzzing loudly around the body. The trapped, unattended cats had eaten the flesh from her dangling left hand.

Driving home that evening, Brian noticed the stench of death was still with him. He rolled down the windows in the car, and when he arrived at his apartment, he stripped nude in the kitchen. After sealing his clothes in a plastic trash sack, he took a long shower. He did not eat that night.

Early the next day, they were called to the scene of the second stinker. A heavy-set woman suffered a heart attack while soaking in the bathtub. She'd last been seen five days before. The flesh above the soupy gray water was swelled beyond recognition and split open. Floating on the surface of tub water was a thick pasty foam, the remains of dissolved flesh. Brian held out until JD and the Coroner's deputy pulled the hulk from the tub and a partly dissolved hand fell off the body. Bolting from the apartment, he leaned against a wall in the rear alley as his stomach knotted and spilled its contents. Brian Culpepper was learning the grim realities of a Homicide assignment.

Eager to handle a real homicide, Brian continued to

study the unsolved cases left behind by Ketch. He found the man hadn't been the best report writer. From the logbook and case histories, Brian learned Ketch had been a follower. For the most part, he simply allowed himself to be carried along by his partner, Lasski, and the other men in the unit.

When Brian went to work on one of the unsolved homicides, scheduling witnesses for a follow-up interview—a basic tactic—and talking to Boone, who had been at the scene with Ketch, he met resistance. Boone didn't have time to talk, and the tape room was not available for witness interviews. Brian recognized the resistance. The other men in the unit didn't want Ketch's memory, or image, tarnished by the new guy.

Determined to be accepted, Brian fell in line. He held back on his efforts and played the role the established members of the Homicide unit wanted him to play. He knew the memory of Ketch would fade. He knew he'd eventually become one of the Storm Troopers, and when he did, he'd do it his way.

15 BLOOD BROTHERS

Brian was getting used to usual hours, overtime, death in more forms than he could have imagined, and the fact death in the ghetto was usually not news, just a number. Boone and Hauser were in San Francisco bringing back a murder suspect, and Roberts and Delgado were tied up in court with a jury trial. All which meant every human life that came to an end under unusual, suspicious, or criminal circumstances in the densely populated eleven square miles of the LAPD's Southwest Area belonged primarily to Sergeants JD Kent and Brian Culpepper.

It was these odds that brought Brian Culpepper to the station early. He was surprised to find he wasn't the first to arrive.

David Lasski had returned from his time off. With his jacket off and coffee in hand he had the look of having been there a while.

"Morning," the surprised Brian said, entering the Homicide Complex.

Lasski paused from his reading of the of the reports spread over his desktop and looked to Brian. "You sure made a fucking mess of my desk," Lasski said.

"Interesting," Brian said. "That's exactly what I said to JD when I got here."

Lasski smiled and stood up, extending an open hand to Brian. "You must be Culpepper?"

"You must be Lasski."

They shook hands, evaluating, judging, wondering. It was a firm handshake. "How was the time off?"

"Can't say taking time off because my partner got dead was fun, but I got some rest. Cleaned the garage. Got caught up on my honey do's. You know? Honey do this, honey do that. You married, Culpepper?"

"No."

"Divorced?"

"No."

"You do like girls?"

"Now you're getting personal."

"You bet I am," Lasski defended, "You're my partner. I'm gonna spend as much time with you as I do with my wife. Maybe a little bit more. So, I wanna know who you are."

"From what I've heard of you," Brian said, "you already know who and what I am."

Lasski granted him a smile. "You've been doing your homework, too. You're right, I asked around. I didn't want any surprises down the line."

"There won't be any," Brian said.

"Then I need the telephone number of the DA you're shacking with," Lasski said bluntly.

Brian reacted. Lasski saw it. "If you don't want people saying it. Don't do it."

"I'm old school. I think what I do off duty is my business."

"School's out...What you do off duty is our business. I don't care who you sleep with as long as it's not my wife, but when I need to find you, I want to know where you are."

The two men studied each other. It was a silent probing, a feeling out, a search for the definition of the role each would play in their pairing. "Her Name is Pamela Moss," Brian finally answered.

Lasski pulled a small notebook form his jacket, which was hanging on the chairback. "My wife's name is Julia.

We've been married eight years. She teaches Junior High. We've got two kids. Four and six. And a pool. We like to bar-b-que. This DA of yours, is she social?"

"Very. Her cell is three-two-three-oh-eight-oh-nine."

The difficult moment between them had passed.

Lasski was three years older than Brian. At thirty-two, in police terms, he was an old man. He was pushy, noisy, and seemingly always in a rush, racing toward some goal only he knew about and which always remained just out of his reach. He had a quick disarming smile, but it could quickly give way to his blue-eyed Polish rage.

It wasn't that Lasski was a particularly good detective, but his seemingly endless energy and drive simply wore suspects down. He would press a case so hard and long that eventually the right lead would be bared and the case solved. His reverence for life made him an excellent Homicide detective. It never entered Lasski's mind that the force that drove him to pursue those who killed was the fear of his own mortality.

Senior in years and experience, it was acknowledged Lasski would be the leader in the partnership. He would not dictate, nor decree; he would simply lead. They would be like a team of horses sharing a harness. Both would pull their share of the load, but Lasski, the more experienced, had the right and the responsibility to choose the path.

"Get yourself some coffee," Lasski told Brian, "and I'll try to teach you something about working Homicide."

Brian took his cup to the coffee urn in the reception area. He had already decided he liked Lasski. The man was open, unpretentious, and enjoyed his work. Anything more, Brian knew, was a bonus.

"You ever heard of a crook named Nation Wyde?" Lasski called from his desk.

Brian returned to their desk and sat down across from Lasski.

"Nation Wyde. LA's Robin Hood. Yeah, heard about him. Read about him. Why?"

"Then you know we've got a murder warrant for him?"

"Veronica Washington," Brian said with a glance at the open file in front of f Lasski.

"Ketch and Boone did the preliminary on scene. I was off."

"Problem with it?" Brian asked.

"I'm not sure." Lasski shrugged, "It's a paper murder."

"Paper Murder?"

"Yeah, all we got is paper. I wasn't at the scene. Everything we do has to be based on what Ketch and Boone did. If they missed something, we'll never know it."

"There is something," Brian said.

"What?"

"Nation Wyde was made as the one in the bank the day of my shooting."

"What! I'll be a son of a bitch. That was you? You're the lady killer?"

"I don't celebrate it as much as you may think," Brian said.

"Well, there was a riot and shit," Lasski countered.

"I know. I was there," Brian said.

"So, what you're saying is, you'd like to find this motherfucker?"

"We were talking about Veronica Washington and the crime scene," Brian reminded him, signaling the talk about his shooting was over.

"Yeah, okay, the crime scene," Lasski said. "Not criticizing. I wasn't there, but why would you shoot someone and then toss your gun in the sink? Guns are symbols. They make you bad. You don't leave your gun behind."

"You think there's a chance Nation Wyde didn't do her?"

"Maybe, but there's as much of a chance he did," Lasski said. "Every time you try to use logic on one of these bad guys, they deny it, but Nation is a robber. He doesn't act like a killer. Get this..." Lasski picked up a computer printout. "Last night, he hit The Boys' market on Crenshaw. Nine shots fired. Got eighteen hundred dollars from two cash registers. Then outside the market, he gives a hundred bucks to some homeless dude. Robbery makes him from the video. They want his ass, more than we do. Nation had a gun, he did a lot of shooting, but he didn't shoot anybody. He's a loose end. Messy. Storm doesn't like messy," Lasski said. "Storm argues the best time to find a killer is before the blood dries. He says it looks bad when someone we should have put in jail is still out there stirring shit."

"So, we gotta find Nation Wyde?"

"Well..." Lasski dangled the teletype again. "When the lieutenant sees this, he's not going to like it."

The hall door opened, and Lieutenant Storm came in carrying a computer printout. He looked angry. "You seen this?" He waved the paper as he moved to his office.

"Yes, sir," Lasski answered for both.

"Get the file," Storm ordered. "And get in my office. Both of you."

Lasski pushed out of his chair, gathering the file. "Honeymoon's over, Lady Killer. Welcome to the Storm Troopers."

16 LIFE'S A CIRCLE

There were eleven calls waiting when Deputy Chief Taylor Searcy arrived at his office in the LAPD Headquarters Building at 100 West First Street in downtown Los Angeles. Word had spread quickly through the city's newsrooms and social media; Robin Hood had struck again.

Chief of Police James Peck, annoyed by the attention the press was giving Nation Wyde, had told deputy Chief Searcy to take care of the matter. Searcy in turn had summoned the commander of Metro and ordered a task force formed. Twelve of the department's best surveillance and robbery investigators were assembled and assigned the task of tracking down Nation Wyde. It was done quietly, without fanfare, but a story in *The Los Angeles Times* the next morning was captioned: SHERIFF SENDS THE DIRTY DOZEN AFTER ROBIN HOOD.

Forwarded by the press, Nation Wyde knew continuing to rob banks or savings and loans would be hazardous to his health, so he turned to supermarkets. After the shoot out and successful get away on South Crenshaw, Nation's legend took on new dimensions. It seemed the police would never catch him. At least that's what Chuck Henry, the handsome evening anchor on Channel Four predicted.

Deputy Chief Searcy made a call to the executive producer of the news cast. "What the hell's wrong with you people? This man is wanted for a dozen robberies and the murder of his common law wife. You're treating him like he's the star of some new reality TV series!"

"He's caught the public's attention," the news producer defended. "I think the public feels they've been ripped off themselves by the places he's robbing. It's a common touch thread."

"Jesus Christ," Searcy growled and hung up.

Frustrated with the comic book treatment by the press, Searcy refused any further comment about Nathaniel Wyde. He refused to refer to the suspect as Nation Wyde or Robbin Hood. By mid-morning, a special order was distributed department wide advising everyone else to follow those standards:

Referring to criminal suspects by popular street, pet, or nick-names, is unprofessional and against departmental policy. Inquiries regarding suspects using such street, pet, or nicknames, shall be disregarded until proper identification of the concerned suspect(s) or individual, is provided.

A detective in Hollywood Area Robbery predicted the special order would have, *Nation Wyde impact.* The following morning, the LA Times carried a follow up story—*LAPD Launches a Nation Wyde Hunt.*

Lieutenant Storm knew the pressure would be quick in coming, so he was ready when Captain Winslow summoned him to his office.

"Lieutenant," Captain Winslow said from behind his desk.

When a captain sat behind a desk and used rank addressing a subordinate Storm knew shit was being passed downhill.

"Word is out in the police building that we dropped the ball on this Nation Wyde thing."

"Captain, we conducted an investigation, identified a suspect and sought a warrant. We continue to pursue all leads to locate him. I've got seven men investigating—year to date—forty-two homicides. That's fourteen murders for each of my teams. We don't investigate just some murders, we investigate them all. Fucking Nation Wyde among them. Instead of the police building kicking our ass why aren't they putting out the video from last night's robbery, or how about a nice head shot of Nation Wyde from his last arrest. Let's get that in the news."

"I don't run Press Relations," Winslow said. "I just know the compass is pointing in our direction, and before it taints anyone's reputation, we need to cover the bases."

Storm understood they were talking appearances instead of policies. "I've already got Lasski and Culpepper looking at it. Kent and I will stay on it too."

"Have you got anything? Something I can send downtown?"

"No," Storm was blunt. "Maybe you could remind them we've got nearly four million people in LA. Another ten in LA county. All we have to do is find one Black man."

"Damn."

"JD is writing up a request to the bureau commander. We want a twenty-five-thousand-dollar bounty on Nation Wyde."

"A reward," Winslow scoffed. "The bureau will never give us that much. Plus, no one's going to snitch him off. Hell, everyone loves him."

"Let me remind you, Captain. This is the ghetto. People get snitched off for a hell of a lot less."

"Alright, alright." Winslow waved him off with an annoyed hand. Somehow the pressure had got turned around. "When it's ready bring it over. I'll take it downtown."

"Thank you, Captain."

After being told by Storm to find *Fucking Nation Wyde*, Lasski and Culpepper spent the day searching. They talked with Nation Wyde's mother, his three aunts, two cousins and four known friends. Nation's mother was ashamed of him, while most of the others were in awe. They were all quick to admit knowing Nation, in fact proud, but none had any idea where he might be. Lasski thought they were all lying. Culpepper did not. Brian knew it took more than luck to keep Nation Wyde going as long as he had. Nation, it seemed to Brian, had become a cunning, street wise criminal. With that in mind, Brian decided Nation would be stupid to contact family or friends. He did not think Nation Wyde was stupid.

Lieutenant Storm and JD Kent pursued the *paper* Nathaniel Wyde, poring over arrest reports, jail records, rap sheets, telephone records, and security videos, searching for new leads. They found none.

Late in the day, the three teams gathered in the Homicide Office. Boone and Howser had returned from San Francisco, Roberts and Delgado were back from court, and Lasski and Culpepper were eating a late lunch of Popeyes Fried Chicken.

"Hey," Lasski said, licking a finger, "We're in there showing Nation's mug shot and the manager says, you want some chicken? We didn't wanna insult her, so..."

Lieutenant Storm took them step by step over everything they knew of Nathaniel Wyde. Thirty-one year's old, Nation was the only son of Otis and Mabel Wyde. Born in Mount Union, Pennsylvania, Nation and his parents moved to Los Angeles when he was eleven. Life was good for the family until Otis Wyde died from a sniper's bullet during the Rodney King riots.

Nation believed the police killed his father. He hated them for it. White bastards. After the death of his father, Nation, over the objection of his mother, quit school to find work. The job he found was with a white used car dealer on South Figueroa. Nation drove cars south to a second car lot in San Diego. He was paid ten dollars a trip and he usually made three a day. Nation did not know he was driving stolen cars. Once delivered, the cars were quickly driven into Mexico.

When he was finally stopped on the freeway and arrested by the California Highway Patrol both his cousin and the used car dealer denied knowing him. Nation was convicted of GTA—Grand Theft Auto—and sentenced to a year in the county jail. When released six months later, he tracked down and beat his cousin and the car dealer. Promptly arrested, Nation went back to jail for two years, convicted of assault with a deadly weapon. He had used a tire iron.

After serving a total of thirty months for the two offenses, Nation found life in the Los Angeles ghetto grim. He looked for a fulltime job, but never found one. The problem may have been Nation Wyde had no experience or skills, other than jailtime. He found his good looks coupled with his smooth talk got him interviews, but never the job.

He found lying about having a job, in the absence of really having one, was better than reality. Although living in Los Angeles, Nation had never seen the fabled Hollywood sign, but after seeing it on TV, he decided he was going to work in Hollywood. He became an agent, or he was a close friend of an agent, which was closer to reality than Nation may have thought. As an agent he found he could hustle. Everyone, especially women, wanted to believe they could make it in Hollywood. After successful recruitment and the money was gone, Nation would have his girls shoplift, street walk, hustle old men, steal or rob. It was always more rewarding, when in addition to using a gun, you used an attractive woman.

The paper history of Nathaniel Wyde took Lieutenant Storm and the others to the threshold of Veronica Washington's apartment. There the facts got blurry. Only conjecture could take the Strom Troopers any further. Although there were four human beings present the night of the shooting, there were no *witnesses*.

Veronica Washington was not a witness. She was a victim, and her knowledge of the event died with her. Eleven-month-old Angela Washington and her two year old brother, Lovell, both saw what happened, but the innocence of youth locked the ghastly sight forever deep in the subconscious corner of their infant minds.

The only living being to carry a haunting memory of that evening on South Hoover was Nathaniel Wyde—and he was not a witness, he was a suspect. As a suspect, Nation's version of what happened was tainted. It was a defense, a lie, a self-serving story. A story told by an ex-con that carried as much clout as a fart in a courtroom.

In addition to the stark outline of Nation Wyde's life, the Storm Troopers had a wealth of personal information about him. They knew Nation favored hats and black three-quarter length jackets. They knew when he had money, he spent it first on clothes and then attractive women. He ate only one meal a day. Usually Popeyes Chicken. He smoked Kool's and sometimes grass. In liquor, he preferred Christian Brothers and soda. He slept during the day, liked porn movies and Penthouse magazine. He always carried a forty-five automatic, favored black cars, and loved the limelight.

The investigators also had six prior address, three former cell mates, and a female by the name of Vickie C, who had once visited Nation Wyde at the Chino Prison where he served most of his second prison sentence.

"Thanks to a fucking prison guard who was too lazy to write down a last name we're up the creek," Storm complained when they called it a day near eleven PM. "Let's get an early start tomorrow. We know he sleeps during the day. Get here at six AM."

The marathon efforts continued for two weeks.

"This son-of-a-bitch ain't human," a fatigued Lasski complained at the end of the first week after the untiring Storm announced they'd be working through the weekend.

"Which son-of-a-bitch are you talking about?" Boone asked. "The one we're looking for, or the one we're working for?"

Brian was to see Pamela twice during the fourteen days. On both occasions it was between the hours of two and five A.M.

While the Strom Troopers searched the ghetto for Nation Wyde, the twelve-man robbery task force were being guided by the dictates of the 2200 ML6 computer.

The complex machine was hidden deep in the bowels of the police headquarters building and had been fed all the known facts on Nation Wyde's MOs and whereabouts. The computer predicted six targets, which they staked-out.

The sum result was they arrested two juveniles and one adult for shop lifting, and a would-be robber who tried to rob a liquor store using a black comb concealed in his pocket as a gun. When the Black man was arrested, there was a fever of excitement. It was short-lived. The man was six years younger and three inches shorter than Nation Wyde.

The Storm Troopers, who held a collective breath when they heard the news, breathed a sigh of relief. They wanted to solve Robbery's problem. They didn't want Robbery solving theirs. Nation Wyde was theirs and they were determined to find him—first.

Fifteen days after the request for secret service funds was submitted it was approved. The Storm Troopers got their twenty-thousand dollars to offer as a reward for information leading to the arrest of Nathaniel Wyde. It was a meager amount compared to that offered by the banks Nation had robbed. Western Federal was offering twenty-five thousand and Coast Federal was offering thirty-five thousand. Nation had robbed three of their branches. He liked their hours. They were open late on Fridays. Although the banks were offering more money no one really believed they would pay it. Bullshit to discourage robberies was the common belief, but it was common knowledge the police did pay, and they didn't tell. The Storm Troopers spread the word. Money was waiting for the person who gave them Nathaniel Wyde.

The nighttime burglar that bludgeoned sixty-seven-year-old Bessie Mills to death on South La Salle took, among other things, two pairs of diamond earrings. The less than professional entry, smashing a side window, and the brutal murder told Lasski and Culpepper, who were investigating the case, that the suspect was a beginner. It was likely he would convert the diamonds to cash as quickly as possible and the likely place for quick money was a pawn shop.

Armed with a description of the diamond earrings, Brian and Lasski made the rounds of the pawn shops in the neighborhood. Lasski drove while Brian watched the store fronts sweep by. He spotted a stooped older woman pushing a cart as she disappeared into a market. It made him think of the helpless old woman with a smashed head who they had just spent five hours with.

Brian was surprised. Murder was no longer shocking, disturbing, or frightening. Most times it wasn't even news. Murder was business. His business, and here he was, at work, just like other working men. It was an insane thought and Brian briefly considered telling Lasski about it, but then decided not to. Lasski was a dedicated man who had been in Homicide for three years. It wasn't likely he would share his view.

Brian tried to focus on what he thought of death. It was the end of life. Murder made it the ultimate theft. What more could one human take from another? That was it. His job was to find the life thieves. And what then when they found the life thief? Would the thief have the life he stole with him? No, it was gone. All that could be done was to take the thief's life. The circle was complete. An eye for an eye. It was a maddening, frustrating thought and Brian could find no logic in it.

Sun was warming the palms and waking Los Angeles. Soon the playgrounds would be filling with children, and in a city with more cars than citizens, the freeways would be, as always, slow and crowded. The Dodgers would be warming up for their afternoon game against Cincinnati. The beaches would slowly swell with crowds. And life would go on. Murder, like death itself, had been accepted. It was an item found deep in the pages of the *LA Times*, or thirty seconds on a local newscast in the evening.

Brian tried to remember what number the old lady was. How many murder scenes had he seen since transferring to Homicide? Fifty-two, no fifty-three, or was it sixty-three, he wasn't sure. At first, he had been shocked and horrified to see what ghastly things one human being could do to another. He promised himself he would never forget, but he had. The montage of murder scenes he carried in his mind now blurred and spilled over one another until they became one huge, mutilated pile of human pulp, which in his mind, in defense of sanity, he rejected.

Fifty-two murders, eighteen suicides, and thirteen naturals had numbed Brian Culpepper's sense. Watching a pathologist at the Coroner's Office pull skin from a face like plastic wrap from a melon or cut the sternum with stainless steel bone snips to open the chest cavity, did not allow the luxury of emotion. The dead bodies were no longer humans. They couldn't be. They were cases, statistics, reports, investigations, anything but fellow human beings. It was Brian's way of coping. A balance that kept him from being touched by it, comprehend it, without being changed.

He didn't have an answer. He promised himself he'd ask Lasski about. Lasski had been in Homicide for almost four years. How many murders how he investigated? How many bodies had he seen? How did he drive home to a wife and child and live a normal life? He looked to Lasski with the questions in his mind.

Lasski, behind the wheel of their unmarked car caught Brian's look. "What are you staring at? I got something on my face?"

They were leaving Kings' Small Appliance Store and Loans on West Jefferson, after another inquiry for the diamond earrings, when Brian saw the man. His name was Blue Nobles. He was Black, in his late thirties and he walked with a limp. It was the limp Brian recognized. The slight twist of the right foot, the accented bend of the knee. He hadn't seen Blue since leaving Southwest Patrol. "Ski," Brian said, using Lasski's shorthand name, "I know that man."

They paused as Brian stared across the street.

Blue Nobles, dressed in a plaid shirt and a tattered military field jacket, was walking from the mouth of a liquor store. He had a bottle of wine wrapped in a paper sack under his arm.

"Who is he?" Lasski asked.

"A snitch. A good one."

"You wanna talk to him, go ahead. I'll bring the car around."

Brian darted across the busy street, dodging passing cars. He caught up with the man just as he was reaching a cluttered vacant lot where several other men sat deep in the lot near an abandoned wheelless hulk of a car.

"Blue," Brian called taking him by the arm. Blue's blood-shot eyes twisted to Brian. They were wide with alarm, and then they relaxed. Blue smiled, baring yellowing teeth.

"Officer Culpepper."

"Detective Culpepper," Brian corrected, shaking Blue's hand.

Blue sobered, pulled his hand away. "We got eyes watching."

Brian glanced at the men in the lot. He understood. He stiff armed Blue away. "Get your hands in the air," he barked.

Blue stiffened and raised both arms into the air. Brian quickly patted him down from behind and then reached to take the paper bag from his hand.

"Careful," Blue whispered. Brian carefully dropped the bottle to the ground.

"Somebody watching?"

"There's always somebody watching," Blue answered as Brian took him by the shoulders and turned him to him. Now they stood face to face. "So, you're a big ass detective now. Took you long enough."

"You weren't around to help," Brian said and smiled.

"What's you working now?"

"Homicide. Couple months now."

"Big time shit," Blue said with obvious pride. "It looks good on you."

"Thanks...You still with Nell?"

Blue's eyes went to the dirt. "Naw, she OD'ed a while back. Got some bad shit somewhere."

Brian could see the pain on Blue's face. He had aged poorly. Heroin. The muscle tone was fading from his unshaved face, dotted with a graying beard. When Brian first met Blue, he was fresh out the VA Hospital in Loma Linda. The fifth operation on Blue's mangled leg had reduced the Iraq war souvenir to a limp. Blue, a warrant officer and helicopter pilot was shot out of the sky on his second combat tour.

Three quarters of an inch of bone from the tibia of his right leg put an end to Blue's military career and his love of flying. After fourteen months he was discharged with four hundred and eight dollars, a dependence on morphine, and a Silver Star. The continued constant pain and the distance to the VA hospital turned Blue's morphine dependance into a heroin addiction.

He was arrested the first time just after hocking his Silver Star. Twenty-two other arrests were to follow. Brian had met Blue when he caught him breaking into a car at the LA Colosseum. The crowd inside was watching a football game while Brian and seven other cops in plain clothes looked for *car clouts*. Blue was one of four arrested.

At the station Brian filled out Blue's arrest report. "Military service?" Brian asked.

"Army," Blue said.

"Combat?"

"No, thanks. I've had my share."

"Where?" Brian asked.

"Afghanistan. Iraq. Little bit of both."

"Outfit?"

"Hundred and First."

"You a jumper?"

"No. I flew."

"Crew chief?"

"Pilot," Blue answered in a matter-of-fact tone.

Brian had studied Blue. They were close in years. Both spoke of places where they served, bases they knew, towns and cities they saw that were no longer cities. They had shared a war, fought a common enemy, bore the scars from wounds that would never really heal, but now they sat on opposite sides of a desk in a police station. The Marine

Corps infantry man and the Army helicopter pilot had been reduced to the cop and the crook.

Blue understood why Brian was a cop, and Brian understood why Blue was an addict, and out of that the bond was formed. It was more than the typical policeman informant relationship. It was more of a business relationship. Brian provided Blue with money and Blue provided Brian with information from the streets. The relationship benefited both. Blue with money in his pocket was less apt to steal to feed his habit, and Brian armed with information Blue provided ferreted out long sought suspects. Their partnership blossomed until Brian's successes led to a transfer. The old adage, A policeman is only as good as his informants, rang true, and leaving Southwest, Brian not only left behind an informant but a valued friend.

Their time apart hung on Blue's ravaged frame. He looked tired and hungry.

Studying him, Brian said, "Blue, don't take it personal, but you look like shit."

"It's part of my disguise," Blue answered with a short-lived smile.

"VA will take you back, you know," Brian said.

Blue shook his head. "It ain't the same. The old crew is gone. Last time I was there they made me piss in a bottle. Then they called my probation officer."

A car pulled to the curb not far from them. Brian glanced at it. "It's my partner. Lasski."

"A Polack, huh?"

"For certain," Brian agreed.

"Got a weak spot for minorities, don't you?"

"Guilt complex, I guess. Listen, Blue, I've gotta run, but can we pick up where we left off?"

"I think we should."

"Good," Brian said. "You heard of Robin Hood? His real name is Nation Wyde."

"Nation Wyde! Yeah, I pulled some county time with him a year or so ago. Been a while since I seen him. Word is, lots of people looking for him."

"Me among them. He's worth twenty grand."

"I'll keep an ear open."

"Come by Southwest when you can. I'll leave an envelope at the front desk."

"Appreciate that."

"You got a phone?"

"Got a nice cellphone," Blue patted a pocket. "All I have to do is convince Verizon to connect me."

Brian patted Blue on the shoulder. "I'll leave a number where we can connect."

The two men studied each other for a moment. Both wanted to say more. Both knew they couldn't. It was an awkward heavy moment. Finally, Brian spoke, "You take care of your ass."

"You, too, home boy." Blue winked.

Brian turned away to the waiting car.

Blue sniffed, dug a crumpled pack of cigarettes from a jacket pocket and lit up as he watched Brian climb into the detective car. When it pulled away, Blue reached down to gather his bottle of wine in the paper sack.

Several hours later, at the station, Brian wrote *Blue Nobles* on a white envelope and sealed it. He left it with the crew manning the front desk. Inside, folded carefully between several sheets of plain white paper, were two twenty-dollar bills and a ten. The twenties were Brian's. The ten he borrowed from Lasski. Along with the money was an LAPD business card. On it were three telephone numbers. Brian did not want Blue's calls to go unanswered.

When he went EOW at ten o'clock he went to the front desk to check. The envelope was still there. He checked again when they returned for duty in the morning. The envelope was gone.

18 NOW YOU SEE HIM

Banks, supermarkets, liquor stores, a shoe store, and the recent addition of a florist shop, were all wary of Robin Hood. He had hit one or more and he had the frightening habit of coming back for seconds. All had developed a policy of keeping as little cash as possible on hand until Robin Hood was captured, or someone killed the son-of-a-bitch. Nation knew it was all true because he watched it all on the local news. "Motherfuckers are trying to kill the small businessman," Nation complained.

Popularity and fame had its price, and although Nation Wyde was enjoying the mantle of a contemporary Robin Hood, he hadn't forgotten the sheriff's men were combing the forest. The streets seemed to teem with cops and word was out there a treasure in cash waiting on whoever delivered Nathaniel Wyde.

The story of the betrayal of Jesus by Judas he'd heard long ago in a Watt's Sunday School class kept coming back to him. If they betrayed Jesus, and they had, they wouldn't hesitate to betray him. Nation gave up his comfortable suite at the Pear Tree Inn in Compton under the name of Miles Stewart. Whores and parties, even under the guise of a textile salesman from Canton, Ohio, were a luxury he could no longer afford. His mouth had set his own trap. Hell, it was hard not to tell a five-hundred-dollar blonde who she was having the good fortune to fuck. Fear made him run and without notice to friend, foe, or the front desk, Nation Wyde simply disappeared.

Nation Wyde believed in luck, but he had more confidence in planning, and he had a plan. What he needed was anonymity. In the Black community he was known, and known well, but north of the Santa Monica Freeway, in the buffer between Black LA and the wealthy Wilshire District, was Korea Town. The Koreans with their eyes and sloped shoulders lived in an almost closed society. Shunned by both Black and white they clung to their Oriental heritage like a shield. Many of them spoke little English or had valid immigration papers. There, few, if any, had heard of, or cared about, LA's Robin Hood. So, there is where he went.

Nation sat in a coin laundromat on Olympic Boulevard for two days before he spotted the girl. You want to meet women try a laundromat. There was something different about this woman in addition to the fact she was pregnant. The usual black hair was a softer brown, and her eyes were green. She just wasn't as Korean as the others and finally Nation realized what it was. It even explained why others seemed to shun her. She was a Kamerican, a cross between Korean and gringo.

In less than an hour, the handsome Nation Wyde knew her name and when she left the laundromat, he carried her basket full of clothes. "My mother taught me to always help a lady." Nation smiled. When he left her at the door of her second-floor apartment she had accepted his invitation to dinner. "I know this little place just a block away," he assured.

It was over dinner that Nation learned Su Linn's pregnancy was the result of a rape. "When I refused an abortion, my parents throw me out. They still give me money. My father, he owns three gift shops."

Nation was impressed. Three gift shops meant money. He told his story. It was very convincing. His young wife and infant son had recently died in an automobile accident. Torn by grief he hadn't been able to work and lost his home.

Life on the street was difficult, but he knew someday it would end. Su Linn invited him to stay in her apartment. He spent the first night on her couch. The next night he was in her bed.

On that same night, a team of six Robbery detectives stormed into room twelve-twenty at the Pear Tree Inn in Compton. They found two pairs of shoes, a pair of green Jockey shorts, a tube of lipstick, a packet of unused Trojan condoms and Nathaniel Wyde's fingerprints. "That lucky, son-of-a-bitch," Bud Johnson, the senior Robbery detective complained.

The long days across the street from the Louisiana Bottle Shop in Su Linn's apartment, provided Nation Wyde an answer. With little else to do while Su Linn made a trip to her doctor, he watched the street. Watching, Nation complimented himself, that was the key—*you got to look at what you're seeing*—and in his watching, he saw an endless stream of customers in and out of the liquor store. The flashing neon sign above their window confirmed his belief. It winked a steady message, *Payroll Checks Cashed*, and Nation knew to cash checks you needed money—lots of money.

The more Nation thought about it, the more he was sure it was the right decision. It had been a long time since he'd done a liquor store. Ghetto liquor stores were white gold mines. The Louisiana Bottle Shop had a nice ethnic ring to its name, but Nation, like everyone else, knew it belonged to an old attorney living in Beverly Hills. The Cotton Brothers' Shop on South Normandie was another. It was owned by a Greek that came around on Mondays to inspect the books. Blacks didn't own liquor stores, they worked in them, they shopped in them, and Nation knew not many would die for them.

The decision made, liquor stores the choice, Nation still needed a plan. He learned from those experienced in such matters while in jail, that most liquor stores were robbed at night, and usually on weekends. He'd be different. He'd strike when the police were changing shifts, in the morning.

If not then, at lunch, cops had to eat too. Ten to one he wouldn't meet any resistance. Hell, odds were, he'd be recognized, and they'd co-operate. After all, wasn't he *Robin Hoo Robin Hood?*

And he wasn't robbing Blacks. He was robbing the poachers, the leaches. The ones that charged two bucks for a can of Coke while, in the white Valley, the same can cost a dollar. He was robbin' the rich. Hell, man, that's how Robin Hood got his start. Nation was excited. He figured a single hit might get him a couple thousand. A hit like that and he could move on, without the girl.

When Nation decided to go out, he had to make a painful decision, but he knew wearing the stingy-brim hat, the black leather jacket, and carrying the forty-five was a risk even his ego must surrender to. He hid the gun in the back of Su-Linn's closet.

Nation filled a plastic bag with refundable bottles after he dumped all the soda in a sink. He headed for the door. Not a cop in L.A. would expect to find Robin Hood walking the streets in broad daylight with a bag full of plastic bottles, and he was right.

It was a bright sunny day and the streets seemed crisp and alive. Nation enjoyed the sight, the sounds, the smells, the freedom as he walked east on Adams Boulevard. He was waiting to cross the street at Montclair Avenue when a black and white patrol car rolled by. Nation smiled. He was confident. The patrol car never slowed. To the two uniformed officers Nation Wyde was invisible, and he felt it. When the light changed, he walked on with a confident strut.

The decision to rob the Louisiana Bottle Shop on West Adams came easy and Nation found himself walking to it. He decided he didn't like Greeks. He didn't know any, but he was sure if he did, he wouldn't like them. They had no business in the ghetto. Greeks had no soul, Nation told himself. Their music sucked. People that had bad music couldn't be trusted. Ever hear anyone snapping their fingers to a Greek song? The Greek that owned the store probably didn't even know anybody from Louisiana. Ten to one he never ate a hotlink. The prick was asking for it.

The Louisiana Bottle Shop was on West Adams at Montclair Avenue. As Nation approached it, he promised himself one of the things he'd do before he robbed the store was steal a car. *This walking shit is for poor folks.*

Bag of bottles under arm, Nation Wyde pushed through the double glass doors into the air-conditioned interior of the liquor store. A Coors clock above a glass doored refrigerator read eleven-fifty. Nation and a Black clerk behind the counter were the only two in the store. Nation damned himself for not bringing his gun.

"Can I help you?" the clerk asked. He was eating a beef stick and its rich aroma reminded Nation Wyde he was hungry.

"Got some bottles to return." Nation smiled, setting the sack on the counter.

The clerk, chewing his beef stick, did not return Nation's smile. "You buy them here?"

"My girl did."

"What's her name?"

"What's that have to do with my bottles?"

"Cause," the clerk explained, "I don't know you, and if I don't know her, I ain't takin' the bottles. That's policy."

"Shit," Nation hissed, baring his teeth. "Whose policy, that mother-fuckin' Greek?"

The two men studied each other. The clerk was in his fifties, Nation guessed, but there was no sign of fear on his sober, chewing face. An electronic chime sounded as a woman with a child in her arms entered. Nation gathered his sack of bottles and moved for the door.

"Try the market on Jefferson," the clerk called after him, "they take anyone's."

"Fuck you." Nation pushed out the door and was gone. Silently promising he'd be back, with his gun.

The clerk behind the counter was Amos Moses and he had been at work since six A.M. Amos had opened the store every morning for the past nine years. He was a full partner of Tommy Kazantzakis, the seventy-seven-year-old Greek immigrant who first opened the store eighteen years ago. It was called the Louisiana Bottle Shop because, Tommy's first employee, Amos Moses told him no one would ever say, "Hey, I'm gonna run down to Kazantzakis' Liquor." Tommy agreed and renamed the store.

Amos was granted a full partnership in the liquor store after a stroke fell Tommy two days after his sixty-ninth birthday. Tommy had promised that upon his death, Amos would have the first option to buy the remaining share. Tommy, partially paralyzed from his stroke, still visited the store every Monday morning and pretended to help Amos with the books. They would sit in the back and drink Greek Metaxa and talk of the old days. When Tommy grew tired, he would tell Amos the books looked fine and leave. The store was the only life the widowed Tommy Kazantzakis had, and Amos understood that.

It was only nine o'clock when the two detectives from Robbery-Homicide came into the store. Amos was uneasy, cops, particularly white cops made him nervous. He was worried about the sawed-off shotgun he kept hidden behind the counter, but the two men seemed friendly, sympathetic. They bought a bottle of Star Bucks and an orange juice. They seemed to hate robbers as much as Amos did.

LeBlanc, the detective with the thick moustache, even recommended Amos get a gun. It was then Amos confessed he had one, a shotgun. LeBlanc told Amos to pack the barrel with carpet tacks and chili pepper to give it a little extra punch.

The two Robbery detectives explained they were searching for Nathaniel Wyde, AKA, Nation Wyde, and Robin Hood. Nation was wanted for numerous counts of armed robbery, grand theft auto, assault with a deadly weapon, and murder. They showed Amos a variety of mug shots featuring Nation Wyde, and asked if he'd seen the man.

Amos studied the photos. He'd heard of Nation Wyde, but the pictures didn't look familiar. Detective LeBlanc told

Amos that Nation liked Christian Brothers Brandy and if he ever saw him to please call. Amos promised he would. The two detectives gave Amos a business card and left.

When Nation Wyde walked into the store two hours later, with the sack of bottles, Amos recognized him instantly. Amos watched Nation closely, staying near the shotgun hidden beneath the counter, but the man never made a move. Now with him gone, Amos was on the phone.

"Robbery-Homicide, this is Sergeant Hanson."

"Hey, Sergeant, are Detective LeBlanc or Drum there?"

"Sorry, they're in the field. Can I take a message?"

"Ah, yeah. Tell 'em Amos Moses called from the Louisiana Bottle Shop."

"Got it."

Amos was nervous. Why was Nation Wyde in the store with a bag of refundable bottles? He didn't need money. He couldn't need money. Was he planning to rob the store? Why weren't the police calling back? Did they know something they weren't telling him? Did they know Nation Wyde was going to rob the store? Is that why they told him to pack the shotgun with tacks and chili pepper? Were they staked outside waiting for it to happen? Was that why they weren't calling back?

Amos walked to the front windows and searched the block in both directions. There was a street maintenance crew working a half block away. Were they the police? Just as Amos' fears ballooned, his sixteen-year-old niece, Shelly, arrived. She worked parttime, three days a week, stocking shelves and dusting the bottle stock. Amos warned Shelly there may be trouble and if he gave the word, she was to hide in the back room. Shelly smiled and teased that her uncle was watching too much television.

The worried Amos returned to the telephone. He as angry now. The police had no right to put him in the middle of this damned thing. He called the Robbery-Homicide number on the business card again. A different voice answered. He left a second message for LeBlanc and Drum, stressing it was urgent. The voice on the other end of the line expressed little concern and promised to deliver the message. Amos hung up in anger.

Amos checked the shotgun. It was loaded and waiting. Twenty minutes went by. Customers came and went. Shelly busied herself, humming as she worked. It all seemed so normal, but Amos knew it wasn't. He could feel it and the feeling made him stay close to the counter and the gun.

Shelly was a talkative girl, tall and mature for her sixteen years. She wore her hair in a natural and although her body was still lanky in appearance, what she lacked in natural beauty was compensated for by her aura of energy and happiness. She was, in her Uncle Moses' words, a *tease*.

Usually when Shelly was in the store the banter between her and Uncle Amos entertained not only themselves, but the stream of customers, many of whom were familiar faces. This day was different. Amos was nervous and quiet. Finally, Shelly said, "You're really serious about this trouble thing, aren't you, Uncle Amos?"

Amos was at the front window looking out. The street maintenance crew was still there, just standing around, pretending to work. Amos knew he was right. He glanced at Shelly. "I'm serious, girl. You know who was in, not more than an hour ago?"

"Who?"

"Nation Wyde," he answered.

Shelly's expression brightened. "Nation Wyde! Robin Hood! He was here?"

"Yeah, and I think he's coming back."

"Is he handsome? Did he have a gun? What did he say?" Her questions came in a rush.

"He's a thief," Amos spat at her. "He robs liquor stores." When he said it out loud, the thought came to mind. He moved to the telephone near the cash register. If the detectives from downtown wouldn't tell him what was going on, he'd ask someone else. He'd heard about the Storm Troopers offering thousands of dollars for Nation Wyde. Screw those Robbery guys. He wasn't gonna sit back and wait for his store to get shot up. He picked up the telephone and dialed.

"Operator, I need the number for the Southwest Area of the L.A.P.D."

Brian Culpepper was at his desk in the Homicide office. Lasski was in court on a case he'd shared with Ketch. Brian punched the blinking light on the phone console and picked up the receiver. "This is Detective Culpepper."

"Yeah, Sergeant, this is Amos Moses from the Louisiana Bottle Shop on West Adams. You looking for Nation Wyde?"

Brian's interest, like his reaction, had been dulled by the hundreds of telephone calls proceeding this one, and his question was mechanical, "Have you seen him?"

"This morning," Amos answered. "He came in my store."

Brian reacted, straightening in his chair. "What time was this?"

"Eleven-thirty, or so."

The man had Brian's interest, but he was skeptical. "How do you know it was him?"

"'Cause some detectives came in, showed me his picture, just before he came in."

"Can I have your name again, sir?" Brian's skepticism was gone. He readied a pen.

"Moses. Amos Moses."

"Mr. Moses, I'd like to come by and talk to you about this."

"I'd like that."

"I'll be there in a few minutes. My name is Culpepper."

"Thank you, Detective. I'll be waiting."

Brian hung up, grabbed his jacket. Boone glanced up "Gonna be a hero," he asked sarcastically. "Capture Robin Hood single handed? Bet you a case of beer."

Brian didn't answer as he moved for the door.

19 THE LADY KILLER

Driving north on Western Avenue Brian thought about Nation Wyde. If it was him who had been in the Louisiana Bottle Shop, it was a safe bet he was living nearby. Nation was an arrogant fugitive who kept showing up everywhere. Speeding by several slower cars, Brian pushed the detective car faster. He was in a hurry to settle an old score.

At the Louisiana Bottle Shop, Shelly was sweeping the long aisles with a push broom. Her mind was full of thoughts about Robin Hood. Amos Moses was behind the counter near the register, his back to Shelly, restocking a cigarette rack.

"Uncle Amos," Shelly called as she pushed a fine line of dust and debris over the polished tile with her broom.

"Can't you see I'm busy, girl."

"Tell me what Robin Hood looks like?"

Amos continued his work with the cigarette rack without turning. "He's a Black man. You know what they say about us Black men?"

Shelly paused. She took the bait, "What do they say?"

"They say we all look alike."

Shelly laughed and picked up her broom to point its black handle like a shotgun at her uncle's back.

Outside, Detective Brian Culpepper parked his detective car at the curb in front of the shop. He was at the double glass door entry, pushing the door in when he heard the voice. "Okay, dude, tell me what I want, or I blow you in half."

Brian stopped cold. The glass doors were covered with sticker advertisements and reflections. It was difficult to get a clear view, but he saw the clerk behind the counter. He was facing the wall with both arms in the air.

Brian's heart pounded in his ears. He reached for his Glock pistol. Pushing the door slowly open He looked through glass, seeing the dark shape of the barrel of a shotgun. It was pointed at the clerk from the mouth of an aisle. He couldn't see who was holding the gun, but he knew where he would be standing. Brian knew what he had to do. He stiff armed the door open, aiming his gun. "Police, Freeze!"

Brian's shout startled Shelly. She swung the broom toward the shout.

Brian saw the barrel of the shotgun moving toward him. He was aiming where the robber stood hidden by the shelves. He already had pressure on the trigger. He squeezed three times in rapid succession. The noise from the shots was deafening. BOOM, BOOM, BOOM!

The bullets ripped through the shelves sending glass and debris flying. The barrel of the shotgun disappeared. Brian took a step in. The clerk, an older man, was screaming and running toward where the man with the shotgun had stood.

Brian, his pistol aimed at the two, moved closer.

Amos Moses was on his knees in the broken glass and debris knocked from the shelves. He was screaming, crying as he pulled Shelly's bloody body into his arms. Her chest was covered with blood where the shots had torn through her. Her head and neck bobbed as Amos wrapped his arms around her. Her lifeless eyes were wide as if staring into the distance. Blood bubbled out of her mouth in gulps like a hiccup. Brian saw the barrel of the shotgun lying beside the young Black woman. It was the handle of her broom.

Brian tried to breathe as he holstered his gun and moved

to the telephone beside the cash register. Amos's screams were continuing. Brian dialed 911.

"911," a female voice answered. "What is your emergency?"

"I'm a police officer. I'm at the Louisiana Bottle shop on West Adams."

Amos's screams filled the air in the background, "You killer her. You killed my niece."

"I need help," Brian gasped into the receiver over Amos's cries. "Shots fired. One down. Get me an ambulance here!"

"Where are you, Officer?"

"Montclair and Adams. I'm white and in soft clothes."

Only seconds passed before the broadcast reached out into patrol cars across the city. "Southwest units, any unit able to handle, officer needs help. Shots fired. Adams and Montclair. Use caution, plain clothed officer on scene. Any unit able to handle, identify and handle code 3."

Brian dropped the telephone and moved to Amos and the fallen girl. Amos buried his face against the girl's torso, crying uncontrollably. Brian grabbed Amos by the shoulders and jerked him away from the girl. She fell limp, awkwardly into her own blood. Brian knelt over her, reached for her neck, ignoring the blood, glass, and debris. He searched for a pulse. "Come on, breathe," Brian pled. He did not notice Amos grabbing a bottle of wine from a shelf in the aisle.

"You bastard," he swung the bottle hard striking Brian on the back of the head. The glass bottle exploded sending wine and glass flying. Brian fell forward, arms limp, onto the body of the bloody girl.

Amos bolted to the counter and reached behind it grabbing his shotgun. He unlocked the weapon and in three steps was back to where Brian lay atop Shelly. He sobbed and raised the shotgun, aiming at Brian's back.

Brian moaned, reached for the pain at the back of his head. He pushed up off the girl with effort; blood seeped between the fingers he held on the back of his head. He was stunned, soaked with Shelly's blood. Amos's arms were trembling. He tried to hold the shotgun steady in his own bloody hands. His face was a mask of torment and anger.

"Drop the gun!" a uniformed officer barked from the open door of the liquor store. He was aiming a gray 12-gauge shotgun at Amos. "Drop it or die."

"Drop it." A second officer aimed a pistol over his partner's shoulder at Amos.

Amos looked to them. "He killed her."

"Drop the gun or die," the officer with the shotgun repeated slow and deliberate.

Amos sniffed, tears streamed down his face, dropping from his chin. He let the shotgun sag, and then he released it. It clunked to the floor.

The distant call of a chorus of sirens wailed in the distance. Amos turned, leaned into a shelf to cover his face and wept. More officers were arriving, pushing inside with guns drawn. One of the first moved to Amos and shackled his wrists behind his back.

"No, no, you don't understand," Amos cried as he was grabbed by two officers and muscled toward the front door.

Two others went quickly to Brian who was staggering to his feet. "You hit? You alright?" They helped him to stand and find his balance. Brian looked down at the girl. Sightless dead eyes were staring up at him. Brian grimaced and looked away.

"That's Culpepper," Brian heard a voice say among those crowding in.

A LAFD ambulance with paramedics arrived as Brian staggered to the sidewalk with the help of two officers. Six police cars, emergency lights flashing, sat parked at hard angles to one another in front of the liquor store. Distant sirens warned more were on the way. A help call, from a fellow officer, with shots fired, was taken seriously.

Brian was escorted to the ambulance where he was helped up into the back. One of the paramedics, a young blonde woman helped him lay down. She took a quick look at the back of his head and reached for a compress. "Can you tell me your name?" she asked, wanting to see how responsive he was. Her partner had already disappeared into the store with a duty bag.

A uniformed sergeant arrived on the scene. It was the Black Sergeant Taylor. He quickly got the others out of the liquor store and posted an officer at the door. "No one goes in without me knowing it. Start a log."

Brian was back from the edge. "I don't know what happened," he said to the blonde paramedic.

"I'm not a detective, but I'm guessing you were hit in the head," she said, holding the compress to the back of his neck. "How's your pain on a scale of one to ten?"

Brian ignored the question and asked, "What's happening with the girl?" He knew already and the question came as almost a sob.

"My partner is with her."

JD Kent and Lieutenant Storm arrived along with Boone and Roberts. Their first stop was at the ambulance to see Culpepper.

"What's his condition?" Storm asked.

Brian, laying on the stretcher inside the cabin of the ambulance, the compress still on the back of his neck, heard the lieutenant's question. He didn't look to him. He was flushing with guilt.

"Bleeding has slowed. He's got a hematoma. Possible concussion, to be determined. We'll go to Centinela in Inglewood."

Brian reached, moved the girl's hand and compress from his neck. He pushed upon an elbow, looked to Storm, JD, and the others. "I'm okay."

"You fire your weapon?" Storm asked.

"Yes," Brian answered.

"Boone, take his gun," the lieutenant ordered.

Brian raised his arm and jacket to expose his holstered Glock. Boone climbed in, reached, took the gun, aimed it at the ground and cleared the weapon. He released the magazine and with a glance at the ammo clip he said, "Looks like he fired three."

"JD, go with Culpepper. Keep us advised," Storm added,

196

reaching out to pat Brian on the leg. "Glad you're alright, Sergeant."

Shock, Brian learned, could be an ally. Until the ambulance delivered him to the hospital ER all he could think about was the pain on the back of his head and the blood all over the front of his shirt and jacket.

He was beginning to realize where the blood came from. He had shot and killed the girl with a broom. He knew she was dead. He closed his eyes as the ambulance, siren yelping, worked its way through afternoon traffic en route to the hospital. He heard JD and the blonde talking but had no interest in what they were saying. How could the world be normal when he had just shot and killed another girl?

"Goddamnit," he growled as they lifted him from the stretcher onto the gurney in the ER. Here he was bloody with an empty holster. Instead of the flood of anxiety and regret he felt with his first shooting, this one was brinking on anger. How the hell could this be? How could it be another girl? What the fuck was wrong with the world? Brian hoped he wasn't the answer. He wasn't angry at the girl, or the Black man. He was angry at the situation. How in the hell could this happen? How could he be in the middle of it?

People were touching him. He closed his eyes. He was nauseous. He had no answer. Maybe there was no answer. Suddenly anger yielded to exhaustion. He felt lonely and tired. Three masked nurses and two doctors quickly surrounded him. JD was escorted away.

"I'll be right outside, dude," JD called. A nurse offered him Brian's empty holster and badge from his belt. The remainder of Brian's bloody clothes were quickly cut away and bagged as biohazard. He felt vulnerable in only a hospital gown and socks. They examined his head, removing bits of glass. The wound was examined and cleaned, before he was wheeled off to Xray. He had no way of knowing what was going on in the lobby outside the ER.

Captain Winslow, after visiting the scene of the shooting, arrived at the ER, along with the area commander,

Jason Langley. A telephone call from Boone to Lasski's cellphone brought Lasski from court to the hospital where he cursed and swore and damned himself for not being with Brian. JD calmed him down and filled him in on what little he knew of the shooting.

"Son-of-a-bitch," Lasski complained as he made the call to Deputy District Attorney Pamela Moss to inform her of Brian's injury. It was a call he thought he'd never have to make. Pulling up Pamela's number on his cell phone took him back to the night Ketch died, and the knock on his front door.

Pamela answered, listened, and promised she be there in thirty minutes. She arrived nearly an hour later. Damned LA rush hour traffic. Pamela drew looks from the collection of cops. Lasski took Pamela's hand and led her away from the others. Lasski introduced himself.

"My name is Lasski. David Lasski. I'm the one who called. I'm Brian's partner," he said almost apologetically. "I should have been with him. I was in fucking...I'm sorry, I was in court."

"Me too," Pamela said forcing a smile. "How is he?"

"Nothing life threatening is all they've said. I wasn't there, but they say he got hit in the head with a bottle."

"I heard on the radio a young Black girl was shot."

"Yeah, I heard too. All I know I got from these guys," he gestured with his head toward the others. "Not likely they want me talking about it."

"I understand," Pamela said, tears welling in her eyes.

Boone and Howser as well as Roberts and Delgado joined the wait as well as the uniformed day watch commander. Deputy Chief Searcy and Chief of Police Peck both called Captain Winslow asking for an update on Culpepper's condition.

Word of the shooting death of a teenage Black girl by an LAPD Officer had already found its way onto the Internet as well as becoming *Breaking News* on four of LA's hungry early newscasts.

The scene at the Louisiana Bottle Shop on West Adams

was now being covered by two noisy orbiting news helicopters. Three mini-cam vans joined the crowd on the street, which was jammed with patrol cars, a Coroner's van, four unmarked cars from SID, OIS and RHD. Adding to the tempo of excitement surrounding the Bottle Shop was a growing crowd of curious, offering cat calls and insults.

Sergeant Taylor, still on the scene, was watching them. He knew there was a fine line between provoking a crowd and controlling one. He would soon have to call for reinforcements as he knew the body being carried out was going to be a volatile moment. Now, on-scene reporters were milling in the crowd with their camera operators trying to get fill for a live broadcast.

Brian was given an IV along with more shots than he could count or remember. The film from X-ray finally arrived, and the doctors looked at it on an illuminated screen in the ER. Brian lay prone on the treatment table in his hospital gown and socks. He could hear their voices, but not clear enough to understand. Finally, they turned from the screen and moved to Brian's side. The older of the two doctors removed his mask. "How are you feeling?"

"Good enough to go home," Brian answered looking up at the two.

"Who is the vice president of the United States?" the younger of the two doctors asked.

Brian considered the questioned carefully before he spoke. "Vice president? It was Pence. Now it's a Black woman." Brian cursed his failing memory.

The two doctors exchanged a look. The older took the lead.

"X-ray shows no sign of internal hemorrhaging, but it's just an X-ray. We want to follow it up with a CT scan as well as some other tests. With blunt force to the skull sometimes we simply must wait and observe. Which is what we recommend tonight."

Brian looked up into the bright light above him. He felt helpless.

"I'm his captain," Winslow said as the doctors came into the waiting room to the collection of cops. The others crowded around. Pamela pushed her way to the captain's shoulder.

"There is no evidence of anything beyond a mild concussion. Nevertheless, for his wellbeing, we would like to keep him overnight for observation."

"May I see him?" Pamela asked before Captain Winslow could speak.

"Yes, if you'll keep it brief."

Brian had his eyes closed. He lay half-covered with a sheet. He was watching the barrel of the shotgun in the liquor store, which in reality was the dark handle of a push broom. He was at the door again, remembering the sight of the gun. When it swung toward him, he knew he was going to die...but he didn't die. Instead, he shot and killed a girl with a broom. A young Black girl. *Fucking hell*, he didn't even know her name. What would anybody else have done? Would any other cop have done it differently? The answer was a resounding painful, *yes*! What if he just stepped inside with his gun aimed, waiting for another two or three seconds. *Maybe! Fucking maybes.*

"Brian," Pamela whispered as she laid a hand on his. He opened his eyes and looked up into hers. She smiled and leaned to kiss him on the forehead. "We have to stop meeting like this."

Her hand was warm on his. Brian took her hand and cupped it in both of his. "I'm sorry," he said, not knowing what else to say. She placed the forefinger of her free hand on his mouth.

Brian was admitted. He was placed in a private room. The PM watch commander assigned two officers to protect his privacy. It was an order from the chief of police. Chief Peck was savvy enough to know the shooting death of an unarmed sixteen-year Black girl by one of his officers would already have put the City of Angels on the edge. The chief cursed and kicked a chair in the conference room after Deputy Chief Searcy told him the shooter was Brian Culpepper. "Goddammit, this is going to get ugly."

Pamela was at Brian's side when Captain Winslow and Lieutenant Storm came in. Knowing there should be no talk of the shooting they tried small talk. It didn't go very well.

"If they let you go in the morning," Lieutenant Storm said, "give me a heads-up. I'll be on duty. OIS needs to get a statement from you. They said they could come out to your place after you're released."

"He'll be at my place," Pamela said, interjecting herself into the conversation. She and Lasski were standing on either side of Brian's bed. Brian said nothing. He was being strangely quiet.

Lieutenant Storm tried his annoyed *go to hell look* on Pamela, but it didn't work.

"I'll give you a call when he's available, Lieutenant."

Storm continued his mad dog stare. "You know, Miss Moss it would be inappropriate, considering who you are, to be a witness to the interview."

"I'm familiar with the law," Pamela assured.

"Well, Detective," Captain Winslow said with a look to Culpepper. He was trying to end the contest between the two wannabe alpha dogs. "After your interview, you'll be on administrative leave until we get a ruling from the shooting review board. Use it as a time to get some rest." He patted Culpepper's blanket covered foot.

Storm chose to say nothing. He followed Captain Winslow out the door.

"Well, wasn't that fucking special?" Lasski smiled.

Lasski stayed while Pamela left with a promise to return with clothes for Brian's early morning release. It was Brian and Lasski's first private moment.

Lasski reached and took Brian's hand in his. "Listen, you gung ho fuck, I'm really sorry I wasn't with you."

Brian pulled his hand from Lasski's. "You're not going to cry, are you?"

"You know this girl, Pamela Moss. What the hell does

she see in you? I know your dick must be about the size of your little finger."

Brian turned the exchange serious. "I hope I haven't screwed the pooch?"

"Any wits? Anyone else there?"

"Yes," Brian said. "There was a wit. He was behind the counter. He's the one that hit me."

"And he saw it all?" Lasski asked.

"I don't know. He had his back to the girl," his words came in a rush. Almost like a plea. "I didn't know it was a girl. I thought she had a shotgun. I thought she was a guy. All she had was a fucking broom?"

The detectives from RHD, OIS, SID and Use of Force were busy at the scene. They were concerned about the growing crowd outside the liquor store. Shouts, insults, and then pieces of bricks and concrete resulted in the officers stationed outside putting on their helmets. The County Coroner's van suffered a broken windshield as it pulled away. There were no arrests.

Hanson, one of the detectives from RHD, gathered the money from the cash register—eight-hundred and sixteen dollars in cash and coin. They locked it in the open safe they found in a back room. Hanson and his partner, Mattingly, were the last two in the store. They used a set of keys found in the safe to lock the front door. The keys were then dropped through the mail slot in the door.

In addition to scale drawings, measurements, prints, digital and video imagery, physical evidence—including a bullet recovered from an interior wall—they found gold. The Louisiana Bottle Shop had five strategically placed security cameras. All were operational and recording to an HD/CD.

Hanson was the first to play the recording. He watched it on a computer screen in the rear of the store. There was no audio, but the silent images told the story.

"Son-of-a-bitch," he whispered, watching the girl pick up her wide floor broom and point the dark handle at the man behind the counter at the front of the store. The video switched to a second angle showing Detective Sergeant Brian Culpepper pushing the glass front door partially open, reacting to something, draw his weapon, shout silently, aim and then fire. His Glock jerked and spewed flame. One, two, three times in rapid succession. It was like a motion picture. The security cameras had been set to motion detection sequencing. In the next frame Hanson watched the young Black girl fall as if struck by lightning. He grimaced and turned off the video.

The City of Angels has many faces. The day was beginning to fade as the afternoon light turned the western shy to a light gold. The temperature was in the mid-seventies and lights were beginning to wink on across the face of the city. The freeways were jammed with those inching their way home. Crowded airliners thundered overhead as they slid through the sky toward LAX. For most of the city's nearly four million people another workday was ending, the city seeming to draw a sigh of relief, but for some there would be no relief.

Karen Simpson, the mother of sixteen-year-old Shelly Simpson, learned the police had shot and killed her daughter when an emotional neighbor burst in crying, "Turn on your TV."

Dianna Moses, the fifty-four-year-old wife of Amos Moses, learned something was very wrong at the Bottle Shop when a Budweiser delivery truck driver called. "I'm at the store," the driver said on the phone. "Amos gave me this number to call if ever there's a problem. There's a problem. People here are saying there was a shooting."

Dianna drove to the store only to find it locked and surrounded with a crowd of curious. She dialed 911. A police car arrived four minutes later.

"I can't find my husband. Our store is locked, and people here are saying there was a shooting," Dianna cried.

"I'm sorry ma'am," the Black policewoman said after climbing out from behind the wheel. "He's been arrested."

A bottle clanged and bounced off the hood of the police car.

"Come on, partner," the officer in the car called. "Let's get the hell outta here."

Dianna's next stop was the Southwest Area police station at 1546 West Martin Luther King Boulevard. She parked in a red zone in front of the station and went in the front door to where two officers were stationed behind the front desk. One of them was working with a *walk-in* making a report. Two young children were pressed close to their mother's legs as she spoke with the female officer behind the desk.

"Where's my husband?" the emotional Dianna screamed at the second officer slapping the surface of counter. The woman with the two children moved away.

"Ma'am, what's your husband's name?" the desk officer asked in a quiet tone hoping to calm Dianna.

"You got him. He's here. I want to see him," she screamed in response.

The PM watch commander, hearing the disturbance, appeared at the desk officer's side. "What's the issue?"

"You killed my niece and arrested my husband. He's here. I want to see him," her demand was even louder. The woman with the two children hurried them toward the door.

"Are you talking about Amos Moses?" the watch commander asked.

"Where is he?" Dianna shouted.

Boone and Delgado, hearing the disturbance, and knowing what the woman wanted, came from the Homicide office to answer Dianna's questions. "He been arrested for battery on a police officer," Delgado said.

"He wouldn't do that. Where is he?"

Dianna Moses did not calm down. She demanded to see whoever was in charge. She threatened to sue all of them. Her shouting continued for another eight minutes. Finally, the watch commander warned her, "Ma'am, if you don't lower your voice and calm down, you're going to be arrested."

Dianna swung her purse at the lieutenant. She missed, but she was arrested for creating a public disturbance. Her car was impounded. The towing fee would be ninety-six dollars and thirty-eight cents. Daily storage fee would be another sixty-eight dollars.

Dianna Moses was handcuffed and transported to Sybil Brand Institute, the women's jail in East Los Angeles. Her purse was taken from her and booked as personal property. Finally, able to make a call, five hours after her arrest, she telephoned Tommy Kazantzakis, their Greek partner and owner of the liquor store.

Tommy was shocked. He told the emotional Dianna not to worry, he'd get help for her and Amos both. Initial bail and attorney's fees for both would total $6,374.00.

Dianna would be the first to be released the following morning at 9 AM. She was twelve miles from her home in a part of the city she had never seen. She had eight dollars in her purse.

Amos would be released from the men's county jail at two in the afternoon. He had no wallet and no money. The Louisiana Bottle Shop would remain closed for three days. Amos Moses went back to the store two days later. Shelly's blood had dried and turned a near dark brown. Amos couldn't go near it. He called a disaster clean-up crew. They cost eighteen hundred dollars.

Brian was released from the hospital in the morning. Pamela had brought him clothes the night before. She stayed late and came back early. Brian was glad to be released, although a nurse insisted on pushing him out in a wheelchair. Pamela drove as they wormed their way through the early morning crush of traffic toward her condo. Brian's cell phone rang. He looked at the caller ID. The number 213-486-1000 appeared. He recognized it as an LAPD number.

"This is Culpepper."

"Detective, this is Stew Baxter, OIS. We've talked before." Brian remembered who he was. "We're scheduled to see you today. I understand the interview was going to take place at the residence of Pamela Moss."

"That's correct."

"Well, we think that may be an issue?"

"An issue? Why?"

"We're told she's a deputy district attorney."

"Correct."

"Well, that's the issue. Conducting a post shooting interview in the residence of a deputy district attorney could become an issue when and if the matter went to trial. You must see the connection. We'd like the interview to take place here, at PAB."

Brian was angry. He knew the OIS detective was right, but the bias against Pamela made him stiffen. "What time?"

"Timing is important," Baxter said in Brian's ear. "How are you feeling? Can you do it today?"

"What time today?" Brian asked, feeling control was once again slipping away.

"Can be you here by eleven?"

Brian tried to tactfully explain to Pamala that the OIC detectives did not want to interview him at her condo. "They're concerned about aftershocks."

"And they're right," Pamela agreed. They had talked the night before. Pamela knew it would be wrong for Brian to tell her the details of the shooting. As a deputy district attorney, who foreseeably could, in the course of her duties someday, become involved in the case. "Okay, plan B," Pamela said. "I'll drive you to Southwest. You can pick up your truck."

"Welcome to my world," Brian said sarcastically as they turned south on Western Avenue.

After reaching the station and being waved into the employee parking area they kissed. "Don't let them hurt you," Pamela said.

Brian smiled, climbed out. "I'll buy you dinner tonight."

"Jury trial. Remember?" Pamela said. "If I'm late, I'll bring fish and chips from that place on Hill."

"Love you." Brian nodded, closing the car door. Pamela drove away. He regretted not inviting her into the station. Their bias could go to hell he thought with a glance at the personnel entrance.

"Hey, it's the shit stirrer, Brian Culpepper," Detective Howser called when Brian opened the door to Homicide.

Lasski, Fran Cox, Boone, Howser, Delgado, and JD Kent all crowded around him. They patted him on the back and shoulders, looked at the bandage on the back of his head.

"I heard the X-ray of your head showed nothing," Lasski said.

They all laughed. Brian felt comfortable in their midst. This was where he belonged. Here he was wearing more than a gown and socks. Here, at least for the moment, he was with those who cared. They joked, made small talk, and then Brian, with a glance at his watch, told them OIS was waiting for him at PAB.

Lasski walked to the parking lot with Brian. "So, you're gonna get paid to sit around and do nothing. Can I come over and help?"

"Sit at home and think?"

They reached Brian's black pickup.

"You wanna take a city ride down to PAB?"

"Naw, I'm going home after the interview. If I drive mine, I won't have to come back down here." He climbed up into the pickup with its oversized mud tires.

"Home? You mean over to the den of that fox you're living with?" Lasski teased as he walked away.

At the headquarters building of the LAPD, Brian presented his ID card and was waved into the employee parking area. The massive building was covered with reflective glass. It made Brian think of a fish tank. He was about to swim in a fish tank. He hoped the sharks weren't hungry. Walking toward the entrance, he tried to calm himself. He was there because he had shot and killed another girl.

"God, help me," he prayed. It was sincere.

20 A CITY ON FIRE

Chief of Police James Peck, his uniformed Executive Assistant Renna Lincoln, Deputy Chief Searcy, and Commander Hays sat in the chief's conference room watching the video from the Louisiana Bottle Shop's security cameras on a large screen. Commander Hays had brought the CD to the chief after the OIS team called him to review it.

"Let's reserve comment until we've looked at it," Hays said.

They watched it three times. When the commander finally switched off the CD they looked to the chief.

Chief Peck rocked back in his chair and took in a deep breath before he spoke. "I'll defer to whatever the shooting review board decides, but clearly you can see why Culpepper fired. He thought she had a gun."

"A picture is worth a thousand words," Searcy said. "Instead of saying what our investigation, our conclusion, or our evidence suggests, let's put the video out. It tells a story that can't be denied. We didn't produce it. It came from the store. It shows exactly what happened."

"You don't think the world seeing an LAPD detective shooting a sixteen-year-old to death isn't going to be the spark that will set the city on fire?" Commander Hays said.

"They'll find out we have this," Searcy said. "If we don't release it, they'll say we're hiding something."

"To compound the situation, isn't Culpepper the officer involved in the shooting of the woman at the bank on Wilshire when it turned into a civil disturbance?"

"Yeah," Searcy said. "And that's something the world will soon connect the dots on."

Chief Peck rocked forward to rest his elbows on the conference table. "After an incident like this, I usually have calls from Congresswoman Irene Waters, the head of the NAACP, the Urban League, the ACLU, Councilman Gates, and every other civil rights group west of the Mississippi. So far nothing. Not one call."

"They're waiting," Deputy Chief Searcy said.

"Or angry," the chief said. "They simply don't care what we have to say."

"So, who do we give this to? How about *TicToc*?" Commander Hays said pulling the CD out of the computer.

"Don't be a smart ass, Jim," the chief said. "Is Culpepper being interviewed today?"

"As we speak," the commander answered.

"Then before EOW," Chief Peck said, "I want to know what he has to say, and then, maybe? We put it out."

Brian was isolated in a spartan interrogation room deep in the heart of the Police Headquarters Building. He couldn't see the camera or microphone, but he knew they were somewhere. His watch told him he had been waiting for thirty-eight minutes. Pricks. He knew what they were doing. They wanted him eager to talk. What did they know that he didn't? The truth he reminded himself. It didn't matter what they said what they put in front of him he was going to speak nothing but the truth. Talking about shooting a girl armed with nothing but a broom wasn't going to be easy, but he knew it had to be done. He wondered if he would ever face it again. Would there be a third girl? Would he have to shoot another? Would he choke on it? The thoughts disappeared as the door to the room opened. Detectives Baxter and Connelly stepped in. Brian looked at the two men and remembered them from the hours they had spent grilling him about the shooting of the girl at the bank. Damn, were they doing this on purpose? Did they know how it unnerved him. He decided they knew.

"Damn, Culpepper," Detective Connelly said sitting down across the table from Brian. "This is just like your first shooting. Why don't we just give you the forms and you can fill in the blanks."

Baxter laughed at his partner's attempt at humor as he too sat down across from Brian. Brian did not laugh.

Baxter had carried two paper cups into the room. He pushed one across to Brian. "I remembered. Diet Coke, right."

"Right," Brian granted him.

Brian was reminded that as a sworn LAPD officer he did not have a right to remain silent. He could, if he so desired, have an attorney, or another sworn officer of his choice, sit in on the interview, but that would not change the fact he was obligated to answer their questions. And so, it began.

What time did you come on duty the day of the shooting? What weapon were you carrying? Was your Glock an LAPD issue firearm? Why did you go to the Louisiana Bottle Shop? Why did you go alone? Did you ask anyone to go with you? Why not? Have you ever been there before? Do you know a man by the name of Amos Moses? Where did you park? What did you see? What did you hear?

Did you hear anyone speak in the store? What did the voice say? Was it a male or female voice? Why did you believe the person you thought had a gun was going to shoot you? Were you in fear of your life? Did you believe others were about to be shot? How many shots did you fire? Are you certain of the number of shots you fired? What did you say before you fired your weapon? What did you do after you fired your weapon?

When did you realize the girl did not have a gun? Did you touch the girl after she was shot? What did you do? Do you know who hit you in the head with a bottle? Did you call anyone other than the 911 operator after the shots were fired? Did you speak to the man you say was kneeling over the girl? Have you discussed this incident in detail with anyone else?

The questions continued for three and a half hours. The two detectives had left the room together after the first hour. Brian decided they were using a tactic he and Lasski used. It was called *cooking the suspect*. Let them *cook* after questioning and then come back and ask the same exact questions all over again.

The truth Brian kept reminding himself. The truth and nothing but the truth. He smiled, remembering Pamela at the Blue Moon after they had thrown coins into the restaurant's wishing well. She wanted to know what he had wished for.

"The truth, Brian Culpepper, nothing but the truth," she had said.

Pamela wasn't there in the interrogation room with him, but her love was, and he was clinging to it.

As morning yielded to afternoon, Brian was offered a bathroom break and lunch if he wanted. He declined. The questions continued.

When was the last time he qualified with the gun used in the shooting? Did he think having a partner with him may have prevented the shooting? When he fired his weapon was it his intent to kill the person hidden from his view? Did he believe he had the lawful right to shoot at a person aiming a broom at him? Why did he believe it was a shotgun aimed at him? Should he have waited longer before firing?

The two OIS detectives took another break leaving Brian alone in the room. He was tiring. His butt ached. His head itched. He massaged the bandage on the back of his head, but not while his interrogators were in the room. The chair was uncomfortable. An eighth of an inch had been deliberately cut from one of the legs to make it even more uncomfortable.

The door opened. It was Detective Baxter. He was alone. "We're all done, Brian. You know the drill. We'll put a summary together. It'll go to the chief and the shooting review board. You may or may not be called before the board. Either way, you will be informed of their decision. Until then you'll remain on paid administrative leave. Do you have any questions?"

Brian pushed out of his chair. "What was her name?"

_____

Brian was glad to get away from the Police Headquarters Building. In his mind—and seemingly in the mind of every cop working south of the Santa Monica Freeway—those individuals who worked in the LAPD Headquarters, and the number had to be in the thousands, were part of some other department. A department that many times they couldn't recognize or believe, and a department they never really felt part of. He was assigned to Southwest. There they knew him and knew him well. There he was assigned duties, supervised, trusted, but when something went wrong, or someone thought it may be wrong, the downtown cops in the police building took over. It sucked. Brian was glad he wasn't part of the downtown crowd. He was glad he was a ghetto cop, even though he was white and driving home to a condo in West LA.

It was a draw, Brian decided, arriving at Pamela's condo early, and she was going to be late. He took off his shoes and carefully pulled the bandage from the back of his head before fixing himself a drink from a bottle of Jack he had bought. No guilt over that.

Next came the spot he favored on Pamela's sectional couch in front of her wide screen HDTV. Picking up the remote, Brian wondered what deputy district attorneys earned. Looking at the furnishings in the condo, he made a mental comparison with his apartment. It humbled him. Pamela was obviously earning more. She was the one with the law degree. Was that what fate had in mind? Was that how the score would be settled?

His growing anxiety reminded him of her complaints about his schedule and assignment. Was that going to get worse? And there was her talk about the conflict between their professions. He was a ghetto cop, and she was a deputy DA? What was wrong with that picture? When was the fact he'd shot and killed two women going to become an obstacle between them? Hell, it already was. He aimed the remote and switched on the TV, refusing to think of any more maybes. *Fucking Maybes.*

Channel 7's *Early Eyewitness News* lit up the screen as Brian raised his feet, pushed back in the pillows on the couch, took a deep relaxing breath and sipped his Jack and Coke. Finally, he was feeling relaxed. It was to be short lived.

On screen an attractive anchor announced, "Funeral arrangements have been made for sixteen-year-old, Sally Simpson, shot and killed by Los Angeles police earlier this week. Gina Parks is at the scene in south LA. Gina, fill us in."

The scene switched to a reporter standing in front of an alabaster church where a line of Black men and women filed into the open doors. The sound of an organ and the church choir reached out to underscore the reporter's words. "As you can see, Karen, the Black community is feeling the pain from this senseless shooting. A large crowd is expected here tonight for Shelly Simpson's memorial. They've been arriving for over an hour now, while even bigger protests are planned for tomorrow at the LAPD's headquarters in downtown Los Angeles, where Shelly Simpson's mother is scheduled to appear. A private family funeral is planned for next week after Shelly's body is released by the county coroner. All this…"

Brian switched channels to find another a Black reporter standing in front of the Louisiana Bottle Shop. The sidewalk behind the reporter was piled with an assortment of colorful flower arrangements, cards, toys, and placards taped to the windows and doors. Hand painting on the placards read, *Baby killers, Stop shotting children, shoot a cop, save a child!*

The reporter spoke into his microphone over shouts and calls coming from the crowd of Black faces surrounding him, "The store where Shelly Simpson was shot and killed by the police is still closed. We have word from the family that until the funeral..."

A third channel found yet another remote report with an attractive blonde reporter standing in front of the sprawling Police Headquarters Building.

"Media relations from the Department is saying there is an intense investigation going on behind the scenes. We're told Chief Peck is expected to make a statement sometime tomorrow."

Brian jerked forward from his relaxed position on the couch, splashing his Jack and Coke onto the front of his pants and the couch. "Damn it," he growled. He was angry.

He switched off the television and tossed the remote to a coffee table. The shooting had followed him home. His relaxed, shoes off, feet in the air afternoon was gone, and a flood of guilt was washing over. The three reports he saw, and he knew there were more, did everything but spell his name.

They were talking about him and what he had done. Maybe they didn't know his name yet, but they soon would, and wasn't that fair. They knew Amos Moses' name, they knew his wife was arrested, they knew her name, they knew the store was closed, they knew his niece, sixteen-year-old Shelly Simpson had been shot dead, but all they knew about the cop that caused all of this was—*The officer is on paid administrative leave.*

Brian's confidence in the idea he had done nothing wrong was slipping. If he had done nothing wrong, why was Shelly's family awaiting her body to be released by the County Coroner? She hadn't done anything wrong either. He walked to the kitchen, set his drink on the counter, and used a paper towel to wipe at the spill on his pants. The wet stain on the front of his pants made him laugh, or was it a cry? He was a marked man.

Brian was pretending to read one of Pamela's coffee table books entitled, *Birds of the Southwest.* He had not turned the television on again. Pamela, as promised, brought dinner. Brian had no appetite, but he faked it for Pamela's sake. After they ate, Brian excused himself to go to the bathroom. When he returned to the living room, he found Pamela had turned on the television.

A reporter was interviewing a Black councilman. The councilman was outraged an yet another innocent Black youth had died at the hands of the police. He was demanding the district attorney's office conduct an independent investigation into what he called a *senseless police shooting*. Pamela turned the television off and looked to Brian.

"It's politics, Brian, not the law. You haven't done anything wrong."

Her words did little to help. Brian Culpepper felt he had done something wrong. Nation Wyde, that son-of-a-bitch, had once again set it all in motion. Wherever he was he was having the last laugh.

Commander Hays and Deputy Chief Searcy brought the CD of Brian Culpepper's interview to the conference room. They also brought the two OIS investigators who had done the questioning. Lieutenant Lincoln, the chief's aid came in from an adjoining office. "The chief will be with us in a moment."

They sat quietly until the door opened again and Chief Peck led a serious looking balding man in glasses into the room. "Most of you know Dan Hawks, our city attorney."

The chief gestured for Hawks to sit down. "Dan and I were looking at the video from the security cameras. I want him in on our every step. There is little doubt the victim's family will be, no, already have been, hustled by an army of high-profile attorneys all claiming they can get millions from the city."

"Chief," Renna Lincoln said with a look at the two OIS detectives, "these are the two men who interviewed Detective Culpepper this morning—Sergeants Baxter and Connelly."

The chief sat down at the head of the table. "Gentlemen, thanks for coming. I listened to some of the tape you sent up and went through most of your notes, but let's cut to the chase. Tell us what you think, not what you think we want to hear."

Baxter and Connelly exchanged a look. Baxter took the cue. "The shooting is tragic. There was no crime or criminal conduct by any of the parties involved."

Connelly glanced at a report he carried. "Our conclusion regarding Detective Culpepper's actions are that his actions were based on reasonable observations, thus, the resulting action he took was justified."

"Our report shows," Baxter continued, "we found that when Detective Culpepper fired his weapon, he believed a shotgun was being pointed at him and that he had walked into a robbery in progress."

"All of which shows," Connelly added, "tragic as it may be, the shooting is well within the policy of the Los Angeles Police Department."

The chief offered a subtle nod of appreciation to the OIS detectives and then looked to City Attorney Dan Hawks.

Hawks knew the chief wanted his reaction.

"Your findings underscore what I saw in the video the chief showed me. And as an attorney I agree no one had criminal intent and the officer acted reasonably." He paused for a moment. The silence in the room held them. "But the fact remains, and it's a grim one, a police officer shot and killed an unarmed sixteen-year-old Black girl."

Renna Lincoln, along with Media Relations, spent nearly two hours reaching out to the press, including print, television news agencies, social media, bloggers, and a couple friendly podcasts to announce that Chief of Police James Peck would be holding a press conference at eight PM to announce the results of the investigation into the shooting death of Shelly Simpson.

Chief Peck called his wife, Cindy, at six-thirty to tell her he was going to be late. "I've got a news conference at eight."

"This on the sixteen-year-old?" his wife asked.

"Yeah."

"I may be late, too. We've got three coming in from a crash on the East bound Ten." His wife was a surgeon at the LA County Hospital.

"Jackie at home?" They had a nineteen-year-old daughter living at home while studying at Caltech. The chief was hoping his daughter would not be watching.

"Don't worry. She'll be on her phone." His wife knew why he was asking.

"Be careful driving home," the chief said.

"Be sure to tell your driver I said hello," Cindy said.

"Love you, bye."

After hanging up, the chief looked to his notes and the CD laying on his desk. He was worried. The city was on the edge and he knew it. He had ten thousand cops at his command. The city had nearly four million people. People who were shocked at what happened to George Floyd in Minneapolis. Nine minutes that changed the world.

There the cops acted with reckless criminal abandonment. An innocent man died. Tragic. Here, a sixteen-year-old Black girl with a broom was shot to death. It sounded worse and James Peck knew it. He glanced at his watch. Thirty-eight minutes and he would have to sell a bucket of shit.

He wondered who this Detective Culpepper was. Had he met him? Perhaps at some banquet, an event at the academy, passed him in the hallway. He had no way of knowing. The Chief knew how he felt about this shooting. He wished the hell it had never happened, but it had. He wondered what Culpepper thought. This was the second shooting where he had to take a human life. Did that change a man. Hell, yes.

As a cop in LA with over thirty years on the job, the chief had never had to kill a man, or a woman. Afghanistan was different. There he remembered the man who fired an AR-15 killing two men in his platoon as they walked into the village of Ab Bala. The man, who later turned out to be a mere fourteen years old, ran into a ragged hut to hide.

The chief—then Lieutenant Peck, Platoon Leader of the Third Platoon, H Company, Second Battalion, Fifth Marines—took the killings personally. Angry, he ordered his men to surround the hut. Once it was surrounded, he gave the Marines the order to fire.

In the *After Action Report*, the estimate would be a total of four hundred and fifty six rounds were fired. When one of his squad leaders went into the hut, he promptly came out and threw up. In the hut they were to discover the dead fifteen-year-old with his rifle—as well as his mother, two sisters and an infant.

War was hell, but it turned out LA was almost as bloody as Afghanistan. In his case, some Marine Corps colonel had to sell the shooting death of five Afghan natives—three of which were women—to the gatekeeps at the Pentagon. Now, he was faced with selling the shooting death of Shelly Simpson in LA by one of his men. Life was a circle.

His aide, Renna Lincoln, ended his thoughts by knocking on his office door and opening it slightly.

"Showtime," she said, and gave him a consoling smile.

The chief relieved himself in his private bathroom, washed his hands, gathered his notes, and the CD and walked with Renna to an elevator. On the elevator, he studied his Black aide. She was an attractive shapely forty-something Black woman. He had hired her after seeing her when she was a patrol sergeant in Hollywood. She was directing the dealings with a hostile riotous mob after George Floyd was killed. He had been impressed with her tact under pressure. She became his aide two months later. Six months after that, she was promoted to Lieutenant.

"Renna," Peck asked, "what do you think of this?"

The elevator stopped and the doors parted to reveal two uniformed officers. Renna raised a hand to stop them from stepping in.

"Take the next car, please." She smiled at the two. The officers recognized the chief and stepped back. The doors closed and the elevator resumed. Renna returned her attention to the chief.

"I was angry when I first heard about it. Suspicious of Culpepper. Maybe because I knew it was his second shooting. Killing a Black girl armed with a broom? Who would do that? Then I saw the video. I'm glad I wasn't the one walking into that store. If you want someone to blame in all this, blame fate."

The captain in charge of Media Relations met the chief and his aide in the off-stage wing of the press room. The two OIS detectives, Baxter and Connelly, looking worried and apprehensive, were also waiting.

"We've had a good response," the captain said over the buzz coming from the auditorium. "Whenever you're ready, Chief, I'll turn down the lights in the auditorium. That will warn them we're ready. Once you walk out onto the stage, I'll bring your lights up. We've got the security cam video all set to play."

Chief Peck nodded, looked to the two tense OIS men. "I know this is unusual, gentlemen, but I need you on this one. Either we get this right or we fuel a fire that's already burning. You were both at the scene. You interviewed the officer firing the shots. You've studied the video tape. There isn't a question out there you can't answer. The shooting review board agrees with your conclusions. We had them meet this afternoon to review your summary and look at the video. This is not something that can wait. The only thing I don't want is to give up Culpepper's name. He's got a life, a career, dreams. His administrative leave ended today. Other than that, tell the truth."

Neither of the two men seemed relieved by the chief's encouragement.

"I'll make some opening remarks, introduce the video, play it, and then it's all yours. You'll do fine," the chief said. He turned to the captain, "Okay, let's roll."

"This just in," Chris Comma, an evening anchor on CNN, announced as a *Breaking News* logo momentarily filled the screen. "Police in Los Angeles have just released a shocking video of the deadly shooting death of sixteen-year-old Shelly Simpson earlier this week. We must warn you some of the images you are about to see may be disturbing."

Five LA television stations made similar interruptions in their programming to show the video. FOX, MSNBC, and News World all followed shortly. The internet acted even faster with the video seen again and again on Instagram, Facebook, Google, and countless other social media platforms. The viewers, and they numbered in the millions, regardless of whether they hated cops, believed them, supported Black Lives or Blue Lives, all were shocked, but as their shock wore off, bias, opinions and prejudices returned. Not many hearts or minds were changed. They were simply numbed.

———

Brian and Pamela sat together on the couch in the living room while Brian told her about the shooting. She knew he had to talk about it. Neither were worried about the probability of a down-the-line conflict.

"Screw down-the-line," Pamela had told him. "Tell me about it."

Pamela held Brian's hand as he talked. It was if he was walking her through a movie and then she realized it was cop talk. He was testifying, but not in a court room. He was in her living room. It was told nearly in real time and when he finished, she held him. They were on the couch, sitting in the darkness when Brian's cell phone rang. Brian had to hunt for it. He finally found it in the kitchen.

"Hello."

"Hey," Lasski said in his ear. "You got your TV on?"

"We don't watch *Wheel of Fortune*."

"Well, you just got your life back, Dude."

"Don't mess with me, Ski. What are you talking about?"

"Chief Peck was on. A news conference. He released the video from the Bottle Shop, then he put Mutt and Jeff from OIS on to take questions. Chief said they found no wrongdoing on your part. You've been cleared. I think it's because I'm your partner."

"You're being straight with me?"

"That sounds like something my wife said to me last night."

Pamela held Brian through the night. If he slept, she wasn't aware of it. When the first light of dawn began to show on curtains in the bedroom, Brian welcomed it as excuse to get out of bed.

He was tired and anxious. A shower did little to help. They drank Starbucks and sat at the kitchen counter. Pamela was chatty while reading a trial transcript, but he heard little she said. Finally, the call he hoped for came. His cell phone rang. It was Lieutenant Storm.

"Culpepper, your administrative leave has been lifted. We'd like you in this morning."

"Thanks, Lieutenant. I'll be in."

Pamela was first to leave. Brian kissed her at the door. Her arms were loaded with a handbag, folded transcripts, a lunch bag, and a briefcase her parents bought her. She had been worried about him, but she could see the change on his face after his call to duty.

"Have a good day keeping the forces of darkness out of LA," Brian said to her at the door.

"You too, Detective."

And then she was gone.

Brian decided not to turn the radio on as he drove his pickup from Pamela's condo in West LA, where the resident population was eighty-eight per cent white.

His self-confidence was returning as he moved with the flow of morning traffic. He was going to work. Back to the ghetto. The department he served and loved had closed ranks and stood behind him. Most of LA's cops didn't know his name, weren't sure what the controversy was, but he carried a badge like theirs, and whatever the issue was, they were with him. It was the *Brotherhood of the Badge*.

Brian was shocked when he turned from South bound Western Avenue onto Martin Luther King Boulevard. Southwest Area station a short two block ahead was surrounded by hundreds of pickets, a surprising mix of both Black and white, young, and old.

Placards waved in the air in front of an army of TV cameras—*Black Lives Matter, Eye for an Eye, Cops Kill Kids, Black Justice*—but the most prominent was, *Culpepper, the Lady Killer*.

The words sprang from the placard stabbing Brian's senses. Brian drove slowly, looking at their faces. They returned his look, but none seemed to react. They may hate him. They may want justice. They may call him *The Lady Killer*, but none seemed to know who he was.

It was a strange anger to be the focus of and it unnerved him. Right or wrong, just, or unjust, he was *The Lady Killer*. It made him shudder and grimace. He was unnerved by the number of protestors. A nightmare was unfolding in front of him, a nightmare that had followed him to the one place he, and every other cop felt secure, the police station.

There were armed uniformed officers inside the station's low perimeter wall watching the pickets. There more on the roof with long guns and binoculars. One held a video camera. The officers at the open driveway onto the station's parking lot stopped a car ahead of Brian. It was driven by a Black man. Brian stopped behind the car and watched. He could see the two officers were being cautious. The Black man in the car presented ID. One officer took it, examined it, and then waved the car in. Brian pulled up, stopped. He was ready to reach for his wallet and police ID. The uniformed officer looked at him and waved him through.

Lasski was waiting for him in the Homicide office. Captain Winslow was calling for an all hands meeting in the patrol roll call room. Brian, Lasski, and the other Storm Troopers climbed the stairs to the roll call room on the second floor. Detectives, patrol officers, Vice, Narcotics and all the station's civilian support staff were there. The large room was packed, and although Brian was in their midst, he felt strangely alone.

A hush fell over the room when the thirty-nine-year-old Captain Winslow came in. He was handsome in his tailored shirt with a gun and gold badge worn at his side. He looked like he was in charge, and Brian knew the LAPD put high value on what among the rank and file was called, command presence.

Winslow had it. He stepped to the raised platform at the head of the room. Stepping on it made him taller than the others in the room, more imposing. The captain paused, prayer like, allowing his eyes to drift over the armed force crowded shoulder to shoulder in front of him.

What little noise there was in the room ceased. Captain Winslow began by saying he was proud to be the commander of Southwest Area. He claimed there wasn't one woman or man in the room, sworn or civilian, that he didn't have confidence in. He spoke of loyalty and duty with the zeal of an evangelist. He warned of what he feared were long hard days ahead for the Area, claiming it was time to join hands and stand united.

The captain said several television stations were setting up mobile units to cover the demonstration.

"We gave them truth," Winslow said in a convincing tone, "and they turned truth to lies."

He told them to expect every bleeding heart in the country to respond. He blamed the economy, unemployment, the season's heat, and inflation for the mood on the street. He said the shooting at the Louisiana Bottle Shop had just triggered what was certain to come anyway.

People were angry and frustrated, Winslow told them. But few really understood what they were angry about. The most visible arm of the government was the police, he explained, so the police became their target.

Winslow concluded his remarks by bluntly stating that any man or woman, who thought they could not stand behind a fellow officer, could transfer out with no questions asked.

He paused. The only response was silence.

The captain offered the room a nod, then turned and marched out. The room hung in a heavy awkward silence after his departure as if they were expecting, perhaps wanting, more. Finally, the uniformed watch commander stood up and barked, "Okay, let's get back to work."

The captain's speech made it official. Everyone knew who he was, and that he was the epicenter of all their problems. By now the chief of police and the mayor were reading summaries of the shooting. Detective Brian Culpepper was the one who shot and killed the teenager. He brought the pickets outside. Brian knew of no other policeman who had survived such exposure without being exiled to a do-nothing area and a desk. He couldn't take it all over again.

Captain Winslow's prediction was accurate. By late afternoon, the station was ringed with a thousand chanting Blacks. "Lady Killer...Lady Killer...Lady Killer," they called in a loud endless cadence. The TV cameras and the Internet drew more and more people and the swelling crowd played to them.

The day inside was long and nerve racking for Brian. Restricted from field work, he sat, idle and alone, in the Homicide office. Lasski was in court, and the other Storm Troopers came up with reasons to get away from the station. There were no windows to show the crowd outside, but their muffled chant hammered at the walls—*Lady Killer...Lady Killer...Lady Killer*.

Too much coffee and no lunch knotted Brian's stomach. He walked the hallways of the station but could find no one to talk with. Everyone who could, had fled to avoid the din that continued outside. Late in the afternoon he called Pamela. She was in court. He left no message.

Lieutenant Storm, speaking to Brian for the first time that day, told him two of the Storm Troopers would drive him home. Undercover officers had learned that the crowd now knew what he looked like and what car he drove. Someone had found pictures online. There had also been numerous threats on his life.

His cell phone was ringing when they reached his apartment. When Brian answered the caller said, "We know where you live, Lady Killer, and you're gonna die." He ended the call. The cell phone rang again. He didn't accept the call.

Holcomb called Lieutenant Storm and told him about the calls. Storm instructed Holcomb to stay with Brian until he called back. It was several hours until the call came, and Storm advised them that members of the SWAT team were being dispatched to provide protection for Brian.

It was nearly seven o'clock when Brian finally reached Pamela. She was relieved to hear his voice. She was worried having watched the demonstration on television. Brian assured her he was all right. He had protection, but because of the threats, he didn't want her involved. So, he told her that until things calmed down, the phone would have to do. Pamela argued against it. She didn't care about the threats, she wanted to see him. Brian nearly gave in but fought it.

"Wait," he told her. "This will pass." He said it but doubted his own words.

"I love you," Pamela said at the end.

"I love you too," Brian answered.

21 RUN AWAY HOME

During the days that followed, Brian Culpepper felt like a prisoner under guard. At work he never left the station. At home, several SWAT team members shared his apartment, while others stood guard outside. Policemen drove him to the station in the morning, and home at night, always in a different car and always over a random, unpredictable course. It was ordered, he could not go out at night, or invite anyone to his apartment, which offered little refuge anyway. His cellphone never stopped ringing. Most of the voice mail messages were obscene or threatening. The ones that weren't were from the press. Brian never answered and told Pamela not to call. Two days after paint was splattered on the apartment building, Brian received an eviction notice in the mail. He tore it up and threw it in the trash.

At home Brian spent most of his time in his bedroom although he could not sleep. He simply had nothing to say to his guards. They weren't fellow policemen, they were guards. He wondered what would happen if he ordered them out of his apartment. He did not like the answer that came to mind. He was angry, but he couldn't really find a target for his anger. Was it the faceless sea of chanting picketers at the station, the police department, Nation Wyde...fate? He couldn't find an answer.

The organizers of the demonstration at the station

labeled it a pro-life boycott. Their efforts gained momentum and publicity as the days passed. Dozens of picketers were arrested for blocking the station's driveways. The A.C.L.U. immediately provided them with bail and promised a defense that would carry the case to the Supreme Court if necessary.

During the night thousands of nails were scattered in the streets surrounding the station. Workers from street maintenance were called in to clean them up but refused to do so after being threatened by the angry picketers. Finally, a street sweeper driven by a policeman got the job done. That night the streets were again salted with nails. The nerves of the rank and file at Southwest Area were growing raw.

Brian, depressed and isolated, requested his vacation thinking it would give him a chance to see Pamela, as well as escape from the pressures at the station. Lieutenant Storm promptly denied the request, saying it would look like they were giving in to the boycott pressures.

"I don't give a shit what they think," Brian spat at Storm.

"The answer is still no," Storm said flatly.

"Then I'm requesting a meeting with the captain," Brian argued. "It's my vacation and I'll take it when I goddamn please."

Within the hour, Brian was standing in Captain Winslow's office. The captain carefully explained how sensitive the situation was. Those who were behind the organization of the boycott were the same people who were campaigning for a civilian police review board. It was important that the Area, to a man, stand united in resisting their efforts. "With the best interests of the Area, the entire department, for that matter, I have to deny your request."

"What about my interests?" Brian asked.

"You have to look at the big picture, Detective."

"Fuck the big picture. I wanna see the area commander." Brian was near his breaking point.

Chief of Police James Peck delayed the start of a scheduled press conference on the Southwest Area boycott after receiving the call from Deputy Chief Searcy. "It's about Culpepper, Jim, and it can't wait."

They met in the chief's office and talked for forty minutes. "He's requested his vacation, Jim, and he won't take no for an answer. Captain Winslow thinks he's about to snap."

"No wonder," Chief Peck said pointing a finger at a stack of intelligence bulletins on his desk. "Eighteen threatening cell phone messages yesterday alone. Living under guard."

"If we hide him," Searcy argued, "every time they decide they don't like a cop, we'll see the same tactics used."

"I know that. You know that, but neither of us are living in the hell Culpepper is."

Searcy didn't answer, because there was no answer.

"Who's providing his security?"

"Metro, SWAT, PDID," Searcy answered.

"Get rid of them," the chief ordered. "Let's surround him with people he knows and likes. His partner. Others from the unit. Tell 'em to take the pressure off. Get him drunk. We're supposed to be protecting him, not imprisoning him."

Searcy nodded agreement. "Okay, what do we do about his vacation request?"

The chief walked to his window, looked at the skyline, drew in a breath and let it out slowly. Then with a glance to his deputy, "Pass the word down that the request has to come to my desk. In writing. Make him write it six times and reject five of them. In short—stall."

At EOW Brian was driven home by Lasski and JD Kent.

"My truck is back there in the parking lot," Brian complained.

"Hey," Lasski said from behind the wheel of the detective car they rode in. "We're saving you gas money. Shut up."

The SWAT team members standing guard at the apartment withdrew. They didn't go far, but at least they were out of sight. Brian thanked and shook the hand of each. Brian worked on the third version of his fifteen-seven vacation request while JD Kent went out to buy chicken. Both Brian and JD passed on Lasski's offer to cook something.

Brian labored with the language of his request while Lasski watched an exercise program on television. "Check this broad. You ever see such a set of jugs?"

"Jugs aren't everything," Brian said from where he worked at the kitchen table.

"Did you ever notice guys who say that are the ones that have women with big jugs?" Lasski said, without taking his eyes off the television.

Brian paused from his writing and thought about Lasski's comment. It was true, he decided. Pamela did have large breasts. He recalled watching her once as she walked nude from her bed to the bathroom. Her breasts danced as she walked. Smooth jelled mounds he loved to touch, hold, and kiss. How long had it been? The discomfort in his groin told him it had been a long time.

He had spoken with her earlier in the day, told her about his vacation request. She was excited about it. When his was approved she planned to request hers. They talked about the beaches in Mexico, maybe Hawaii, Vegas. His thoughts of Pamela comforted him. Part of his life was still real. A knock on the door put an end to that delusion.

Lasski turned off the volume on the television, drew his gun and moved to the door. Brian paused from his writing to watch. "Who's there?"

"Chicken man," JD's voice answered from outside.

Lasski opened the door to reveal JD with his arm loaded with three sacks. Along with the chicken for eight, JD brought two bottles of Canadian whiskey, several bottles of mix, an assortment of chips and pretzels. "Some of this may go outside to Metro. That is if there's any left," JD said as he dumped the bags on the table.

Lasski prepared a bag of chicken, some soft drinks and pork rinds and went outside in search of the Metro cops sitting on the block. When Lasski returned, he joined Brian and JD at the kitchen table. "You know, I heard if a Metro cop doesn't eat pork rinds everyday his dick falls off."

They ate the chicken and drank whiskey, and for the moment, the shit storm haunting all of them seemed to fade. Brian knew he was getting drunk, but he felt good and silly and couldn't think of a reason why he shouldn't. When the El Pollo and rice was gone, they started on the chips and pretzels.

More whiskey flowed and talk came easy. They talked about religion. Lasski was a Catholic, Brian a Methodist, and JD a Baptist. They spent an hour trying to convert one another and then gave up and turned to politics. Lasski argued that a man wasn't qualified to be president unless he had police experience. "Did either of you know Teddy Roosevelt was the police commissioner in New York City?"

"That's bullshit," Brian countered.

"Is not," Lasski slurred. "JD, tell his ignorant Methodist ass."

"It's true," JD said. "That's where Teddy learned to carry a big stick. It was a fucking billy club."

Sex followed politics and they each talked of how they lost their virginity. JD held the record with his first sexual encounter at age twelve, although Lasski disputed the claim saying cousins didn't count. The first bottle of whiskey was emptied, and the cap was twisted off the second. Heavy glasses were poured.

The mix was ignored. They drank, knowing they were drunk and loud and boisterous. They laughed and joked and teased and any trouble any of the three had was drowned in the liquor.

"Hey, hey," Lasski said, raising a finger to his mouth to quiet Brian and JD.

"Wait, wait," Brian said to JD, "I've seen him like this. He's wants to speak."

"I was just going to say," Lasski cautioned, being as sober and serious as he could. "Either we get quiet, or some neighbor is going to call the police."

Brian and JD roared with laughter.

When half the second bottle was gone JD quieted his two drunken companions with an outstretched hand. "You know why our party isn't perfect?" he spoke slowly and deliberately.

"Why?" Brian asked, taking the bait.

"Cause there ain't no pussy here," JD said.

"Hey, hey, a wait a minute," Lasski pled.

"A wait a minute?" JD said. "What the hell is that a new Polish expression?"

"I mean a minute," Lasski corrected, trying to maintain his serious tone. "I don't want any pussy."

"What?" JD gave Lasski a suspicious look.

"It's okay, JD." Brian smiled. "He's one of those Polish heterosexuals."

Lasski pointed a finger at Brian. "The hell I am," he growled. "It's just I am a married faithful person. Married to another happily married person, my wife."

"OK, so we prove one out of three of cops is a faithful married person. Brian, what color hair would you like on the whore I order for you?"

Brian shook his head. "No thanks, JD. I'm sort of waiting. You know...Pamela and me."

"Waiting?" JD complained. "That's like saying pussy and a bus are the same."

"Hey, wait a minute, you've been married three times," Lasski said to JD. "You think maybe you're the problem?"

"Pussy has never been a problem for me." JD smiled.

"There's another thing," Lasski said with a look at Brian and then JD.

"What?" JD asked.

"You were going to invite ladies into this apartment?"

"Basically, you've got the idea."

Lasski shook his head. "You can't do that."

"Bet me. I'll have a skirt here in twenty minutes."

"You can't. 'Cause the Lady Killer lives here."

A knife could have cut the charged electric air hanging between the three men. Brian sat rigid, stunned. Every muscle in his body was tight and then he understood. It was a ridiculous, macabre thought. He was a Lady Killer in every sense of the word. It was true. It was real and it was all right to say it, feel it, laugh at it because it was true. The laughter spilled from Brian in a burst of emotion. "I am the

Lady Killer!" he roared, slapping the table, their glasses danced.

JD and Lasski saw it too. They knew why Brian was laughing. It was alright to laugh with him and they did. They laughed until their sides hurt, and tears ran down their faces.

Brian slept that night for the first time in days. Although he slept on the floor of the living room, when he awoke in the morning he felt as though something had passed, something was different. He wasn't sure what it was, but he knew he felt different, better. The thought of shooting the girl in the bottle shop was still with him. He still felt remorse. He still wished it hadn't happened, but the crushing guilt was gone. That was it, he decided. He was sorry he shot the girl, but the jury Brian carried in his heart and mind had found him not guilty. He wasn't innocent. He realized that, but he wasn't guilty either. It was bizarre morning-after logic, but he clung to it.

At Lasski's urging, Brian called Pamela from the station to warn her that Lasski and JD had a plan for their Friday night. When the long day ended, Brian still hadn't finished his vacation request. It just didn't seem important anymore. The unnerving chanting protestors still lined the street in front of the station, but the fact they still didn't recognize him baffled Brian. At EOW Brian left the station with JD.

JD drove north on the Harbor Freeway. It was Friday evening, and the traffic was heavy, but finally they found the exit for Elysian Park near Dodger Stadium. JD wheeled the detective car into the green wooded park and followed a narrow winding road deep into the park until they spotted a parked detective car. JD pulled in behind it and stopped. "Enjoy yourself," JD said to Brian.

Brian climbed out and walked to the parked detective car. Boone got out from the passenger's side. He patted Brian on the shoulder. Brian smiled. Climbed in and the car pulled away.

Near the front of Brian's apartment complex two SWAT team officers, assigned to protect him, sat in the back of a white van. On the side of the van a metallic sign read—*Carpet Cleaning*. One of the SWAT officers watched with binoculars as a detective car slowed and swung into the subterranean drive of the apartment building. After the detective car disappeared inside the officer with the binoculars said, "He's home."

"R-David-90, this is Point Charlie, the primary just arrived home."

Pamela Moss was waiting with Julia Lasski in the living room of the Lasski home in Huntington Beach. "They're here," Julia said as a detective car swung into their driveway. The automatic garage door went up and the car disappeared inside. Julia took Pamela by the arm. "Come on."

Pamela grabbed Brian by the neck when he stepped in from the garage. She cried. So did Julia Lasski. The two women made dinner and the four of them dined in candlelight. Brian loved it. Afterwards, they sat, talked, and played Crazy Eight. It was a relaxed quiet evening and the troubled days at Southwest seemed far away. The Lasski kids, Garth, six, and Jill, age four, were spending a night with their grandparents. Brian and Pamela were invited to stay. They spent the night in the Lasski's guestroom. Hungry for one another they made love, talked, touched, and made love again. Neither wanted to sleep.

In the morning, the Lasskis, pretending they had plans, went out leaving Brian and Pamela alone. "Yesterday, at work I heard the DA was going to make some sort of public announcement today at eleven," Pamela told Brian.

"And you being a dedicated public servant don't want to miss it."

"Well..." Pamela smiled.

They sat in the living room and she turned on the wide screen TV. The DA's announcement was just beginning. Pamela stiffened when she saw the Black Congress Woman Irene Waters standing beside the district attorney. The DA, standing at a microphone was flanked by a collection of sober faced Black men and women. "I am announcing today," District Attorney Jason Stone said to the collection of microphones in front of him, "as District Attorney of the County of Los Angeles, the appointment of a special prosecutor to investigate the shooting death of Shelly Simpson."

Pamela looked to Brian. He was listening soberly.

"Our investigation is not intended to cast doubt on the report provided by the Los Angeles Police, but to end the fear of bias, or prejudice, that result in matters when the police investigate themselves. I feel it necessary to conduct this independent investigation. When our investigation is complete, and if the facts merit, I will present the matter to a Grand Jury."

The spell was broken and the warm glow holding them together was dulled. Brian was sullen and quiet. Pamela tried to assure him the district attorney's action was purely political. He had to do this to be reelected. The words made little difference.

Brian looked to Pamela. "Let's hope he doesn't appoint you the lead prosecutor."

22 A PASSING STORM

It was the beginning of the second week of the boycott when the Reverend James McAlister arrived from Chicago. He was known worldwide for his role in promoting and protecting Black rights. His appearance did not go unnoticed. The ranks of the pickets swelled with new volunteers. The placards took on a more professional look. The television cameras returned and by late afternoon the protestors numbered twenty-five hundred and growing. The Southwest station of the LAPD was surrounded. Chief of Police Peck ordered his department to a full tactical alert. He cautioned his commanders to exercise restraint and maintain a low profile.

Speaking to an array of network cameras from the back of a flatbed trailer brought in to act as a platform, the Reverend McAlister called for a total boycott of Southwest station until the Lady Killer was brought to trial for the unprovoked, unwarranted, reckless, cowardly killing of the young, innocent, helpless, unarmed young Black woman, Shelly Jackson. The Reverend was reminded later the girl's last name was really Simpson. "Names are not important," McAlister defended. "Issues are."

The reverend McAlister called on all people to honor the boycott, police officers and civilian alike. "If your eye shall offend thee, cast it out...if one among you has offended thee, cast him out."

The next morning only four of the station's civilian staff reported for work. The result was a severe overload of administrative tasks. Paperwork quickly back logged, as hallways became littered and dirty, trash cans overflowed. The absent garage mechanics caused disabled patrol and detective cars in need of service to sit idle and out of service.

Patrol officers as well as detectives were pulled off regular assignments to fill in for missing staff. There was grumbling. Several men refused to empty trash from restrooms. More pitched in after Captain Winslow took a broom and began sweeping hallways, but still morale remained critical.

Late Tuesday night, Commander Hays met with Chief of Police James Peck. Hays played a video of the ABC evening news. A full six-minute segment of the broadcast was devoted to the boycott. *Storm Troopers in Los Angeles*, the network anchor had tagged the story. The internet picked up on the story and soon had its own horror stories on the abuses of the Storm Troopers. The police department's switchboard lit up with complaints and threats.

"Who in the hell does Lieutenant Storm think he is?" Commander Hays said. "This is a public embarrassment, an ugly scab on the face of the department. Remember, Jim, it was the Storm Troopers that got us into that mess in Blythe."

Wednesday morning the Storm Troopers were shattered by the news. Lieutenant Storm was gone. The area commander had given the order during the night, but the Storm Troopers, like everyone else, knew it was the chief of police that made the decision. Storm Troopers, a name coined by some forgotten policeman and intended as a compliment to a dedicated police lieutenant, backfired and the legend came to an abrupt bitter end.

Word came from the Office of the Chief of Police later in the morning.

Personnel are advised to refer to the various tactical units of the department by official assigned designations only. The use of slang terms, substituted names, or reference to specific individuals heading such units, is expressly prohibited.

Lieutenant Storm had been the eye of the hurricane. He had seemed oblivious to the chanting protestors, carrying on with normal routine which was no longer normal.

The Storm Troopers had no doubt the trouble would pass. Lieutenant Storm had told them it would. They believed him, but now he was gone, and they were shaken.

Sergeant JD Kent became the acting OIC, but he was openly talking about finding another assignment. They were all snake bit. Delgado had already set up a transfer to Hollenbeck Area. The Storm Troopers were like rats on a sinking ship. Once proud of their identities and work, they now tried to find a way out. The telephones in the Homicide office rang incessantly. None of the men would answer. Finally, Fran Cox, sickened with the insults and threats pouring in over the lines took all the telephones off their hooks. The Storm Troopers, like the rest of the station, were finally paralyzed. The chanting continued to hammer the walls.

Several of the station's windows were shattered by rocks. Captain Winslow called Deputy Chief Searcy for approval to clear the streets. Word came back through an assistant—*Take no action.* Captain Winslow was told not to provoke an incident. The officers manning the station were angry, insulted and tense. The protestors continued their insults and taunts. Both sides were like smoldering, charred embers about to burst into flame, and both sides knew it could not go on.

At the Hall of Justice, Pamela Moss returned from lunch to find a note waiting on her desk. It was brief—*Ms. Moss: The District Attorney would like to see you at 1:45 PM. Thanx, Marge (Secretary of)**

Waiting in the district attorney's reception office Pamela was nervous. She wasn't working on any case of any importance. The alternatives worried her.

The intercom on the secretary's desk buzzed. She picked up the telephone. "Yes, sir." The woman hung up and looked to Pamela. "You may go in now."

District Attorney Stone stood when Pamela entered his office. He was in his shirt sleeves and tie. His jacket hung on a coat rack with several others. The book lined shelves and thick curtains made the plush office look more like a retreat than a law office. An oval carpet framed two comfortable chairs, a table with a decorative lamp, a coffee table with several carefully placed law books, and a wall full of awards and framed photos added to the décor. Pamela noticed one of the larger framed pictures was of the DA and former President Donald Trump. It reminded Pamela she was in the presence of power. The DA smiled, gestured to the two comfortable chairs.

"Pamela, thanks for coming up. Please, let's sit over here."

"Mister District Attorney," Pamela said, sitting down in the chair and smoothing her skirt. The DA rounded his desk and sat down across from Pamela.

"First, I'd like to thank you for the job you've been doing down in one-oh-six. You handled some very demanding cases. I know they've been challenging."

"Thank you."

The DA rocked forward in his chair to rest his elbows on his knees. She sensed he was uncertain. He picked his word carefully. "Pamela, I reached out to you because there is a very sensitive matter we need to discuss."

Pamela tensed. She drew in a breath. She knew what was coming. She chose to say nothing.

"The subject is your relationship with Sergeant Culpepper of the LAPD."

Pamela felt herself stiffen. She chose not to respond.

"I'm sure you're aware our office is conducting an investigation into the shooting death of Shelly Simpson."

"Yes, I'm aware."

The DA rocked back in his chair. He seemed annoyed with Pamela's lack of response. "Then you must understand the position I find myself in. One of my deputies, you in particular, have a close personal romantic relationship with the individual who is the focal point of our investigation."

"And your source for this relationship information is?" Pamela asked. Her heart was racing.

"Do you deny the relationship?"

"No."

"Then there's no need to discuss the source. What you do need to recognize is how volatile this could be in the press."

Again, Pamela chose not to answer.

The DA joined his hands in a tight grip. "To eliminate the real possibility of the press, or a judge, or anyone else pointing an accusing finger at us, or you, and saying our investigation was compromised by a personal relationship, we've got to do something about it."

Pamela's mind raced. "Judge Donnelly in two-twelve is married to a Los Angeles Police captain."

The DA nodded. "The key word there is married. You're not married to Brian Culpepper, are you?"

"No."

"Then it's called an affair and it's a threat. I know this must be difficult for you. I can see that, but nevertheless, your relationship with Brian Culpepper, for your welfare and for the good of our office, must come to an immediate end. Perhaps after some time…"

Pamela stood up. She was angry. "There are two things important to me, Mr. Stone. First, is my love for Brian Culpepper. The second is my love for the law. You've asked that I choose between the two. Alright, I have. I quit."

The district attorney stood up. He was concerned. "I can't accept that, Pamela. Your response is emotional. I don't want that. I wish I had an answer, but I don't. It's more than a problem for you. It's a problem for us. I don't want to lose a valued employee. Give the matter thought. Life in the courts has taught us there's always a compromise."

"Love knows no compromise," Pamela said and turned for the door.

The tense confrontation dragged on and the city waited for an explosion everyone knew must come. Chief of Police James Peck spent his days in the EMC, the Emergency Control center, and the nights in his office. He had silently vowed the Reverend McAlister from Chicago, was not going to succeed with his litany of threats to turn *The City of Angels into a City of Ashes.*

The chief had ordered every cop in the city to turn the other cheek. He had even attended to two patrol roll call briefings at Southwest Area to ensure his message was reaching the front lines. While there the chief got a first-hand view of the Reverend as he stood preaching to his crowd of admirers across the street. The chanting from the protestors was much more unnerving in person than on television.

Meetings in the police building became tense. The department's leadership was divided. Culpepper should be placed on administrative leave, he should be transferred, he should be suspended without pay, he should be hidden, he should be fired. Chief Peck knew transferring Culpepper would accomplish nothing. Culpepper was no longer the issue. He was simply the excuse. The department could not knuckle under to pressure from a mob.

Los Angeles was a city of Law and order. Protests and demonstrations were legal, and as Chief of Police, James Peck would protect the protestor's rights. He would not have his authority compromised by threats of civil distur-bance. He did not want a fight and was determined not to start one, but by God, if it came, he'd show them who was in command. The chief knew Culpepper was not the only one being blamed for the death of a sixteen-year-old. James Peck was always among the accused.

A telephone call from the mayor added to the chief's worries. The mayor was worried. Things were getting out of hand. He didn't want a riot in LA like they had in

Minneapolis after the killing of George Floyd. "How important can this man Culpepper be?"

"How important is justice?" the chief answered.

"Jim," the mayor warned, "you're worried about a department with ten thousand employees. I'm responsible for the management of the second largest municipality in the United States. I have fifty-thousand employees looking to me for answers, and I'm now looking to you. I've watched this situation for nearly two weeks. I haven't seen any improvement. Quite the contrary, it seems to be getting worse. As mayor it's my responsibility to defuse this time bomb if I can. This is no longer just a police problem. If the situation hasn't improved by Monday, I'll be forced to take action."

Chief of Police James Peck understood his ass was on the line. He hung up without further comment.

Fran Cox, the Black Administrative Aide from Southwest Homicide was among the few civilian employees who continued to cross the protestors lines every day. Three kids and an unemployed husband helped drive her. Thursday morning was to be her last crossing. Pushing through a crush of protestors, Fran was crossing the street for the front door of Southwest Station when the bottle arced through the air and hit her on the cheekbone. Fran went down hard. The crowd behind her cheered. She pushed up bloody, a hand to her face. She was quickly pulled inside.

The two officers on security at the front door gave pursuit of the youth who threw the bottle. A uniformed lieutenant quickly ordered them to stop. Again, the crowd roared its approval.

Sergeant JD Kent held the bloodied Fran as they waited in the front lobby for the ambulance. The towel he held to her face was filled with blood that now ran down her neck. Brian knelt near JD and Fran. He tried to apologize to her.

He felt responsible.

Fran, slipping into shock, went into a hysterical rage. "You," she pointed at Brian. "You did this. Nothing like this ever happened. It's your goddamned fault."

Brian retreated to the Homicide Office. He felt very White and very alone. He spent his day waiting in the office. He was waiting on the DA's investigators. He'd been waiting since Monday. Lasski had learned from an inside source that one of the DA's Investigators was a former cop from Oakland and the other was a retired Sheriff's Deputy from Riverside County. Well, he was thankful they were at least cops, but how the hell were they investigating anything without him?

No one talked in Brian's presence anymore, not even the officers assigned to protect him, and that number had doubled. Desperate to talk to someone he called Pamela. Her voice mail answered, "I'm not able to take your call at the moment, but if you'll leave a brief message, I'll return your call as soon as possible." Brian knew it meant she was in a court room. He left no message. A chill swept over him as he hung up. He was cold and anxious, and a growing sense of doom was settling over him.

Sergeant JD Kent did not like being the OIC of South-west Homicide. He felt like he was the captain of the Titanic. He was a sergeant doing a lieutenant's job but getting a sergeant's pay. They could take their job and wipe their asses with it. The LAPD in JD Kent's mind had become a ball-less outfit.

Five years ago, ten pickets wouldn't have been tolerated in front of the station. What was the latest count? Seven hundred plus. Seven hundred assholes. They weren't Black. JD knew who they were. They were assholes. The Black men from the Hood were at work. The assholes were outside with their store-bought professional looking fucking placards. They had been there for nearly two weeks. Where did they sleep? Who was buying them the hundreds of sandwiches that were passed out every few hours? Who was buying the bottles of soda, water, and Starbucks? Who paid for the buses that brought protestors from San Diego and Oakland? Who paid for Reverend McAlister's airfare from Chicago? Who was paying for his suite at the Beverly Hilton where he was staying? There were many Black men and women who were still slaves, JD thought...they just didn't know it.

Sometimes, JD reasoned, assholes were assholes just because no one told them they were assholes. Only an asshole would throw a bottle at a young woman. Why did they all cheer. It came over JD in a rush. It had been building since Lieutenant Storm was removed. He was angry, frustrated, and ready for a fight. He was not one to be fucked with. JD headed for the front door.

The line of protesters was on the Northside of Martin Luther King Boulevard, the wide six-lane street that separated them from Southwest station directly across the street. Traffic on the boulevard was light. Motorists had quickly learned driving by might mean something thrown at your vehicle or a delay by the crowd pushing into the street. There was a near circus atmosphere among the mix of young and old making up the protestors. All were waiting for the ax to fall. "The ax that will cut away the cancer growing in your city," Reverend McAlister had predicted.

JD Kent, wearing soft clothes along with a badge and a gun strapped on his waist bolted out the double glass doors of Southwest Station and marched to the center of the street to face the crush of protestors. A hush fell over the crowd as they looked to the lone Black policeman standing in the street facing them. JD recognized Reverend Macalister standing in their midst.

"You recognize me? I live just a couple blocks from here," JD shouted. "I'm the one you call when someone breaks into your house, or your car goes missing. I'm the one that keeps the gangs off your street. I'm the one that gets shot at where your corner store gets robbed." He paused to let his eyes survey the faces. They were listening, so were the television cameras. "I am Sergeant JD Kent. You're gonna call me, if not today, tomorrow, or the next day, when your ass is on the line, you're going to call me. And you know what? I'm going to come. No matter who you are when you need help, no matter what for. I'm going to be there. You know that. So, what the hell are you doing here? Who is that standing beside you? Is he a neighbor or is he here to stir things and get in front of all these cameras?" And the cameras had found him. "You need to think about me." He patted the silver and gold badge hooked to his belt near his holstered pistol.

JD was getting louder with each of his words. "Yeah, me, I'm Black just like you. And like me, every cop carrying a badge in this city is on your side. I took an oath to die for you. Anyone standing out here in this crowd with you going to do that?"

Suddenly JD was grabbed from behind. It was Captain Winslow, the day watch lieutenant, Lasski and Boone. "Come on, Sergeant," Winslow ordered.

They muscled the reluctant JD toward the south curb and the station. "You're all in the wrong fucking place!" he shouted at the crowd. "You need to find where you belong."

The crowd roared. The noise rattled nearby windows. The cops in the station tensed.

"I'm sorry," JD told Captain Winslow. "I'm really fucking sorry."

Captain Winslow, proving JD had no lock on stress, paced back and forth in the near deserted detective squad room. "This is really fucking great. Your speech will be world news tonight. The only thing the chief will remember is that I'm supposed to be in charge down here. "

The captain was wrong. JD's street speech was already on the internet. Captain Winslow ordered two detectives from the Burglary team to drive JD home.

Late in the day, just before Brian left for his escorted rush from the station, Lasski took him aside. "You want to plan something for the weekend? Maybe Lake Arrowhead, get away with the girls?"

"Maybe you haven't noticed, but I've got armed guards."

244

"Minor detail. I know the OIC of the SWAT detail."

Brian was uncertain. The day had been long, and JD going off the rail was alarming.

"Let me see if I can set it up," Lasski said in a hushed tone. "We need to get out of this fucking city and breathe some fresh air." He slapped Brian on the shoulder.

The protestors lining the street had been throwing rocks, bottles, bricks, anything they could lay their hands on, at every car exiting the police station, but when Brian and his three Metro SWAT team members drove out ten minutes later, they were surprised when the crowd reminded quiet, nothing was thrown at their car.

23 THE BEST LAID SCHEMES

Nation Wyde was certain his luck had returned. The shooting at the Louisiana Bottle Shop had occurred just an hour after his visit. The turmoil that followed pushed any mention of L.A.'s Robin Hood from the news. Now the city was plagued with protests. Streets everywhere were filled with chaos and confusion. The city was his for the picking. Liquor stores were always fat with money to cash payroll checks. Thirty minutes after a robbery he'd be on a jet to New York City.

Su Linn talked of marriage and life in San Francisco, but Nation had a different idea, and it didn't include a pregnant Oriental. He was tired of her swelled stomach. He longed for a firm flat one, and it was high on the list of things to do when he arrived in New York.

It was a one-way trip. Nation knew staying in L.A. meant eventual arrest. And no matter how much he liked California; the thought of prison soured any plan to stay. Plus, New York wouldn't be that bad, and when it finally did turn cold, he could winter in Miami. All in all, not a bad plan.

Nation called his cousin Vern. He needed a ride to his mother's house on the east side. Vern was shocked when Nation called but promised to pick him up. Nation was now waiting. He did not tell Su Linn where he was going, only that he'd be back.

"I gotta go, woman. See you at nine or so." Nation moved for the door.

"I'll get some packing done," the pregnant Su Linn promised as Nation stepped out the door.

"Yeah, okay. Do that."

Ten minutes after Nation Wyde left, Su Linn had her first cramp. It was sharp and deep in her pelvis and it frightened her.

Brian was stretched on his back in his bedroom watching a hockey game. It was eight o'clock. He could hear the SWAT team officers in the kitchen. They were playing a game on a laptop. Brian envied them, remembering the days when he enjoyed being a cop. It seemed long ago.

Staring at the ceiling, Brian accepted the fact he had to do something to change his situation. The LAPD stood ready to fight and die for him, and with each passing day that became more and more probable. There were already casualties. Fran Cox took sixteen stitches in a face that would never be the same. Lieutenant Storm was gone, exiled to a area he hated. The Storm Troopers were leaderless, disgraced, embarrassed and disbanded. Brian couldn't allow it to go on.

Tomorrow, he would resign. News of his resignation would spread quickly, and when it did, the howling mobs would cheer and celebrate then move on to its next cause. It would be over. It was not as painful as he thought it might be and now the decision was made, he felt peaceful. He had found the answer and it was simple. His police career was over, but he still young. He was not leaving in shame...he was leaving to end it. He was the only one that could.

Brian savored his decision. For the first time since the shots rang out in the Louisiana Bottle Shop, there was hope. He wasn't worried about the district attorney's investigation. Pamela was right. The D.A. was doing what he had to do. Brian knew his conduct would stand the test any Grand Jury might put it to. He would gladly tell the Grand Jury how sorry he was, but he was not wrong, only mistaken.

He had nearly seventeen thousand in the credit union. That would get him through the weeks while he decided what to do. A vacation was high on the list of considerations. Maybe Hawaii. Pamela liked Hawaii. Why not a honeymoon? Hell, that was it! He'd ask Pamela to marry him. Wait. Shouldn't he have a job first? No, why wait? He was talented enough to find a job. He was thinking about calling Pamela when the doorbell rang. Brian heard a chair scrape against the kitchen floor. There was a rush of movement as the SWAT officers reached for their weapons. Brian pushed off the bed as one of the officers pulled the bedroom door shut.

The three SWAT team officers crouched behind chairs and the counter that divided the living room from the kitchen. When they were ready with their automatic weapons leveled at the door, the senior officer called. "Who is it?"

"Huntley," a voice answered from outside.

"Serial number?"

"Four-six-seven-three-oh."

The senior officer gestured for one of the others to open the door. A blonde-haired female officer wearing a plaid shirt and a bullet proof vest pushed up from behind a chair in the living room and crossed to the door. Standing beside it, she reached, unsnapped the dead bolt lock, and pulled the door open.

The door swung wide revealing a frightened Pamela and another SWAT officer in a baseball cap. The three men inside relaxed and set their weapons aside.

"She wouldn't take no for an answer," the officer holding Pamela's arm told the others. "Says she's a deputy D.A."

"Figures," the senior officer said. "You got any ID?"

"She doesn't need any," Brian said as he stepped out of the bedroom.

"Brian." Pamela bolted to him. Brian took her in his arms and led her into the bedroom. He closed the door behind them. The SWAT officers went back to their game.

In the dim light of the bedroom, Pamela and Brian held each other and kissed and tasted and kissed again. They had been apart four days.

"Hold me, Brian. Just hold me."

He covered her face, her neck and her eyes with his kisses and held her close. She was warm and soft and perfumed. "What are you doing here?"

"I'm sick of cellphone and text messages, Brian." Pamela sighed as he bit gently at her neck. "I'm sick of not being able to see you. I'm sick of sleeping alone, I'm sick of the whole damn mess."

"It'll be over soon," Brian promised, finding her mouth. When the kiss ended, Pamela said, "Brian, sit down. I want to talk."

They sat down on the edge of the bed. Pamela pushed her jacket from her shoulders. "I've been doing a lot of thinking," she said, taking his hands in hers.

"I have too," he said.

"I want you to listen to me," she said, raising a finger to his lips. "I think you're too close to the problem to understand it. It's only a problem for me because you're involved. I think I'm being more objective."

"You sound like an attorney," he said and smiled.

"Brian, listen to me," Pamela scolded.

"Sorry."

She squeezed his hands and went on, picking her words carefully. "You can't win, Brian... All you can do is stall defeat...but it will come."

Brian didn't answer. Pamela held his look and his hands. "You're no longer important to them, Brian. All that's important now is who wins, and the fact is, nobody will."

Pamela adjusted the grip of his hands. Brian could feel her plea flowing through her hands into him. "I love you, Brian, and it's keeping us apart. I can see the pain it's causing you. Your pain is mine, and I can't stand by and watch it destroy you. Is this insane power play more important than our love? I'll quit my job. I'll go anywhere you want. I'll do anything you want. We don't have to stay in LA. Brian, please...before it's too late."

Brian could see the shimmer of tears rimming Pamela's eyes. He squeezed her hands. "I'm going to resign tomorrow."

Pamela bit her lip. A tear spilled and traced down her cheek. Brian released her hands and drew her against his shoulder.

"It's okay, it's okay," he said, but he knew it wasn't. He heard his own words as he tried to make them a reality. Maybe getting away from the police department, away from Los Angeles, would cleanse him.

Then he remembered Blythe—he'd run once before and failed to escape. Was he running again? Could he escape? Could he be something other than a cop? Did an oath, or a badge, make you a cop? Would it end when he resigned?

How could he be something other than what he was? He was a peace officer. A peace officer for whom there was no peace. Pamela's warmth against him made the conflict even greater.

A rap sounded on the bedroom door. "Sergeant Culpepper?"

Brian was annoyed. "Yeah?"

"R-David-ninety just called. The ODO is on his way over here."

"Okay," Brian answered.

Pamela raised her head from his shoulder. "Who's the ODO?"

"The Operation's Duty Officer. You better go."

"It doesn't matter anymore, does it?" Pamela said.

"Not to me it doesn't, but it does to those guys out there."

Pamela hugged him. "I don't want to leave you."

Brian held her and ran a hand over her hair. "Only a few more hours."

Pamela mopped her eyes with a tissue, and they kissed at

the bedroom door. Brian promised to call her in the morning after his resignation. Pamela told him she'd be waiting at her condo. Brian opened the bedroom door and walked her across the living room to the front door. The three officers in the kitchen pretended not to notice.

They stood at the door for a moment, eyes searching. Brian pushed a wisp of hair from Pamela's cheek. She took his hand. Their fingers laced over one another's. "I love you," Pamela whispered.

"I love you back," Brian answered softly.

They kissed and Pamela stepped out the door.

24 NATION WYDE HUNT

Su Linn was worried and alone in her apartment. The painful contractions had subsided, but she sat on the couch afraid to move, fearing the pain would return. She ran a hand over the child swelling her stomach. It was still and quiet and that worried her, too. She prayed and pleaded with God to keep the child in her womb, sensing that its birth now would mean she and the child would remain behind when Nation moved away.

Nation Wyde's plans to say goodbye to his mother went badly. When he walked into the kitchen of her home and hugged her, she slapped him and ordered him out of her house. When he pleaded with her, she went to her telephone to call the police. Nation made a hasty and embarrassing retreat. She hadn't been right since his father was killed; Nation told his cousin Vern.

Driving back to Su Linn's apartment, Nation made the decision. He couldn't spend another night with her. He'd go back, pack his shit—he didn't have much—and get out. He'd tell Su Linn he'd send money for the baby and he promised himself he would. Maybe. Nation glanced at Vern. "Hey, man, could you come back in a couple hours?"

"What for?"

"I can't be staying with that woman no more, ya know?"

252

"Ha, ha," Vern laughed pulling over to allow a fire truck to pass. "She's trying to marry your ass, huh?"

"Something like that," Nation granted.

"Yeah," Vern said. "I'll come back by. Whadaya wanna do then?"

"Whadaya mean, *do*?"

"You know, *do*. I've been around. I've *done* a few things."

"You mean stick-ups?" Nation was surprised.

"Yeah, that's what I mean. You ain't got no patent on it, do you?"

Nation laughed. "Shit," he hissed. "Here I am ridin' around with a motherfuckin' crook."

"And a goddamned good one, Jack."

They laughed and joked and teased and when Vern pulled the Cadillac to the curb on West Adams it was agreed. They would rob the Mac's Liquor on South Crenshaw. They cashed checks, it was a big store, it was ripe for picking. Nation climbed out of the Cadillac and leaned in to the open window. "You come get me. I'll be ready."

"I'll go change into my stick-up clothes." Vern smiled. "Be a couple hours."

They laughed. Vern pulled the car in gear and was gone.

Nation stood and watched as the Cadillac's taillights faded into the distance. Los Angeles was gonna remember Robin Hood. Maybe just for fun, he'd shoot up the place. Break some bottles. Maybe give a few to the hanger-ons who were always outside the store. Fucking press would love it. He was gonna say goodbye with a major rip. Look out New York, Nation Wyde is on his way. He ran a finger around the brim of his hat, took a final glance around and headed for the stairs to Su Linn's apartment. He did not see the man in the recessed storefront across the street, but the man had seen him.

Blue Nobles did not like the night. He never allowed himself to admit it, but darkness frightened him. Nor was he ever likely to conclude that the roots of his fear were linked to Vietnam and the terror of nights in the jungle after his helicopter plunged into the thick forest. The only thought that was relevant in Blue's drug-starved mind was where he might get some money for a fix. The sweats, chills, and cramps were on him. He was walking the streets, looking for an answer, when he saw the Cadillac slide to the curb. He watched as a tall, smartly dressed Black man in a stingy brim hat climbed from the passenger's side of the car. When the man ran a finger around the brim of his hat, a habit Blue Nobles knew well, he recognized him. It was Nathaniel Wyde. Blue waited until Nation started up the stairs to the apartment before he headed in search of a telephone.

Brian had two suitcases on the bathroom counter. He was busy moving clothes from the bedroom closet to the bathroom to pack them. The bedroom door was closed and even if one of the officers opened it, they wouldn't see the suitcases in the bathroom. His decision was his business, not theirs.

Brian was excited. After signing his resignation in the morning, he planned to stop by his apartment, pick up the suitcases, and then on to Pamela's. Anything else in the apartment could be picked up later. His rent was paid for a month. There was no hurry. Much of his wardrobe was dirty. Clothes were in a pile in the closet. If he needed more, he'd simply buy them. It would be fun shopping with Pamela—she had excellent taste. A rap sounded on the bedroom door and Brian tensed.

"Sergeant Culpepper," a voice called.

"Yeah," Brian answered, stepping out of the bathroom. He crossed to the bedroom door and opened it.

The senior SWAT team officer, a muscular man was waiting. "You know a guy by the name of Blue Nobles?"

"Yeah."

"He called 911 trying to get in touch with you. Says it's an emergency."

Brian thought about Blue. Hell, he hadn't seen him in nearly a month. What did he want?

"He left a number." He offered a slip of paper to Brian.

Brian took the paper, glanced at it. "Thanks."

Brian closed the bedroom door and sat down on the edge of the bed. He had told Blue they wanted Nation Wyde. There were thousands of dollars riding on it. Brian knew that was it. If it were anything else Blue would have waited.

"Shit..." Brian cursed softly. Why now? Why not two weeks ago? Why not before Amos Moses called from the Louisiana Bottle Shop? Nation Wyde was at the root of the whole mess.

There were so many goddamned *ifs!*

If he weren't under armed guard, he'd call Lasski, and they'd go get the sonofabitch.

If!

And then he made a decision. Nation Wyde was the focal point of all Brian's anger and frustration. Nation Wyde was responsible for all of this. The girl at the bank, the girl in the liquor store, the protestors lining the street at the station, Lieutenant Storm, Fran Cox, his resignation. Nation had to pay. You play, you pay. That was the credo of the street, and Nation Wyde had played. It was time for him to pay, and Sergeant Brian Culpepper, as his final act as a Los Angeles Police Officer, was about to see that he did. Brian reached for his cell phone.

"Goddamn," Lasski complained, reaching the cell phone he had pushed deep in his living room chair. The cell phone kept ringing. Julia Lasski gave him a look from where she lay on a couch. They were watching a film on Netflix.

"Yeah," Lasski answered, finally finding the cell phone.

"Dave, it's Brian. Blue Nobles called. He's found Nation Wyde."

"What? Where?"

"Second floor apartment. Adams and Hobart."

"No shit?"

"Let's get 'im."

"Can you get out?"

"I'll get out. Pick me up at Arch Drive and Ventura."

"We can't take him to Southwest," Lasski warned.

"We'll book him at Central," Brian said.

"Arch Drive and Ventura?"

"Right," Brian answered.

"Okay," Lasski agreed. When he turned, Julia was at the mouth of the kitchen. "I gotta go x," he said.

Julia Lasski looked worried.

Brian took off his shoes and walked to the kitchen. The three SWAT officers were still playing with their laptop. Brian yawned, got a drink of orange juice from the refrigerator, and told them he was going to bed.

Closing the bedroom door, Brian braced it with a chair jammed against the doorknob. He dressed, shoved his badge case into a back pocket, and strapped on his Glock. After turned off the lights, he opened the curtains and lifted the screen out. His heart was racing.

Leaning out the window, Brian looked down into the black void below. From his second story perch, he could see nothing but darkness. He had no idea where the officers outside were and a fleeting thought that they may shoot him, raced through his mind. His stomach was in a knot as he climbed into the open window. Unable to bring himself to jump, he hung from the window, prayed, and let go.

Brian fell seven feet and landed on top of the carport. He was shocked and relieved. He walked the length of the building on the rooftop, jumped down into a nearby alley and casually strolled away.

Brian waited on the corner of Ventura Boulevard and Arch Drive. It was the first time he'd been alone in nearly two weeks, and it felt good. A car approached and slowed.

Brian thought it was Lasski. Looking into the headlights it was difficult to tell but as it pulled to the curb, he saw it wasn't. A middle-aged man behind the wheel rolled the window down on the passenger's side and leaned toward it. "Hi, are you looking for a ride?"

Brian shook his head. "No, I'm waiting for a friend." He knew from his Vice experience what the man wanted.

"Why wait?" the man smiled. "A bird in hand."

Brian was offended. "Get the fuck outta here." He kicked the side of the car, which then sped away.

The next car pulled to the curb. It was Lasski. Brian opened the door, climbed in.

"Wanna go on a Nation Wyde hunt?" Lasski asked,

They were eager and excited. Lasski drove the detective car south on the Harbor Freeway at eighty miles an hour. At the Santa Monica Freeway, they turned west. The distant horizon was aglow with the night lights of LA. Lasski raced up the Western Avenue off-ramp.

"Five blocks," Lasski exhaled. "You think he'll be armed?"

Lasski's question made Brian smile. "Would you come down here at night without a gun?"

"That's very White of you," Lasski said.

25 HE WHO LIVES BY THE
SWORD...

"Su Linn," Nation Wyde called from outside the locked bathroom door. He rattled the knob again. It was locked. "Su Linn, you're bein' a pain in the ass. Cryin' ain't gonna solve nothin'.

"Su Linn, I promise I'll send you some money. I'll pay you back double."

Again Su Linn did not answer. Nation could hear moaning and groaning behind the door. It sounded as if she were sick. Damned Oriental. "It's a big job, Su Linn. I'll be able to come down from Frisco on weekends. I promise. We'll do things, you know." There was no answer.

"Shit," Nation hissed and walked away from the door. He wished he had someplace to go, but he had to wait on Vern. By now he had to be on his way. Vern would be his wheel man. After they hit the liquor store, Vern would drive him to the airport. He'd give the sucker three or four hundred. He wouldn't know what he got from the store.

One liquor store Nation remembered over on Central he got eighteen thousand. Pretty good for four minutes in and out. Nation glanced back at the bathroom door. Why couldn't the woman be reasonable. He tried to let her down easy. When he told her about his big job in San Francisco, just in case she decided to tell someone where he went, she said some Oriental shit and ran into the bathroom and wouldn't come out. To make matters worse he had to piss.

In the bathroom Su Linn laid on the floor on her back. Her knees were drawn up and she had pulled a towel from a rack to soak up her water. The painful contractions unrelenting now. She sucked in a breath through flared nostrils. It hissed out through clenched teeth. She was soaked with perspiration.

Each new pain racked her body and sent involuntary animal-like cries from her lips. She wanted to scream, she wanted to cry, she wanted her mother. She would do anything but listen to the man on the other side of the door. He was just like the father of her child. A liar. A cheat. He had taken all her money. Money her mother had given her for the baby. How did she get it so wrong? She vowed her child would never see the man on the other side of the door. The baby was hers. She would bear it, love it, protect it. She prayed God would kill both the lying bastard who impregnated her and the son of a bitch on the other side of the door.

Another groan from the bathroom brought Nation from the living room window where he was watching for Vern to pull to the curb down below. Reaching the bathroom door, he listened. It was quiet. Maybe she was asleep. A board creaked on the landing outside the front door. Nation looked to it. He hoped it was fucking Vern.

The door to the apartment exploded in a shower of splinters and plaster dust as it sprang in wide. Nation's heart rose into his throat as his wide eyes stared at the Detectives Culpepper and Lasski. The finger size barrels of their pistols loomed deadly and they looked straight into Nation's eyes.

"Freeze," they screamed in one voice.

Nation leaped into the alcove between the bathroom and the living room, flattened his back to the wall and pulled the blue steel .45 automatic from his waistband.

Lasski took two steps and dove into the kitchen, landing in front of the refrigerator.

"He's got a gun," Lasski screamed.

Brian stepped out the open door and pressed his back to the wall. Nation aimed at the open door with his .45 and fired. Its sharp bang in the small apartment was thunderous. Bits of plaster and wood spewed from the wall around the door as shot after shot was fired.

Brian's ears rang. He could smell the burned gun oil and powder. It made him think of the academy range. Suddenly there was silence. Brian moved into the open door with his Glock aimed. He held the gun steady as Nation Wyde stepped into view. His eyes found Nation's and time stopped. They were twenty feet apart. Both with guns in their hands and both wishing they were somewhere else. Nation stared at Brian; he was frightened. Brian strangely was not.

"It's over," Brian said.

Nation grimaced. Brian knew it was trigger pressure. He fired. Nation's .45 exploded in reply. Something exploded beside Brian's face and splinters tore into his cheek, but he continued to squeeze the trigger of his Glock. It spit flame time and time again. Lasski reached around the corner from the kitchen. He was no more than ten feet from Nation Wyde. He fired a volley of four shots.

Nation Wyde's body wrenched as the bullets ripped through him. He sagged and sank toward the floor. He had a bewildered confused look on his face. He fired his gun again, reflex. A throw rug sprang up off the floor, sending dust billowing. Nation sank to the floor grasping his chest, blood spurted out between his fingers. He fired the gun once more. It was random. Wood and splinters sprang from the bathroom door.

Brian stepped toward the fallen man, aiming. Nation's legs spasmed. Brian fired into Nation's chest. The hand holding the .45 relaxed, it thumped onto the floor. Both Brian and Lasski held aim as Brian moved to Nation Wyde and kicked the .45 away.

"He's dead." Brian holstered his weapon, breathing hard. He looked to Lasski.

Lasski was pale. He stared at Nation's body.

"You okay?" Brian asked; he was talking loudly. Both men had ringing ears.

"Yeah, I'm okay."

Lasski moved to Brian, still holding his Glock at the ready. "You're bleeding." He pointed to Brian's face.

Brian moved a hand to his cheek, found the blood. His finger touched the tip of a splinter. He grimaced.

"Let's have a look." Lasski said stepping to Brian, putting his gun away. He stopped when they heard the cry. Both men looked the bathroom. They stood frozen, silent. Brian drew his weapon. Lasski did the same. With silent agreement they moved to the punctured splintered bathroom door. The two men exchanged a look, moved shoulder to shoulder, guns aimed, then each raised a foot and kicked in unison.

The thin door broke around the knob and swung open to slam against Su Linn's knees.

"Holy Mother of God!" Lasski gasped.

Su Linn lay with her head against the tub, her feet toward the door.

Her knees were drawn up and wide revealing her swelled and oozing vagina. She coughed and spat out blood. Her eyes were open, staring aimlessly at the ceiling. There was a bullet hole high on chest at the base of her neck. She was littered with bits of wood and paint from the door.

"My God," Brian said as his breath left him.

Lasski grimaced and sagged against the door frame. His knees were failing.

Brian wanted to turn away and run, but he couldn't. He looked to her face. Her eyes found his. They pleaded with him. She tried to speak but coughed again. Syrupy blood ran from her mouth and spilled down her cheek. Brian grimaced and she closed her eyes. He looked to her swelled belly. A contraction rippled over it.

"Dave, she's having the baby."

Brian drew in a breath and sank to his knees between Su Linn's open legs. He could hear Lasski praying. He didn't listen to the words. Su Linn's open vagina spread more and the top of a small, wet, glistening, hairy head appeared.

"Come on, come on," Brian willed. He was nauseous and covered with sweat. Lasski continued his prayer.

"Come on, come on," Brian pleaded, but the head stayed where it was. Brian looked to the woman's face. Her eyes were half open, fixed. Brian hoped she wasn't dead. His stomach convulsed. He clamped his eyes and mouth shut to keep from vomiting. Bitter warm fluids filled his mouth. He swallowed and gasped in a deep breath.

"Damnit, Dave...help me. She's dead."

"I can't."

"You have to," Brian said.

Lasski knelt beside Brian. His eyes were rimmed with tears.

"Push her legs open," Brian ordered.

Reaching across Brian, Lasski put a hand on each of Su-Linn's knees and pushed them apart. He closed his eyes and turned away.

"God help us," Brian breathed. Su Linn's body was warm and wet, and Brian eased his fingers carefully forward until they touched the small head. He could feel hair. An ear. He probed cautiously, biting his lip. There! There was a nose. He worked his fingers in and around both sides of the child's head and then pulled.

"Please...please, come on." The child's head didn't move. Sweat ran down Brian's forehead and spilled into his eyes. His chest was iron tight.

"Please, God, please," he begged. Lasski joined in the prayer.

Brian pushed his fingers in and around the child's head. He knew the seconds must be critical. How long could the child live in a dead womb? He didn't know, but it seemed like an eternity had passed. His hands were wet well beyond his wrists. He gripped the small head carefully, firmly and pulled again. The child moved, but when he released the pressure, Su Linn's body reclaimed it. He gripped again and pulled.

"Come on...come on." He pulled harder, steadily. The head emerged. and suddenly the baby slipped from its mother's body and into his hands.

"Dave!" Brian shouted, "It's here."

Lasski looked at the glistening child in Brian's hands. A girl. Still tied to its mother by the umbilical cord. but alive and moving.

"My God...my God!" Lasski cried.

The baby's nose and mouth were coated and glazed with thick fluids.

"Get me a towel. A wet towel," Brian ordered.

Lasski grabbed a washcloth on the side of the sink. He stabbed it under the faucet and turned the water on. When soaked, he wrung it out and handed it to Brian.

"Holy shit! Can you believe this?" Lasski laughed.

Brian cradled the child and wiped at its face. It waved its arms and feet. He dropped the cloth and tried clear its mouth with his finger.

"It's not breathing," Brian was frantic. He raised the child to his face and opened his mouth.

Covering most of the baby's face, Brian inhaled through his mouth and blew breath gently into the infant. He did it twice. The baby was limp, not making a sound. He tried again.

"Please, God, please," Lasski was praying. He laid a hand on Brian's shoulder as if somehow that would help.

Brian moved his mouth from the infant. A heavy silent second crept by and then the baby gasped. The gasp was followed by another and then a small heartening cry. A tear traced down Brian's cheek.

"I'll be a son-of-a-bitch," Lasski smiled. A gun shot shattered the moment. Lasski never heard it. The bullet struck him low on the left back and sent him crashing headfirst over Su Linn into the gritty bathtub.

Brian dropped the infant between Su Linn's legs and turned. Vern Tucket, Nation Wyde's cousin stood in the open doorway of the apartment with a chromed .357. It was aimed at Brian. "You motherfucker," Vern grated and pulled the trigger.

A violent pain shot through Brian's right leg. The bullet tore through his upper thigh shattering bone. He grabbed his Glock from the bathroom floor and fired as the man in the door pulled the trigger for the second time. The two shots exploded as one.

Brian's shot hit Vern in the center of the chest. The bullet penetrated his heart and lodged against his spine. Vern staggered into the kitchen on dying legs, leaned over the table, cried, "Mother," and was still.

It was quiet after the shooting. Brian knew he was hurt. He was surprised at how little pain he felt. He guessed that was shock. You have to watch shock, he remembered. It could be as deadly as a goddamned bullet. The baby was crying. Brian, sitting with his back to the wall, twisted to look down at it. Blood was pooling around the infant. Christ! Brian tried to move his left arm to reach the child and couldn't. It didn't hurt; he just couldn't move it. He turned his neck to look at his shoulder. There was a jagged tear in his shirt and his arm was soaked with blood.

"Dave, I'm hit," he said, but Lasski didn't answer. Brian closed his eyes and willed himself calm, but his breath was becoming more labored, heart pounding in his ears. The circle was complete, he thought. Along with death had come new life. Brian liked the thought. He tried to hold onto it, but his mind kept drifting, fading. Hang on, hang on. If he could just make it 'til morning. Everything would be all right in the morning. In the morning he would be with Pamela. The baby's cry was faint how. Don't cry baby. Don't cry. Pamela will make everything all right.

His feet were like lead weights and he was tired. He could no longer move. He had to wait for Pamela, she would help. The alarm was ringing beside her bed, but he couldn't reach to turn it off. Damn, it was going to wake her. Wait! It wasn't an alarm it was a siren. Lots of sirens. They were coming closer. Now there were footfalls on the stairs. He tried to fight it but the darkness smothered him. His head sank to his chest.

Uniformed cops, guns in hand, were cautiously making their way up the stairs.

EPILOGUE

JUSTICE FOR ALL

Chief of Police James Peck was notified by telephone of the OIS shortly after midnight. He listened as the captain of RHD briefed him on the details. There were many, but what the chief did remember was the report of two Southwest Detectives being shot and what appeared to be the birth, and presence of a newborn child at the crime scene. Additionally, there are three adults, one woman, two men, all dead of gunshot wounds."

"Tell me about our men. Are they alive?"

"Both critical. Both in surgery."

"Who, Bill?"

"Lasski and Culpepper. Southwest Homicide. I'm at the hospital. They're both in surgery. Culpepper was hit twice. Leg and chest. Lasski middle of the back."

"Culpepper again? Damnit. What hospital?" the chief asked as he swung his feet to the floor. His wife awakened by the call, sat up, switched on a light. She was listening. Notifications were not a new drill.

"Centinela in Inglewood."

The chief's mind was racing. Two cops shot, three others dead, a newborn at the scene. This was going to be a

266

fucking mess. "Any issues at the scene?" He headed for a nearby closet.

"No, darkness worked for us. We limited the number of cars at the scene. It went quietly."

Peck was now at an open closet, rummaging through shirts. His wife appeared at his side. She pushed him aside and took over the search.

"I'm coming out there." The chief accepted the shirt his wife pushed at him.

In less than two hours, news of the shooting appeared on the Internet. There were postings on Twitter, Instagram, YouTube and more. Descriptions were inflammatory— *Robin Hood killed in LA, Massive Police shooting in LA; LA Police shoot and kill three; Five shot in LA Shoot out; Police shooting kills pregnant woman; Baby survives the shooting death of its mother; LA Police bungle leaves five dead.*

The Internet postings seemingly served as a wake-up call for the All-News Networks followed by the glut of LA stations, both television and talk radio. The reports were less than factual—*Robin Hood and his wife, both shot and killed by LA police. Infant child survives.*

The watch commander from Southwest Area was dispatched to the Lasski home to inform Julia Lasski her husband had been shot, and transport her to the hospital. Julia Lasski took the news well. She had been a police wife for eight years. She had taken the long ride to a hospital on two other occasions. Once when a drunk ran a red light and smashed her husband's patrol car, and on another occasion during the George Floyd riotous demonstrations when David was knocked unconscious by a thrown bottle. The two Lasski children, Garth, age six and Jill, age four, both heard the doorbell as well as the news of their father being shot from the sober uniformed Lieutenant Marshal. They were left behind, shaken, and crying. Julia's sister had arrived to watch them.

Both Lasski and Culpepper were in surgery when the Chief of Police arrived.

The chief of surgery had been called in to direct the

sensitive procedures now taking place to save the lives of the two cops.

David Lasski had suffered a gunshot to his lower left back. The .45 caliber bullet impacted left of his spine on the lower back resulting in damage to his liver, bladder, intestines, all exacerbated by a significant blood loss.

Brian Culpepper shot in the right leg suffered a shattered femur just above the knee with significant muscle and soft tissue damage. A major artery supplying blood to the lower leg was severed resulting in heavy bleeding. He had a second wound on his left shoulder, again, resulting in soft tissue damage and broken bones—all which resulted in a loss of consciousness, subsequent stoppage of the heart, and coma. CPR administered by a LAFD paramedic kept Brian Culpepper alive until the ambulance reached the hospital.

The chief of police found himself waiting with twenty-two cops in the hospital's crowded waiting room. There was an assortment of deputy chiefs, commanders, Captain Winslow, RHD detectives, the OIS team, Sergeant JD Kent along with Boone, and Howser as well as Roberts and Delgado from Southwest Homicide, and an assortment of uniformed and plain clothes cops from across the city who were former partners and friends.

As they waited, a young Black uniformed female officer pushed through the crush with two cups from a vending machine in the hallway. Reaching the chief of police, dressed in casual civilian attire, sitting on a bench with other cops, the young woman offered one of the cups she carried. The surprised chief smiled and accepted the cup.

"You look like you need a boost. It's Doctor Pepper." The officer smiled. "Sugar will do it."

"Thank you," the chief smiled sampling the drink.

The young officer not recognizing the chief had simply read his troubled face. When she joined her partner across the crowded room he leaned toward her. "You know that's the chief.?"

"I do now."

The surgeries lasted over five hours. Julia Lasski had been escorted to a private room away from the crowd in the waiting room. Knowing she'd arrived, the chief of police and Captain Winslow visited her to say hello and offer encouragement. Julia thanked them and asked if Pamela Moss had arrived?

Neither man had an answer. It was awkward.

"Who is Pamela Moss?" Captain Winslow asked.

Julia Lasski, already on the edge, was brief, concise, and loud with her answer.

Forty-six minutes later a patrol car, with Captain Winslow as a passenger, pulled to the curb in front of Pamela Moss's condo.

Lasski was first out of surgery. He was critical, but stable. Julia was quickly at her husband's side. Although he was still unconscious, Julia used her iPhone to call her two waiting kids and show them a live picture of their sleeping dad.

Pamela was briefed by Captain Winslow as the black and white patrol car sped across the face of the sleeping city, returning to the hospital. Brian was emerging from surgery when they arrived. The chief of surgery briefed Pamela and the chief of police. "He's critical. He suffered another heart arrythmia during surgery. He's in an induced coma. We're hoping...well, we're hoping."

Pamela was escorted to Brian's room in ICU. A nurse was stationed in the room. Pamela leaned close and carefully kissed Brian's forehead. "Hello, Brian," she whispered as a tear traced down her cheek. "What did I tell you about leaping over tall buildings?"

Gauze taped over both eyes, an oxygen tube inserted in his nose, an IV in his arm and sensors taped all over his bare chest attached to nearby monitors that beeped rhythmically in the quiet, Brian did not answer.

In the weeks that followed, the police conducted an

intensive investigation. Their findings were simply factual without embellishment or conclusions:

Two patrol units responded to 2706 West Adams #3, a two-bedroom second floor apartment after a call reported shots fired. The officers responding discovered two critically wounded Southwest Area Detectives, Sergeants David Lasski and Brian Culpepper. Both men suffered GSWs—gunshot wounds. In addition to the two Detectives, the dead bodies of Nathaniel Wyde, Vern Tucket, and Su Linn Nehi were found to also be victims of GSWs.

Officers also found a newborn infant (female). Evidence at the scene suggested Su Linn Nehi was the probable mother of the child. Officers protected the scene and notified the AM Watch Commander.

RHD & OIS were notified and conducted an on-scene investigation. They recovered two LAPD issued Glock pistols, a .45 caliber automatic pistol, and a .32 Caliber automatic pistol. Preliminary investigation revealed an estimated nineteen gunshots were fired. Individuals in possession of the recovered guns and what guns were fired and how many times was yet to be determined.

Autopsies pending.

The district attorney's office, recognizing the widespread impact of the shooting, and being the Chief Law Enforcement Agency for the County of Los Angeles, announced its intent to conduct an independent investigation.

"We have confidence in the police department's investigation, but there is public concern about the police once again investigating themselves," the elected district attorney said in his announcement to the press.

The DA's investigation was simply an extension of the one the police department started earlier, and its findings were remarkably similar. The district attorney, in a public statement, strongly urged the police department to come up with guidelines that would prevent any chance of such circumstances repeating themselves, even in the face of civil unrest.

When pressed by reporters as to whether there was any

wrongdoing by the police, the district attorney declined comment. "The results of our investigations will be reviewed by a Grand Jury," he promised.

The news headlines soon found other causes, and the shooting became old news. At least until the district attorney's office received the ballistics report from the police department's Scientific Investigation Division. They announced it as if it were their own findings—*Tests have revealed that the bullet killing Su Linn Nehi was fired from a .45 caliber pistol found in the apartment, but who fired the shot has yet to be determined.*

"Isn't this Culpepper, the cop they call the lady killer?" *the LA Times* questioned. "The one that shot a Black girl earlier. Isn't this the third woman he's killed?" There was no mention of the life he had saved.

The district attorney's office made no comment.

It was human interest and editors and news producers alike recognized it. Minor female Nehi, daughter of Su Linn Nehi, born in the midst o blood and bullets, became the symbol of public concern. The tide of urban slaughter had to be stemmed. The shooting and the birth proved nothing was sacred or safe. Editorials and commentaries talked of the child and the tragic times. They damned, rebuked, warned, and demanded those entrusted with public safety to find the answers. They…the accusers, had none.

The public outcry grew, fed by the media. The pressure increased and focused on the District Attorney's Office. It was from there the promise of justice had come. A clever political move had backfired.

The district attorney met with his chief advisors and they carefully reviewed the case. There was no hint of criminal conduct on the part of the two detectives.

"It's obvious," Harold Green pointed out. "If Sergeant Culpepper hadn't been involved, and if the baby hadn't been born, the shooting would still be tragic, but not controversial."

"*If,*" the district attorney replied.

Their meeting lasted well into the night. They knew

action had to be taken. The public demanded it, and finally they found the answer.

Tom Mathews from the Civil Liability Section made the recommendation—"If the officers' actions contributed to the death of an innocent bystander, Su Linn Nehi, the city of Los Angeles, since the officers were its agents, has liability."

So, it was decided. The County of Los Angeles, acting in an Ad Litem capacity, as the minor female's legal guardian, would sue the City of Los Angeles in a wrongful death action.

"The deputy we assign better be a damned good one," Harold Green said.

"Perhaps a woman," Tom Mathews added. "A symbol of motherhood—young, like the child's mother. It'll help with the jury. The press will love it."

The district attorney nodded agreement. "I've got someone in mind."

———

Pamela hadn't worked since the shooting. She hadn't resigned. She just quit going to work. There had been no calls. No visits. Brian was more important. It seemed the District Attorney's Office understood. She spent most of her time at the hospital. Julia Lasski refused to leave her husband's side as he clung to life. Lasski's chest was sewn together with a patchwork of metal clips and black puckering stiches. Finally, with his wife, two kids and Pamela in the room David Lasski opened his eyes and complained," Damn it's cold!" Pamela held Julia as she wept with joy.

When Pamela did go home the condo seemed foreign and empty. She found a pair of Brian's socks in a bedroom closet. She folded them and put them in a drawer. The scent of his aftershave still hung in her bathroom. The sound of her doorbell brought her out of her world of pity.

"Who is it?" Pamela asked at the door.

"The district attorney," a familiar voice answered.

They sat in the kitchen to talk. The district attorney explained what they planned and why. Pamela listened and when he finished, she was candid. "A few weeks ago, you told me I was a risk to your investigation. Now you want me to handle a trial. Why?"

"Two reasons," the DA answered, "Number one, you're best for the task, and number two, I don't want it to become a political trial. If I give it to any other deputy, they'll use it as a stage to make a name for themselves or go after the police like a shark. I know you won't do that."

"You want this to prove the police were wrong."

"Only if they were wrong. I want the truth to be found."

The district attorney left the case file with her.

Pamela spent the night reading. Deep in the report, she found the pages. Traces of blood taken from the shirt sleeves of Brian Culpepper matched the blood of Both Su Linn Nehi and infant Baby Girl Nehi. In addition to blood matches, traces recovered from fingernail clipping of Detective Culpepper revealed body fluids and masses usually associated with female birthing. Baby Girl Nehi also displayed bruising along both jaw lines suggesting finger pressure had been applied. Not something the wounded dying mother could have done. Cumulatively, the facts indicated Brian Culpepper had delivered the child. A fact never reported in the news. Why?

She, like others, thought the dying woman gave birth by herself. The answer was simple—a woman shot while giving birth was, *big news*. A police detective helping a dying woman give birth was interesting, but not as shocking. Who was the censor? The police, with their paranoia about releasing facts. The district attorney with his political self-serving interests in mind. Pamela didn't know, but she did know how to make the truth known.

It was ten minutes to two when Pamela made the call. "I'll take the case," she told the sleepy voice that answered.

The trial was without precedent. It was pushed to the top of the court calendar. Orphaned Baby Girl Nehi, whose mother had died as a result of a police action, now represented by the District Attorney of the County of Los Angeles, acting in an Ad Litem capacity, as the minor female's legal guardian, was suing the City of Los Angeles in a wrongful death action for thirty-eight million dollars.

The press and a sea of spectators packed the court room and spilled into the hallways. They were on the third day of jury selection when Pamela had to admit to herself she was ill. She blamed it on the inordinate time spent at the hospital.

It became especially bad after the noon recess, but she resisted and with the help of another Starbucks made it through the long afternoon.

Late in the day the final jury member was selected, and Pamela was pleased. There were seven women and five men. It was a women's trial and both Pamela and the city attorney, who represented the City of Los Angeles knew it. The city attorney had fought for male dominance, but his bias was becoming obvious to the women already seated, so he surrendered.

Pamela wished she could tell the worried man her plan. She had no intention of damming Brian or Lasski. How could she? She loved them both. She was there to protect them as much as the city attorney was. She wasn't after millions for the child. She was after the same thing Brian was; justice.

Finally, Judge Richard Moore announced from the bench, "Court is in recess until nine AM tomorrow morning. Please have your opening remarks ready."

Relieved the long day was over, Pamela left the courthouse through a back corridor to avoid the crush of waiting reporters.

Pamela had first seen Doctor Parker several days after Brian was shot. She couldn't sleep. The doctor, an attractive woman in her forties, saw the pain and anguish on Pamela's face. Although Pamela simply wanted something for sleep, she got much more. She learned the doctor was a widow. She had lost her Marine husband in the war in Iraq. They talked for several hours. Pamela was bitter and angry at life. The doctor agreed she had reason to be, but what would Brian Culpepper want, she asked. Pamela went away knowing she had made a friend, and it was more than her prescription for Ambien. She was to see Doctor Parker several times after that, just to check on her progress. This time was different. This time her body was telling her something was wrong. Damnit! Why now at the start of the trial?

"I'm not surprised," Doctor Parker said stepping into the treatment room with Pamela's file in hand. "I've got a television. Guess who I see every day on there? Too much too soon, young lady."

Pamela explained how she felt—weak, shaky, nauseous.

"What time did you got to bed last night?"

"About one. I had papers to go over."

"And what time did you get up this morning?"

"Six."

"Breakfast?"

"Starbucks."

"Lunch?"

"Another Starbucks. I didn't have much time."

Doctor Parker stopped making notes, stuck her pen in a pocket on her tunic and frowned at Pamela. "Are you sensing a pattern here?"

Pamela nodded.

"It's called stress. Look at what brought you in here the first time. Now this made for television trial. Your body is telling you to stop the abuse. Get some nourishment and rest."

"I will, Doctor," Pamela pled. "But please help me through the rest of the week. Today was terrible."

"You're very skilled at lying." The doctor smiled. "I can see why they picked you for the trial. OK, here's what we'll do. I want blood and urine, just to make sure you're not fighting some virus. I'll have the nurse give you a vitamin shot. Then I want you to go home and sleep. After you eat something. Got that?"

"Got it," Pamela lied convincingly and then, as she had more days than she had counted she went across the street from the medical center to the hospital and checked in with the nurse on duty in Brian's intensive care unit.

"Any change?" she asked softly. The comatose Brian lay in a slightly inclined position in the railed bed. The sensors were still taped to his bare chest. Thin wires snaked from the sensors to overhead monitors with scopes where green lines beeped with electronic pulse. An IV line traced from a vein on the back of his right hand to a bottle suspended on a chromed beside hanger delivering nourishment and antibiotics. A plastic drain tube protruded from Brian's abdomen and led to an opaque collection bottle hanging on a bed rail. A large patch between neck and shoulder hinted at a serious wound. An exposed and stitched upper leg held together with a variety of clamps, wires and pins added to the evidence of trauma.

Brian's face was dark with beard. His features were softer with bloating from a variety of life sustaining fluids.

"His signs have been stable today," the nurse said to Pamela.

Pamela crossed to the bed and looked at Brian. It was a hungry passionate look.

"I'm here, Brian," Pamela said softly as she lifted his hand into hers.

"The doctor gave him another Glasgow test earlier today."

Pamela turned to her. "And?"

"Somewhat improved but still low. He's scheduled for another EEG tonight."

"What will that show?"

"In lay terms," the nurse answered, "it will tell us if he's still in there."

"And that means what?"

The nurse skirted a direct answer. "We're not certain how deep his coma is or if he's made any progress."

276

Pamela turned her attention to Brian's face. She lifted her hand and ran a polished nail along the stubble on his jaw line. Her eyes rimmed with tears. She didn't notice Doctor Parker stepping in. She offer the nurse a smile and crossed to Pamela's side. "I thought you were going home?"

Pamela's attention stayed on Brian.

"Actually," Doctor Parker continued, "I'm glad I found you here. We got the results of your lab work."

Pamela brushed a tear from her cheek and looked to the doctor. "That was quick."

"Well, you don't have the flu."

"What do I have?" Pamela asked.

"A child to name in about thirty-two weeks." Doctor Parker smiled.

"I'm pregnant!" Pamela blurted, gripping Brian's hand even tighter.

"I'm guessing you may be standing in front of the baby's' father?"

"Yes," Pamela said wiping another tear. In her excitement she didn't realize when she lifted her hand, Brian's hand was now gripping hers.

A LOOK AT: BLOOD BROTHERS: AN ACTION-ADVENTURE THRILLER

WARPAINT IN THE CORRIDORS OF POWER.

In a high-end hotel near the White House, three Mojave Indians sit in silence, cross-legged and bare chested. The two leather-faced elders and the young buck with a ponytail were all big men. Spread on the floor around them was an assortment of colorful modern cosmetics. Powdered charcoal, red clay, and cactus blossoms had been replaced, but the finger-traced swaths of color on red skin still looked ominous. There hadn't been an Indian attack in the United States since the early 1900s. In fifty-three minutes, that would no longer be true.

When the three unarmed Native American warriors breach the fence around the White House, FBI agent John Fox was going to be drawn into a deadly war between the United States and a tribe of Indians with a blood stained hundred-year-old treaty—This time there would be no surrender.

"The idea of full dress in preparation for a battle comes not from a belief that it will add to the fighting ability. The preparation is for death, in case death should be the result of the conflict. Every Indian wants to look his best when he goes to meet the great Spirit." – Wooden Leg—Cheyenne

AVAILABLE NOW

ABOUT THE AUTHOR

Novelist & Screenwriter, Dallas Barnes has written nearly two hundred hours of primetime television drama, as well as seven bestselling novels. His writings have won nominations for EMMY'S, in both primetime and daytime, as well as the famed EDGAR ALAN POE AWARD, the IMAGE AWARD and the HUMANITAS PRIZE. Dallas Barnes along with JoAnne have written for over twenty-three of the highest rated, most successful, prime time, dramatic television series, as well as several motion pictures made for television.

As Writers/ Producers of the acclaimed historical docudrama, "America, You're Too Young to Die," Dallas & JoAnne became the only writers, outside White House staff, to write for, then President, Ronald Reagan.

Along with writing, Dallas Barnes is an executive level hybrid hospitality security professional with a unique blend of management, Law Enforcement and guest services skills. with over a decade of experience in investigations in demanding hospitality and gaming venues linked to a performance in risk management, safety, compliance, and loss prevention.